G.A. HENTY

December 8, 1832 — November 16, 1902

For Name and Fame
Or, Through Afghan Passes

by

G. A. Henty

ILLUSTRATED BY GORDON BROWNE

PrestonSpeed Publications

Pennsylvania

A note about the name PrestonSpeed Publications:
The name PrestonSpeed Publications was chosen in loving memory of our fathers, Preston Louis Schmitt and Lester Herbert Maynard (nicknamed "Speed" for his prowess in baseball).

Originally published by Blackie & Son, Limited,
May 2, 1885
Blackie & Son Title Page Date 1886

For Name and Fame: Or, Through Afghan Passes
by G. A. Henty
© 2002 by PrestonSpeed Publications
Published by PrestonSpeed Publications, 51 Ridge Road, Mill Hall, Pennsylvania 17751.

This book is printed on acid-free paper, and its binding materials have been chosen for strength and durability.

Heirloom Hardcover Edition ISBN 1-931587-12-4
Popular Softcover Edition ISBN 1-931587-13-2

Printed in the United States of America

PRESTONSPEED PUBLICATIONS
51 RIDGE ROAD
MILL HALL, PENNSYLVANIA 17751
(570) 726-7844
www.prestonspeed.com
March, 2002

INTRODUCTION

G. A. Henty's life was filled with exciting adventure. After completing his work at Westminster School, he attended Cambridge University, where he undertook a rigorous course of study and also enjoyed boxing, wrestling, and rowing. The strenuous study and healthy, competitive participation in sports prepared Henty for his adventures. To name just a few, he fought with the British army in the Crimea, served as a war correspondent during Garibaldi's fight for independence in Italy, visited Abyssinia, witnessed the Franco-Prussian war while in Paris, observed the Carlists in Spain, attended the opening of the Suez Canal, toured India with the Prince of Wales (later Edward II), and visited the California gold fields.

G. A. Henty lived during the reign of Queen Victoria (1837-1901) and began his story-telling career with his own children. After dinner it was his custom to spend an hour or two telling them a story that often continued for days. In fact, some stories lasted for weeks! One evening a friend happened to be present during Henty's "story hour." Watching the children as they sat spell-bound, he urged Henty to write down his stories so others could enjoy them. Happily for us, Henty did so. One of his secretaries reported that he often would pace rapidly back and forth in his study dictating stories as fast as the secretary could record them. He became known to his readers as "The Prince of Story-Tellers" and "The Boys Own Historian."

Henty's stories revolve around a fictional boy hero during fascinating periods of history. His heroes are diligent, courageous, intelligent, and dedicated to their country and cause in the face of, at times, great peril. Respected historians have acknowledged his histories, particularly the accounts of battles, for their accuracy. His ability to bring his readers action-packed adventure in an accurate historical setting makes the study of history exciting, and removes the drudgery often associated with such study.

Henty's heroes fight wars, sail the seas, discover new lands, conquer evil empires, prospect for gold, and embark upon a host of other exciting adventures. They meet such famous personages as Josephus, Titus, Hannibal, Robert the Bruce, Sir William Wallace, General Marlborough, General Gordon, General Kichner, Robert E. Lee, Frederick the Great, the Duke of Wellington, Huguenot leader Coligny, the explorer Cortez, King Alfred, Napoleon, and Sir Francis Drake, to name just a few. The heroes experience the fall of Jerusalem, the Roman invasion of Britain, the Crusades, the Viking invasion of Europe, the Reign of Terror in France, and the exciting events of the Reformation in various countries, etc. In short, Henty's heroes live during tumultuous times in history and meet many of the most prominent leaders of those times.

PrestonSpeed is delighted to offer the long-out-of-print works of G. A. Henty to a whole new generation of adults and young people. Our Henty titles contain the complete text and all maps and/or illustrations included in the original editions. Although the books have been newly typeset, the original grammar and spelling remain the same as in the original versions.

Sam Dickson finds little Willie Gale.

PREFACE

MY DEAR LADS,

In following the hero of this story through the last Afghan war, you will be improving your acquaintance with a country which is of supreme importance to the British Empire, and at the same time, be able to trace the operations by which Lord Roberts made his great reputation as a general and a leader of men. Afghanistan stands as a dividing line between the two great empires of England and Russia, and is likely, sooner or later, to become the scene of a tremendous struggle between these nations. Happily, at the present time the Afghans are on our side. It is true that we have warred with and beaten them, but our retirement after victory has at least shown them that we have no desire to take their country; while, on the other hand, they know that for those races upon whom Russia has once laid her hand there is no escape. In these pages you will see the strength and the weakness of these wild people of the mountains; their strength lying in their personal bravery, their determination to preserve their freedom at all costs, and the nature of their country. Their weakness consists in their want of organization, their tribal jealousies and their impatience of regular habits and of the restraint necessary to render them good soldiers. But when led and organized by English officers there are no better soldiers in the world, as is proved by the splendid services which have been rendered by the frontier force, which is composed almost entirely of Afghan tribesmen. Their history shows that defeat has little moral effect upon them. Crushed one day, they will rise again the next; scattered, it would seem hopelessly, they are ready to reassemble and renew the conflict at the first summons of their chiefs. Guided by British advice, led by British officers, and, it may be, paid by British gold, Afghanistan is likely to prove an invaluable ally to us when the day comes that Russia believes herself strong enough to move forward towards the goal of all her hopes and efforts for the last fifty years, the conquest of India.

Yours sincerely,

G. A. HENTY

CONTENTS

ILLUSTRATIONS

FOR NAME AND FAME
A TALE OF THE AFGHAN WAR

CHAPTER I
THE LOST CHILD

"MY poor pets!" a lady exclaimed sorrowfully. "It is too bad! They all knew me so well, and ran to meet me when they saw me coming, and seemed really pleased to see me even when I had no food to give them."

"Which was not often, my dear," Captain Ripon, her husband, said. "However, it is, as you say, too bad, and I will bring the fellow to justice if I can. There are twelve prize fowls worth a couple of guineas apiece, not to mention the fact of their being pets of yours, stolen, probably by tramps, who will eat them, and for whom the commonest barn-door chickens would have done as well. There are marks of blood in two or three places, so they have evidently been killed for food. The house was locked up last night all right, for you see they got in by breaking in a panel of the door. Robson, run down to the village at once, and tell the policeman to come up here, and ask if any gypsies or tramps have been seen in the neighbourhood."

The village lay at the gate of Captain Ripon's park, and the gardener soon returned with the policeman.

"I've heard say there are some gypsies camped on Netherwood Common, four miles away," that functionary said, in answer to Captain Ripon.

"Put the gray mare in the dog-cart, Sam; we will drive over at once. They will hardly expect us so soon. We will pick up another policeman at Netherwood; they may show fight if we are not in strength."

1

FOR NAME AND FAME

Five minutes later Captain Ripon was travelling along the road at the rate of twelve miles an hour, with Sam by his side, and the policeman sitting behind. At Netherwood they took up another policeman, and a few minutes later drove up to the gypsy encampment.

There was a slight stir when they were seen approaching, and then the gypsies went on with their usual work, the women weaving baskets from osiers, the men cutting up gorse into skewers. There were four low tents, and a wagon stood near, a bony horse grazing on the common.

"Now," Captain Ripon said, "I am a magistrate, and I daresay you know what I have come for. My fowl-house has been broken open, and some valuable fowls stolen. Now, policeman, look about and see if you can find any traces of them."

The gypsies rose to their feet with angry gestures.

"Why do you come to us?" one of the men said. "When a fowl is stolen you always suspect us, as if there were no other thieves in the world."

"There are plenty of other thieves, my friend, and we shall not interfere with you if we find nothing suspicious."

"There have been some fowls plucked here," one of the policemen said; "here is a little feather"—and he showed one of only half an inch in length—"and there is another on that woman's hair. They have cleaned them up nicely enough, but it ain't easy to pick up every feather. I'll be bound we find a fowl in the pot."

Two of the gypsies leapt forward, stick in hand; but the oldest man present said a word or two to them in their own dialect.

"You may look in the pot," he said, turning to Captain Ripon, "and maybe you will find a fowl there, with other things; we bought 'em at the market at Hunston yesterday."

The policeman lifted the lid off the great pot which was hanging over the fire, and stirred up the contents with a stick.

"There's rabbits here, two or three of them, I should say, and a fowl, perhaps two, but they are cut up."

THE LOST CHILD

"I cannot swear to that," Captain Ripon said, examining the portions of fowl, "though the plumpness of the breasts and the size show that they are not ordinary fowls." He looked round again at the tents. "But I can pretty well swear to this," he said, as he stooped and picked up a feather which lay half concealed between the edge of one of the tents and the grass. "This is a breast-feather of a Spangled Dorking. These are not birds which would be sold for eating in Hunston market, and it will be for these men to show where they got it from."

A smothered oath broke from one or two of the men. The elder signed to them to be quiet. "That's not proof," he said insolently. "You can't convict five men because the feather of a fowl which you cannot swear to is found in their camp."

"No," Captain Ripon said quietly. "I do not want to convict any one but the thief; but the proof is sufficient for taking you in custody, and we shall find out which was the guilty man afterwards. Now, lads, it will be worse for you if you make trouble. Constables, take them up to Mr. Bailey; he lives half a mile away. Fortunately, we have means of proving which is the fellow concerned. Now, Sam, you and I will go up with the Netherwood constable to Mr. Bailey; and do you," he said to the other policeman, "keep a sharp watch over these women. You say you can find nothing in the tents, but it is likely the other fowls are hid not far off, and I will put all the boys of the village to search when I come back."

The gypsies, with sullen faces, accompanied Captain Ripon and the policeman to the magistrate's.

"Is that feather the only proof you have, Ripon?" Mr. Bailey asked, when he had given his evidence. "I do not think that it will be enough to convict if unsupported; besides, you cannot bring it home to any one of them. But it is sufficient for me to have them locked up for twenty-four hours, and, in the meantime, you may find the other fowls."

"But I have means of identification," Captain Ripon said. "There is a footmark in some earth at the fowl-house door. It is made by a boot which has got hobnails and a horse-shoe heel, and

3

a piece of that heel has been broken off. Now, which of these men has got such a boot on? Whichever has, he is the man." There was a sudden movement among the accused.

"It's of no use," one of them said, when the policeman approached to examine their boots. "I'm the man, I'll admit it. I can't get over the boot;" and he held up his right foot.

"That is the boot! sir," the constable exclaimed. "I can swear that it will fit the impression exactly."

"Very well," the magistrate said. "Constable, take that man to the lock-up, and bring him before the bench to-morrow for final committal for trial. There is no evidence against the other four. They can go."

With surly threatening faces the men left the room, while the constable placed handcuffs on the prisoner.

"Constable," Mr. Bailey said, "you had better not put this man in the village lock-up. The place is of no great strength, and his comrades would as likely as not get him out to-night. Put him in my dog-cart; my groom shall drive you over to Hunston."

Captain Ripon returned with his groom to Netherwood, and set all the children searching the gorse, copses, and hedges near the common by the promise of ten shillings reward if they found the missing fowls.

Half an hour later the gypsies struck their tents, loaded the van, and went off.

Late that afternoon the ten missing fowls were discovered in a small copse by the wayside, half a mile from the common on the road to Captain Ripon's park.

"I cannot bring your fowls back to life, Emma," that gentleman said, when he returned home, "but I have got the thief. It was one of the gypsies on Netherwood Common. We found two of the fowls in their pot. No doubt they thought that they would have plenty of time to get their dinner before anyone came, even if suspicion fell on them; and they have hidden the rest away somewhere, but I expect that we shall find them. They had burnt all the feathers, as they thought; but I found a breast-feather of a

Spangled Dorking, and that was enough for me to give them in custody. Then, when it came to the question of boots, the thief found it no good to deny it any longer."

That evening, Captain Ripon was told that a woman wished to speak to him, and on going out into the hall, he saw a gypsy of some thirty years of age.

"I have come, sir, to beg you not to appear against my husband."

"But, my good woman, I see no reason why I should not do so. If he had only stolen a couple of common fowls for a sick wife or child, I might have been inclined to overlook it, for I am not fond of sending men to prison, but to steal a dozen valuable fowls for the pot is a little too much. Besides, the matter has gone too far now for me to retract, even if I wished to, which I certainly do not."

"He is a good husband, sir."

"He may be," Captain Ripon said, "though that black eye you have got does not speak in his favour. But that has nothing to do with it; matters must take their course."

The woman changed her tone.

"I have asked you fairly, sir; and it will be better for you if you don't prosecute Reuben."

"Oh, nonsense, my good woman! Don't let me have any threats, or it will be worse for you."

"I tell you," the woman exclaimed fiercely, "it will be the worse for you if you appear against my Reuben."

"There, go out," Captain Ripon said, opening the front door of the hall. "As if I cared for your ridiculous threats! Your husband will get what he deserves—five years, if I am not mistaken."

"You will repent this," the gypsy said, as she passed out.

Captain Ripon closed the door after her without a word.

"Well, who was it?" his wife inquired, when he returned to the drawing-room.

"An insolent gypsy woman, wife of the man who stole the fowls. She had the impudence to threaten me if I appeared against him."

"Oh, Robert!" the young wife exclaimed apprehensively. "What could she do? Perhaps you had better not appear."

"Nonsense, my dear!" her husband laughed. "Not appear because an impudent gypsy woman has threatened me? A nice magistrate I should be! Why, half the fellows who are committed swear that they will pay off the magistrate some day, but nothing ever comes of it. Here we have been married six months, and you are wanting me to neglect my duty, especially when it is your pet fowls which have been stolen.

"Why, at the worst, my dear," he went on, seeing that his wife still looked pale, "they could burn down a rick or two on a windy night in winter; and to satisfy you, I will have an extra sharp look-out kept in that direction, and have a watch-dog chained up near them. Come, my love, it is not worth giving a second thought about, and I shall not tell you about my work on the bench if you are going to take matters to heart like this."

The winter came and went, and the ricks were untouched, and Captain Ripon forgot all about the gypsy's threats. At the assizes a previous conviction was proved against her husband, and he got five years' penal servitude, and after the trial was over the matter passed out of the minds of both husband and wife.

They had indeed other matters to think about, for soon after Christmas a baby boy was born and monopolized the greater portion of his mother's thoughts. When in due time he was taken out for walks, the old women of the village, perhaps with an eye to presents from the Park, were unanimous in declaring that he was the finest boy ever seen, and the image both of his father and mother. He certainly was a fine baby, and his mother lamented sorely over the fact that he had a dark blood-mark about the size of a threepenny piece upon his shoulder. Her husband, however, consoled her by pointing out that, as it was a boy, the mark did not matter in the slightest, whereas, had it been a girl, the mark would have been a disfigurement when she attained to the dignified age at which low dresses are worn.

"Yes, of course, that would have been dreadful, Robert; still, you know, it is a pity."

THE LOST CHILD

"I really cannot see that it is even a pity, little woman; and it would have made no great difference if he had been spotted all over like a leopard, so that his face and arms were free; the only drawback would have been he would have got some nickname or other, such as 'the Leopard,' or 'Spotty,' or something of that sort when he went to bathe with his school-fellows. But this little spot does not matter in the slightest. Some day or other Tom will laugh when I tell him what a fuss you made over it."

Mrs. Ripon was silenced, but although she said nothing more about it, she was grieved in her heart at this little blemish on her boy, and lamented that it would spoil his appearance when he began to run about in little short frocks, and she determined at once that he should wear long curls until he got into jackets.

Summer, autumn, and winter came and passed. In the spring Tom Ripon was toddling about, but he had not yet begun to talk, although his mother declared that certain incoherent sounds which he made were quite plain and distinct words; but her husband, while willing to allow that they might be perfectly intelligible to her, insisted that to the male ear they in no way resembled words.

"But he ought to begin to talk, Robert," his wife urged. "He is sixteen months old now, and can run about quite well. He really ought to begin to talk."

"He will talk before long," her husband said carelessly. "Many children do not talk till they are eighteen months old, some not till they are two years. Besides, you say he does begin already."

"Yes, Robert, but not quite plainly."

"No, indeed, not plainly at all," her husband laughed. "Don't trouble, my dear, he will talk soon enough, and if he only talks as loud as he roars sometimes, you will regret the hurry you have been in about it."

"Oh, Robert, how can you talk so? I am sure he does not cry more than other children. Nurse says he is the best child she ever knew."

"Of course she does, my dear; nurses always do. But I don't say he roars more than other children. I only say he roars, and that loudly; so you need not be afraid of there being anything the matter with his tongue or his lungs. What fidgets you young mothers are, to be sure!"

"And what heartless things you young fathers are, to be sure!" his wife retorted, laughing. "Men don't deserve to have children, they do not appreciate them one bit."

"We appreciate them in our way, little woman, but it is not a fussy way. We are content with them as they are, and are not in any hurry for them to run, or to walk, or to cut their first teeth. Tom is a fine little chap, and I am very fond of him in his way, principally, perhaps, because he is your Tom; but I cannot see that he is a prodigy."

"He is a prodigy," Mrs. Ripon said, with a little toss of her head, "and I shall go up to the nursery to admire him." So saying she walked off with dignity, and Captain Ripon went out to look at his horses, and thought to himself what a wonderful dispensation of providence it was that mothers were so fond of their babies.

"I don't know what the poor little beggars would do," he muttered, "if they had only their fathers to look after them; but I suppose we should take to it, just as the old goose in the yard has taken to that brood of chickens whose mother was carried off by the fox. By the way, I must order some wire-netting; I forgot to write for it yesterday."

Another two months. It was June; and now even Captain Ripon allowed that Tom could say "Pa" and "Ma" with tolerable distinctness, but as yet he had got no farther. He could now run about sturdily; and as the season was warm and bright, and Mrs. Ripon believed in fresh air, the child spent a considerable portion of his time in the garden. One day his mother was out with him, and he had been running about for some time. Mrs. Ripon was picking flowers, for she had a dinner-party that evening, and she enjoyed getting her flowers and arranging her vases herself. Presently she looked round, but Tom was missing. There were many clumps of ornamental shrubs on the lawn, and Mrs. Ripon thought nothing of his disappearance.

"Tom," she called, "come to mamma, she wants you," and went on with her work.

A minute or two passed.

"Where is that little pickle?" she said. "Hiding, I suppose;" and she went off in search. Nowhere was Tom to be seen. She called loudly, and searched in the bushes.

"He must have gone up to the house. Oh, here comes nurse. Nurse, have you seen Master Tom? He has just run away," she called.

"No, ma'am, I have seen nothing of him."

"He must be about the garden then, somewhere. Look about, nurse; where can the child have hidden itself?"

Nurse and mother ran about, calling loudly the name of the missing child. Five minutes later Mrs. Ripon ran into the study, where her husband was going through his farm accounts.

"Oh, Robert," she said, "I can't find Tom!" And she burst into tears.

"Not find Tom?" her husband said, rising in surprise. "Why, how long have you missed him?"

"He was out in the garden with me; I was picking flowers for the dinner-table, and when I looked round he was gone. Nurse and I have been looking everywhere, and calling, but we cannot find him."

"Oh, he is all right," Captain Ripon said cheerfully. "Do not alarm yourself, little woman. He must have wandered into the shrubbery; we shall hear him howling directly. But I will come and look for him."

No better success attended Captain Ripon's search than that which his wife had met with. He looked anxious now. The gardeners and servants were called, and soon every place in the garden was ransacked.

"He must have got through the gate somehow into the park," Captain Ripon said, hurrying in that direction. "He certainly is not in the garden or in any of the hothouses."

Some of the men had already gone in that direction. Presently Captain Ripon met one running back.

"I have been down to the gate, sir, and can see nothing of Master Tom; but in the middle of the drive, just by the clump of laurels by the gate, this boot was lying, just as if it had been put there on purpose to be seen."

"Nonsense!" Captain Ripon said. "What can that have to do with it?" Nevertheless he took the boot and looked at it. It was a roughly made heavy boot, such as would be worn by a labouring man. He was about to throw it carelessly aside, and to proceed on his search, when he happened to turn it over. Then he started as if struck. "Good Heaven!" he exclaimed. "It is the gypsy's." Yes, he remembered it now. The man had pleaded not guilty when brought up at the assizes, and the boot had been produced as evidence. He remembered it particularly because, after the man was sentenced, his wife had provoked a smile by asking that the boots might be given up to her in exchange for a better pair for her husband to put on when discharged from prison. Yes, it was clear. The gypsy woman had kept her word, and had taken her revenge. She had stolen the child, and had placed the boot where it would attract attention, in order that the parents might know the hand that struck them. Instantly Captain Ripon ran to the stable, ordered the groom to mount at once, and scour every road and lane, while he himself rode off to Hunston to give notice to the police, and offer a large reward for the child's recovery.

He charged the man who had brought the boot to carry it away, and put it in a place of safety till it was required; and on no account to mention to a soul where he put it.

Before riding off, he ran in to his wife, who was half wild with grief, to tell her that he was going to search outside the park, and that she must keep up her spirits, for no doubt Tom would turn up all right in no time.

He admitted to himself, however, as he galloped away, that he was not altogether sure that Tom would be so speedily recovered. The woman would never have dared to place the boot on the road, and so give a clue against herself, unless she felt very confident that she could get away or conceal herself.

"She has probably some hiding-place close by the park," he said to himself, "where she will lie hid till night, and will then make across country."

He paused at the village, and set the whole population at work by telling them that his child was missing, and had, he believed, been carried off by a gypsy woman; and that he would give fifty pounds to anyone who would find him. She could not be far off, as it was only about half an hour since the child had been missed.

Then he galloped to Hunston, set the police at work; and, going to a printer, told him instantly to set up and strike off placards offering five hundred pounds reward for the recovery of the child. This was to be done in an hour or two, and then taken to the police station for distribution throughout the country round.

Having now done all in his power, Captain Ripon rode back as rapidly as he had come, in hopes that the child might already have been found.

No news had, however, been obtained of him, nor had anyone seen any strange woman in the neighbourhood.

On reaching the house he found his wife prostrated with grief; and, in answer to her questions, he thought it better to tell her about the discovery of the boot.

"We may be some little time before we find the boy," he said, "but we shall find him sooner or later. I have got placards out already, offering five hundred pounds reward; and this evening I will send advertisements to all the papers in this and the neighbouring counties. Do not fret, darling. The woman has done it out of spite, no doubt; but she will not risk putting her neck in a noose by harming the child. It is a terrible grief, but it will only be for a time; we are sure to find him before long."

11

FOR NAME AND FAME

Later in the evening, when Mrs. Ripon had somewhat recovered her composure, she said to her husband, "How strange are God's ways, Robert; how wicked and wrong in us to grumble! I was foolish enough to fret over that mark on the darling's neck, and now the thought of it is my greatest comfort. If it should be God's will that months or years should pass over before we find him, there is a sign by which we shall always know him. No other child can be palmed off upon us as our own; when we find Tom we shall know him, however changed he may be!"

"Yes, dear," her husband said, "God is very good, and this trial may be sent us for the best. As you say, we can take comfort now from what we were disposed to think at the time a little cross. After that, dear, we may surely trust in God. That mark was placed there that we might know our boy again; and were it not decreed that we should again see him, that mark would have been useless."

The thought, for a time, greatly cheered Mrs. Ripon; but gradually the hope that she should ever see her boy again faded away, and Captain Ripon became much alarmed at the manifest change in her health.

In spite of all Captain Ripon could do, no news was obtained of the gypsy or Tom. For weeks he rode about the country asking questions in every village, or hurried away to distant parts of England, where the police thought they had a clue.

It was all in vain. Every gypsy encampment in the kingdom was searched, but without avail; and even the police, sharp-eyed as they are, could not guess that the decent-looking Irishwoman, speaking—when she did speak, which was seldom, for she was a taciturn woman—with a strong brogue, working in a laundry in a small street in the Potteries, Notting Hill, was the gypsy they were looking for; or that the little boy, whose father she said was at sea, was the child for whose discovery a thousand pounds was continually advertised.

CHAPTER II
THE FOUNDLING

IT was a bitterly cold night in January. The wind was roaring across the flats and fens of Cambridgeshire, driving tiny flakes of snow before it. But few people had been about all day, and those whose business compelled them to face the weather had hurried along muffled up to the chin. It was ten at night, and the porter and his wife at the workhouse at Ely had just gone to bed, when the woman exclaimed, "Sam, I hear a child crying."

"Oh, nonsense!" the man replied, drawing the bed-clothes higher over his head. "It is the wind; it's been whistling all day."

The woman was silent, but not convinced. Presently she sat up in bed. "I tell you, Sam, it's a child; don't you hear it, man? It's a child outside the gate. On such a night as this, too. Get up, man, and see; if you won't, I will go myself."

"Lie still, woman, it's all thy fancy."

"You are a fool, Sam Dickson," his wife said sharply. "Do you think I have lived to the age of forty-five, and don't know a child's cry when I hear it? Now are you going to get up, or am I?"

With much grumbling the porter turned out of bed, slipped on a pair of trousers and a greatcoat, took down the key from the wall, lighted a lantern, and went out. He opened the gate and looked out. There was nothing to be seen, and he was about to close the gate again with a curse on his wife's fancies, when a fresh cry broke on his ears. He hurried out now, and, directed by the voice, found lying near the gate a child wrapped in a dark-coloured shawl, which had prevented him from seeing it at his first glance. There was no one else in sight. The man lifted his lantern above his head and gave a shout. There was no answer. Then he raised the child and carried it in, locked the door, and entered the lodge.

13

"You are right for once," he said. "Here is a child, and a pretty heavy one too. It has been deserted by someone; and a heartless creature she must have been, for in another half-hour it would have been frozen to death if you had not heard it."

The woman was out of bed now. "It is a boy," she said, opening the shawl, "about two years old, I should say. Don't cry, my boy— don't cry. It's half-frozen, Sam. The best thing will be to put it into our bed, that has just got warm. I will warm it up a little milk. It's no use taking it into the ward to-night."

Ten minutes later the child was sound asleep, the porter, who was a good-natured man, having gone over to sleep in an empty bed in the house, leaving the child to share his wife's bed.

In the morning the foundling opened its eyes and looked round. Seeing everything strange, it began to cry.

"Don't cry, dear," the woman said. "I will get you some nice breakfast directly."

The kindness of tone at once pacified the child. It looked round.

"Where's mother?" he asked.

"I don't know, dear, we shall find her soon enough, no doubt; don't you fret."

The child did not seem inclined to fret; on the contrary, he brightened up visibly.

"Will she beat Billy when she comes back?"

"No, my dear, she sha'n't beat you. Does she often beat you?"

The child nodded its head several times emphatically.

"Then she's a bad lot," the woman said indignantly.

The child ate its breakfast contentedly, and was then carried by the porter's wife to the master, who had already heard the circumstance of its entry.

"It's of no use asking such a baby whether it has any name," he said; "of course it would not know. It had better go into the infants' ward; the guardians will settle what its name shall be. We will set the police at work and try and find out something about its mother. It is a fine-looking little chap, and she must be either a thoroughly bad one, or terribly pressed, to desert it like this. Most likely it is a tramp, and in that case it's odds we shall never hear further about it. Any distinguishing mark on its clothes?"

"None at all, sir. It is poorly dressed, and seems to have been very bad treated; its skin is dirty, and its little back is black and blue with bruises; but it has a blood-mark on the neck, which will enable its mother to swear to it, if it's fifty years hence; but I don't suppose we shall ever hear of her again."

That afternoon, however, the news came that the body of a tramp had been found frozen to death in a ditch near the town. She had apparently lost her way, and when she had fallen in was so numbed and cold that she was unable to rise, and so had been drowned in the shallow water. When the master heard of it he sent for the porter's wife.

"Mrs. Dickson," he said, "you had better take that child down and let it see the tramp they have found frozen to death. The child is too young to be shocked at death, and will suppose she is asleep. But you will be able to see if he recognizes her."

There was no doubt as to the recognition. The child started in terror when he saw the woman lying in the shed into which she had been carried. It checked its first impulse to cry out, but struggled to get further off: "Moder asleep," he said in a whisper. "If she wake she beat Billy."

That was enough. The woman carried him back to the house. "She's his mother, sir, sure enough," she said to the master, "though how she should be puzzles me. She is dressed in pretty decent clothes, but she is as dark as a gypsy, with black hair. This child is fair, with a skin as white as milk, now he is washed."

"I daresay he takes after his father," the master, who was a practical man, said. "I hear that there is no name on her things, no paper or other article which would identify her in her pockets; but there is £2, 12s. in her purse, so she was not absolutely in want. It will pay the parish for her funeral."

An hour later the guardians assembled, and upon hearing the circumstances of the new-comer's admission and the death of the tramp, they decided that the child should be entered in the books as "William Gale," the name being chosen with a reference to the weather during which he came into the house; and against his name a note was written to the effect that his mother, a tramp, name unknown, had, after leaving him at the door of the workhouse, been found frozen to death next day. William Gale grew and throve. He was a quiet and contented child; accustomed to be shut up all day alone, while his mother was out washing, the companionship of other children in the workhouse was a pleasant novelty; and if the food was not such as a dainty child would fancy, it was at least as good as he had been accustomed to. The porter's wife continued to be the fast friend of the child whom she had saved from death. The fact that she had done so gave her an interest in it. Her own children were out in service or at work in the fields, and the child was a pleasure to her. Scarce a day passed then that she would not go across the yard up to the infants' ward and bring Billy down to the lodge, where he would play contentedly by the hour, or sit watching her and sucking at a cake while she washed or prepared her husband's dinner.

Billy was seldom heard to cry. Perhaps he had wept all his stock of tears away before he entered the house; he had seldom fits of bad temper, and was a really lovable child. Mrs. Dickson never wavered in the opinion she had first formed, that the dead tramp was not Billy's mother; but as no one else agreed with her, she kept her thoughts to herself. The years passed on, and William Gale was now no longer in the infants' ward, but took his place in the boys' school. Here he at once showed an intelligence beyond that of the other boys of his own age. The hours which he had each day spent in the porter's lodge had not been wasted. The affection of the good woman had brightened his life, and he had none of the dull, downcast look so common among children in workhouses. She had encouraged him to talk and play, had taught him the alphabet, and supplied him with an occasional picture-book with easy words; indeed she devoted far more time to him than many mothers in her class of life can give to their children. The guardians, as they went in and out to board meeting, would delight her by remarking:—

THE FOUNDLING

"That is really a fine little fellow, Mrs. Dickson; he really does you credit—a fine sturdy, independent little chap."

The child of course wore the regular uniform of workhouse children; but Mrs. Dickson, who was handy with her needle, used to cut and alter the clothes to fit him, and thus entirely changed their appearance.

"He looks like a gentleman's child," one of the guardians said one day.

"I believe he is a gentleman's child, sir. Look at his white skin; see how upright he is, with his head far back as if he was somebody; he is different altogether from the run of them. I always said he came of good blood, and I shall say so to my dying day."

"It may be so, Mrs. Dickson; but the woman who left him here, if I remember right, did not look as if she had any good blood in her."

"Not likely, sir. She never came by him honestly, I am sure; I couldn't have believed she was his mother, not if she had sworn to it with her dying breath."

Mrs. Dickson's belief was not without influence upon the boy. When he was old enough to understand, she told him the circumstances of his having been found at the workhouse door, and of the discovery of the woman who had brought him there; and impressed upon him her own strong conviction that this was not his mother.

"I believe, Billy," she said over and over again, "that your parents were gentlefolk. Now, mind, it does not make one bit of difference to you, for it ain't likely you will ever hear of them. Still, please God, you may do so; and it is for you to bear it in mind, and to act so as, if you were to meet them, they need not be ashamed of you. You have got to earn your living just like all the other boys here, but you can act right and straight and honourable. Never tell a lie, Billy, not if it's to save yourself from being thrashed ever so much; always speak out manful and straight, no matter what comes of it. Don't never use no bad words, work hard at your books and try to improve yourself. Keep it always before you that you mean to be a good man and a gentleman some day; and, mark my words, you will do it."

"You're spoiling that child," her husband would say, "filling his head with your ridiculous notions."

"No, I am not spoiling him, Sam; I'm doing him good. It will help keep him straight, if he thinks that he is of gentle blood and must not shame it. Why, the matron said only yesterday she could not make him out, he was so different from other boys."

"More's the pity," grumbled the porter; "it mayn't do him harm now—I don't say as it does; but when he leaves the house he'll be above his work, and will be discontented, and never keep a place."

"No, he won't," his wife asserted stoutly, although in her heart she feared that there was some risk of her teaching having that effect. So far, however, there could be no doubt that her teaching had been of great advantage to the boy, and his steadiness and diligence soon attracted the attention of the schoolmaster. Schoolmasters are always ready to help pupils forward who promise to be a credit to them, and William Gale's teacher was no exception. He was not a learned man—very far from it. He had been a grocer who had failed in business, and having no other resource, had accepted the very small salary offered by the guardians of Ely workhouse, as the only means which presented itself of keeping out of one of the pauper wards of that institution. However, he was not a bad reader, and wrote an excellent hand. With books of geography and history before him he could make no blunders in his teaching, and although he might have been failing in method, he was not harsh or unkind; and the boys, therefore, learned as much with him as they might have done with a more learned master of a harsher disposition. He soon recognized not only William's anxiety to learn, but the fearlessness and spirit with which he was always ready to own a fault and to bear its punishment. On several occasions he brought the boy before the notice of the guardians when they came round the school; and when questions had to be asked before visitors, William Gale was always called up as the show boy. This prominence would have made him an object of dislike among the other lads of his own age, had it not been that William was a lively good-tempered boy; and if, as sometimes happened on these occasions, a sixpence or shilling was slipped into his hand by some visitor who was taken by his frank open face and bright intelligent manner, it was always shared among his school-fellows. At one of the examinations, the wife of a guardian, who was present with her husband, said, on returning home:

"It must be very dull for those poor boys: I will pack up some of the boys' books and send them. Now they have gone to college they will never want them again, and they would make quite a library for the workhouse boys. There must be twenty or thirty of them at least."

If ladies could but know what brightness they can infuse into the lives of lads placed like these in Ely workhouse, by a simple act of kindness of this kind, there would not be an institution in the kingdom without a well-supplied library.

The gift infused a new life into the school. Hitherto the world outside had been a sealed book to the boys. They knew of no world save that included within the walls of the house. Their geography told them of other lands and people, but these were mere names until now. Among the books were "Robinson Crusoe," "Midshipman Easy," "Peter Simple," three or four of Cooper's Indian tales, Dana's "Life before the Mast," and several of Kingston's and Ballantyne's books. These opened a wonderland of life and adventure to the boys. The schoolmaster used to give them out at twelve o'clock, and they were returned at two when school recommenced; and only such boys as obtained full marks for their lessons were allowed to have them. In this way, instead of the "library" being a cause of idleness, as some of the guardians predicted when they heard of its presentation, it was an incentive to work. Certainly its perusal filled the minds of most of the boys with an intense longing to go to sea, but as there is always a demand for apprentices for the Yarmouth and Lowestoft smacks, the guardians did not disapprove of this bent being given to their wishes; indeed, as no premium had to be paid with apprentices to smack-owners, while in most trades a premium is required, a preference was given to the sea by the guardians.

When William Gale reached the age of fifteen, and was brought before the board to choose the trade to which he would be apprenticed, he at once said that he would go to sea. There were applications from several smack-masters for apprentices, and he, with the five other boys brought up with him, were all of one opinion in the matter.

"Mind, lads," the chairman said, "the life of an apprentice on board a North Sea smack is a hard one. You will get a great many more kicks than halfpence. It will be no use grumbling when you have once made your choice. It is a rough hard life, none rougher or harder. When you have served your time it will be open to you either to continue as smacksmen or to ship as seamen in sea-going ships. Sailors who hail from the eastern fishing ports are always regarded as amongst the best of our seamen. Still it is a rough life and a dangerous one; the hardest life on shore is easy in comparison. There is time to change your minds before you sign; when you have done so it will be too late. Are you all determined?"

None of them wavered. Their signatures were attached to the indentures, and they were told that the porter would take them to Yarmouth on the following day. William Gale obtained leave to spend his last evening at the porter's lodge, and there he talked very seriously with Mrs. Dickson over his future prospects.

"I know," he said, "from Dana's book, that the life is a very rough one, but that will not matter. A sailor, when he has been four years at sea, can pass his examination as a mate, and I mean to work hard and pass as soon as I can. I don't care how much I am knocked about—that's nothing; there's a good chance of getting on in the end."

"You will meet a great many bad boys, Bill; don't you let them lead you into their ways."

"Don't be afraid of that," he answered, "I won't do anything I should be ashamed of afterwards. You have taught me better."

THE FOUNDLING

"I suppose the guardians gave you a Bible to-day; they always do when boys goes out."

Will nodded.

"Be sure you read it often, my boy. You read that and stick to it, and you won't go far wrong. You know what the parson said last Sunday, 'No one is strong in himself, but God gives strength.'"

"I remember," Will said. "I made up my mind then that I'd bear it in mind and act upon it when I could. I think the thought of God, and the thought that I may meet my parents, and they must not be ashamed of me, will help me to be honest and firm."

"I hope, Bill, you will come sometimes and see me when you are ashore."

"I shall be sure to do that when I can," he answered. "But, of course, I shall have no money at first; and it may be a long time before I can pay my railway fare here; but you may be sure I will come. Whoever may be my real mother, you are the only mother I ever knew, and no mother could have been kinder. When I grow to be a man, and go to sea in big ships, I will bring you all sorts of pretty things from abroad; and if ever you should want it, you may be sure that my wages will be quite as much yours as if I had been really your son!"

Sam Dickson gave a snort. It was very good of the boy, but he considered it his duty to snub him in order to counteract what he considered to be the pernicious counsels and treatment of his wife.

"Fine talk," he said, "fine talk. We shall see."

"You ought to be ashamed of yourself, Sam Dickson," his wife said wrathfully. "The boy means what he says, and I believe him. If anything was to happen to you, and that boy was growed-up, I believe he would come forward to lend me a helping hand, just as he says, as if he were my son. The gals is good gals, but gals in service have plenty to do with their wages, what with dress and one thing or another; we must never look for much help from them; but if Bill is doing well, and I ever come to want, I believe as his heart would be good to help a bit."

"Well," the porter said dryly, "there's time enough to see about it yet. I ain't dead, you ain't a pauper, and he ain't a man, not by a long way."

"Well, you needn't go to be short-tempered over it, Sam. The boy says as he'll be as good as a son to me if the time ever comes as how I may want it. There is no call for you to fly out as if he'd said as he'd poison me if he'd the chance. Anyhow, you'll write to me regular, won't you, Bill?"

"That I will," the boy said. "Every time I gets back to port I'll write; and you'll write sometimes, won't you, and tell me how you are, and how every one is, schoolmaster and all? They have all been very kind to me, and I have nothing to say against any of them."

The next morning William Gale laid aside forever his workhouse dress, and put on a suit of rough blue cloth, fitted for his future work. Then, bidding adieu to all his friends, he, with his five fellow-apprentices, started by rail under charge of Sam Dickson for Yarmouth. The journey itself was to them a most exciting event. They had in all their remembrance never been a mile from the workhouse, and the swift motion of the train, the changing scenery, the villages and stations, were a source of immense interest. As they neared Yarmouth their excitement increased, for now they were nearing the sea, of which they had read so much, but could form so little idea. They were disappointed, however, inasmuch as no glimpse was obtained of it as they crossed the flat country leading to the town; but, failing the sea, Yarmouth itself—the town which was henceforth to be their headquarters—was in the highest degree interesting. Presently the train reached the station, and then Sam Dickson, who had made many annual journeys to Yarmouth on the same errand, at once started off with them to the smack-owners who had written to the workhouse. These lived at Gorleston, a large village on the south side of the river. Walking down from the station, the boys caught a glimpse of the river, and were delighted at the sight of the long line of smacks and coasters lying by the wharves opposite.

THE FOUNDLING

Presently they left the road and made their way down to the river side. Their guardian had great difficulty in getting them along, so interested were they in the smacks lying alongside. Presently they stopped at a large wooden building, over which was the name of "James Eastrey."

"Here we are," Sam Dickson said. "Now stop quietly outside; I will call three of you up when I have spoken to Mr. Eastrey."

Presently the porter re-appeared at the door, and called three of the boys in. William Gale was one of the number, James Eastrey being the name of the owner to whom he had signed his indentures. A smell of tar pervaded the whole place. Nets, sails, and cordage were piled in great heaps in the store; iron bolts and buckets, iron heads for trawls, and ship's stores of all kinds.

Mr. Eastrey came out from a little wooden office.

"So," he said, "you are the three lads who are going to be my apprentices. Well, boys, it is a rough life; but, if you take the ups and downs as they come, it is not a bad one. I always tell my captains to be kind to the boys; but when they are at sea they do not always act as I wish them. When you are on shore, between the voyages, I give you eight shillings a week to keep yourselves, or I put you in the Smack-boys' Home and pay for you there. The last is the best place for you, but some boys prefer to go their own way. I suppose you are all anxious to go to sea—boys always are for the first time. One of my boats is going out to-morrow. You," he said, pointing to William Gale, "shall go in her. What is your name?"

"William Gale, sir."

"Very well, William Gale, then you shall be off first. The others will only have a day or two to wait. I can only send one new hand in each smack. The others will go to the Home till the smacks are ready. I will send a man with them at once. They can have a day to run about the town; I shall find plenty of work for them afterwards. You, Gale, will stop on the smack. I will take you on board in half-an-hour when I have finished my letter."

The three lads said good-bye to their comrades and to Sam Dickson. A sailor was called up and took two off to the Smack-boys' Home, and Will Gale sat down on a coil of rope to wait till his employer was ready to take him down to the craft to which he was henceforth to belong.

CHAPTER III
LIFE ON A SMACK

"NOW come along, Gale," Mr. Eastrey said at last, "the *Kitty* is close by."

Following his master, the lad went out from the store, and along the wharf, and presently stepped upon a smack on which several men and a boy were at work.

"Harvey," Mr. Eastrey said, "I have brought you a new lad. He will sail with you to-morrow. I have a very good account of him, and I think you will find him quick and ready."

"So as he's not up to tricks I shall do very well with him, I don't doubt," the skipper said; "but boys are an awful trouble the first voyage or two. However, I will do my best for him. Are you ready to begin work at once, young 'un? What is your name?"

"William Gale, and I am quite ready."

"Very well, Bill, chuck off your jacket then, and pass those bags along from the wharf."

The boy was soon hard at work. He was a little disappointed at finding that the skipper was in dress and manner in no way superior to the rest of the crew. The *Kitty* was a yawl of forty-five tons, deep in the water and broad in the beam. Her deck was dirty and at present in disorder, and she did not come up to the perfection of neatness and cleanliness which William Gale had read of in the pages of his favourite author. However, as he told himself, there must of course be a good deal of difference between a man-of-war, where the crew have little to do but to keep things neat and bright, and a fishing-smack. The work upon which he was at present engaged was the transferring of the provisions for the voyage from the quay to the hold. These consisted principally of barrels of salt meat and bags of biscuits, but there were a large tin of tea, a keg of sugar, a small barrel of molasses—or treacle—two or three sacks of

25

potatoes, pepper, and salt. Then there was a barrel of oil for the lamps, coils of spare rope of different sizes, and a number of articles of whose use William Gale had not the most remote idea.

After two hours' work the skipper looked at his watch. "Time to knock off work," he said, "and we've got pretty near everything on board. Now be sure you are all here by six in the morning. Tide will begin to run out at eight, and I don't want to lose any of it. Bill, you are to come home with me for the night."

It was but a hundred yards to the sailor's cottage, which stood on the edge of the sharp rise a short distance back from the river.

"Here, wife," he said as he entered, "I've got a new apprentice and I expect he's pretty hungry; I am, I can tell you, and I hope tea's ready. His name's Bill, and he's going to stop here to-night."

"Tea is quite ready, John, and there's plenty of mackerel. I thought you would not be getting them again for a spell. Do you like fish?" she asked the boy.

"I don't know, ma'am—I never tasted them."

"Bless me!" the woman cried in astonishment. "Never tasted fish! To think now!"

"I've been brought up in a workhouse," William said, colouring a little as he spoke, for he knew the prejudice against the House.

"Ah!" she said. "We have had a good many of that sort, and I can't say as I likes 'em for the most part. But you haven't got the look about you. You don't seem that sort."

"I hope I shall turn out none the worse for it," the boy said; "at any rate I'll do my best."

"And none can't do more," the good woman said briskly. "I like your looks, Bill, and you've a nice way of talking; well, we shall see."

In a few minutes tea was upon the table, and Will sat down with the skipper, his wife, and two daughters, girls of ten and twelve. The lad enjoyed his meal immensely, and did full justice to the fish.

"You will have plenty of them before you eat your next tea on shore. We pretty nigh live on them when we are on the fishing grounds."

"The same kind of fish as this?"

"No, mackerel are caught in small boats with a different sort of gear altogether. We get them sometimes in the trawl, not shoals of 'em, but single fish, which we call horse-mackerel."

After tea the skipper lit his pipe, and his wife, after clearing up, took some knitting and sat down and began to question the new apprentice.

"It's lucky for you, you found such a good friend," she said when he had finished his story. "That's how it is you are so different from other boys who have been apprenticed from the House. I should never have thought you had come from there. And she gave you good advice as to how you should go on, I'll be bound."

"Yes, ma'am," Will said, "and I hope I shall act up to it."

"I hope so, Bill; but you'll find it hard work to keep yourself as you should do among them boys. They are an awful lot, them smack-boys."

"Not worse nor other boys," her husband said.

"Not worse than might be looked for, John, but they are most of 'em pretty bad. The language they use make my blood run cold often. They seems to take a delight in it. The hands are bad enough, but the boys are dreadful. I suppose you don't swear, Will; they look too sharp after you in the House; but if you take my advice, boy, don't you ever get into the way of bad language. If you once begin, it will grow on you. There ain't no use in it, and it's awful to hear it."

"I will try not to do so," Will said firmly. "Mother—I always call her mother—told me how bad it was, and I said I'd try."

"That's right, Will, you stick to that, and make up your mind to keep from liquor, and you'll do."

"What's the use of talking that way?" the skipper said. "The boy's sure to do it. They all do."

"Not all, John; there's some teetotalers in the fleet."

"I won't say I'll never touch it," Will said, "for I don't know yet how I may want it; they say when you are cold and wet through at sea it is really good; but I have made up my mind I'll never drink for the sake of drinking. Half the men—ay, nineteen out of twenty in the House—would never have been there, I've heard mother say, if it hadn't been for drink; and I told her she need never fear I'd take to that."

"If you can do without it on shore, you can do without it at sea," the skipper said. "I take it when I'm on shore, but there's not a drop goes out on the *Kitty*. Some boats carries spirits, some don't. We don't. The old man puts chocolate on board instead, and of a wet night a drink of hot chocolate's worth all the rum in the world. As for giving it up altogether, I see no call for it. There are men who can't touch liquor but they must go on till they get drunk. That sort ought to swear off and never touch it at all. It's worse than poison to some. But for a man who is content with his pint of beer with his dinner, and a glass of grog of an evening, I see no harm in it."

"Except that the money might be better spent, John."

"It might be, or it might not. In my case the saving would be of no account. The beer costs threepence, and the rum as much more. That's sixpence a day. I'm only at home ten days once every two months, so it come to thirty shillings a year, and I enjoy my dinner and my evening pipe all the better for them."

"The thing is this, Will, you don't know, when you begin, whether you are going to be one of the men who, like my John, is content with his pint of beer and his glass of grog, or whether you will be one of them as can't touch liquor without wanting to make beasts of themselves. Therefore the safest plan is, don't touch it at all—leastways till you've served your time. The others may laugh at you at first, but they won't like you any the worse for it."

"Thank you, ma'am. I will make up my mind to that—not to touch liquor till I am out of my apprenticeship. After that, I can see for myself."

"That's right, lad. When you come back from your first trip, you can join the lodge if you like. I and my girls are members."

"Thank you, ma'am," Will said; "but I won't take any pledge. I have said I will not do it, and I don't see any use in taking an oath about it. If I am so weak as to break my word, I should break my oath. I don't know why I shouldn't be able to trust myself to do as I am willed, in that way as in any other. If I'd a craving after it, it might be different; but I never have tasted it, and don't want to taste it; so I don't see why I can't trust myself."

"Yes, I think as how you can trust yourself, Will," the woman said, looking at him; "and I've noticed often that it isn't them who say most as do most. Now, I daresay, you are sleepy. There's my boy's bed for you. He is fourth hand in one of the smacks at sea."

The next morning Will was out of bed the instant he was called, excited at the thought that he was going really to sea. The skipper's wife had tea made and the table laid.

"Here," she said, "are some oilskin suits my boy has given up. They will suit you well enough for size; and although they are not as good as they were, they will keep out a good deal of water yet. You will get half-a-crown a week while you are at sea, so by the time you get back you will have enough to buy yourself a fresh suit."

Half an hour later Will was at work getting two spare sails and the last of the stores on board.

"Now, Bill, come below," the skipper said. "I will show you your bunk."

The cabin was larger than Will had expected. It was about twelve feet square, and lofty enough for a tall man to stand upright. By the side of the companion stairs was a grate, on which a kettle was boiling; and this, as he afterwards learned, was a fixture, except when cooking was going on, and the men could have tea whenever they chose. Round three sides of the cabin extended lockers, the tops forming seats. Above, were what looked like cupboards running round the sides, but the skipper pushed open a sliding door and showed a bed-place.

"That is your bunk," he said. "You see there are two at the end, and one each side, above, and as many under them—eight bunks in all. You will have to help Jack, that is the other boy, in cooking, and make yourself useful generally in the day. The crew are divided into two watches, but you will not have much to do on deck. If the night is clear you can sleep, except when the trawl is being got up. Of a thick or stormy night you will keep your watch. Now, as the other lad is more handy on deck than you are, you can take charge here. All you have to do is to see that the kettle is kept boiling. You can come on deck and lend a hand if wanted, but you must come down sometimes and see the fire is all right."

After inspecting the contents of the kettle, and seeing that it was full, Will climbed up the steep ladder again, and was soon working away coiling down the ropes with the other lad, while the crew hoisted sails and got the boat under weigh.

"Are there only two hands under the captain?" he asked the other boy.

"There are two others," the boy said. "They will come on board after we get out of the river, and you'll see they will be just as drunk as they can stand."

"What, drunk at this time in the morning?"

"Yes, they got drunk last night, and as they won't have fairly slept it off, they will be beginning again this morning. The old man will look them up and get them off."

"Who is the old man?"

"Old Eastrey, of course, stupid. I wish they were all on board. There's a fine breeze, and I hate wasting four or five hours off the bar waiting for the hands to come off."

"I wonder the old Man stands it," Will said.

"He can't help it," the other answered. "Scarce a smack goes out of Yarmouth without half the hands being drunk when she starts. They don't get much chance afterwards, you see, and they sleep it off by night, so it don't make any odds. Our skipper is always sober, and that's more than many of them are. I have gone out when me and the other boy were the only two sober on board."

"But isn't it very dangerous?"

"Dangerous! No," the boy said; "one of them is sure to be sober enough to manage to stand at the helm, and though I've bumped pretty heavy on the sands sometimes, we generally strike the channel. There is no fear of anything else. We never start if a gale is blowing, and the smacks are safe in anything but a gale. They are too deep to capsize, and at sea there's no more drinking."

The smack dropped down the river, and stood off and on near its entrance. Will was delighted with the bright sea, dotted with ships and fishing-craft. The sun was shining, and there was just enough wind to send the smack along briskly through the water without raising any waves sufficiently high to give her a perceptible motion. At eight o'clock the captain went on shore in the boat with a man to look after the absent sailors, leaving only one hand and the two boys on board. At ten the boat was again seen coming out.

"One, two, three, four," the boy said, "he has got them both. Now we shall be off."

The boat was soon alongside, the two drunken men were helped on board, and at once went below to sleep themselves sober. Then the boat was hoisted on board, and the second hand taking the helm, the *Kitty* started fairly on her way.

"Now," the captain said, "let us get her a little tidy."

It took some hours' work before the deck was washed, the ropes coiled down, and everything ship-shape. By the time all was done, the low coast of Norfolk had sunk below the horizon, and the smack was far out at sea. There was more motion now, but the wind was still light. The skipper was pleased with the earnestness and alacrity which the new apprentice showed.

"Now, Jack," he said to the other boy, "take Will below with you and show him how to make tea."

The process of tea-making on board a smack is not a difficult one to master; the sole operation consisting in putting a few more spoonfuls of tea into the kettle boiling over the fire when it begins to get low, and filling up with fresh water. But simple as the thing was, William Gale did not learn it on that occasion. He had been feeling somewhat shaky even while on deck, and the heat of the cabin and the smell of some grease which Jack had just put in the frying-pan preparatory to cooking some fish brought off from shore, completed the effect of the rising sea. Until next morning he was not in a condition to care even had the tea remained unmade to the end of time. He did not go below, but lay under the shelter of a tarpaulin on deck. In the morning the skipper roused him up.

"Now, lad, just take off your coat and shirt; here is a bucket of water, put your head in that, and give yourself a good sluice, and then come down and have a cup of tea and a bit of biscuit, and you will find yourself all right again."

Will followed the instructions and found himself wonderfully better.

"Now, lad, lend a hand in tidying up on deck; there is nothing like work for keeping off sea-sickness. Jack shall cook for to-day."

The boy set to work with a will, and felt so refreshed that by one o'clock he was able to go below and take his share of the dinner. At present, while on their way to the fishing-grounds, their meals were taken at the same time as on shore; but once at work, there were only two meals a day: of these the first was taken when the fishing was over, the fish cleaned, picked, weighed, and packed—the hour varying between nine and eleven. The second meal was taken before the trawl was lowered at six or seven o'clock in the evening.

After five days' sailing the smack arrived off the fishing-ground, but another two days were spent in finding the fleet, as the fishing-grounds extend over a distance of some hundreds of miles. When they came up with it, William Gale was astonished at the vast number of boats that dotted the sea.

In the Yarmouth fleet there are between four and five hundred vessels, and, were it not that the most perfect order and discipline reign, the number of accidents which would occur, from so many boats fishing close to each other at night, would be terrible. The fleet is commanded by one of the most experienced skippers, who is termed the admiral. His authority is absolute: he leads the fleet to the grounds he selects for fishing, and, by signals by day and rockets by night, issues his orders: when the nets are to be lowered down and drawn up, the course which is to be steered, and the tack on which they are to stand.

LIFE ON A SMACK

The fishing is entirely done at night. The trawls are let down about dusk, and the fleet, attached to these moving anchors, forge slowly ahead and to leeward until daybreak. Then the trawls are got in and the fleet sail in a body to the spot where the admiral decides that fishing shall be continued in the evening. At 10 o'clock at night the trawls are hauled in and the nets emptied. All hands are called up for this operation; when it is concluded the trawl is again lowered and the fish cleaned and packed, by the light of a torch formed of rope dipped in tar. The watch, who have hitherto been on deck, turn in, and the others remain on deck until morning, when the nets are again hauled in.

There is not, indeed, much for the watch to do, as the smack needs no steering, and the attention of the men on deck is directed chiefly to see that no other smack drifts down upon them. Should there appear any danger of this, a flare is lit to warn the other smacksmen. The trawl rope is slacked out or hauled in as the case may require, and generally volleys of strong language pass between the respective crews. The trawl beam is a heavy pole, some 30 or 35 feet long; at each end are fitted strong iron hoops of about three feet in diameter. These keep the pole from touching the ground and keep open the mouth of the net, one side of which is attached to the pole while the other drags along the bottom.

The net resembles in shape a long deep purse, and has various pockets and other contrivances by which, when a fish has once entered its mouth, it is prevented from returning.

The trawl rope, which is from 40 to 80 yards in length, according to the depth of water, is hauled in by means of a winch, and its great weight taxes the united strength of the crew to get it level with the bulwark. When it is up, the net is hauled on board, the small end is opened, and the fish tumble on to the deck; they are then separated and packed in trunks, as the wooden cases in which they are sent to market are called. Soles fetch by far the highest price, and fortunate are the crew who get a good haul of this fish, for the men work upon shares, an account being kept of all the sales made during the fishing trip. The owner deducts the cost of the provisions and stores which have been put on board and takes one or more shares for the vessel. Each man has one share, the skipper and mate receiving rather a larger proportion than the others; thus the men have a lively interest in each haul, and great is the satisfaction when the net comes up well filled, and there is seen to be a good proportion of soles among the contents.

The coarse fish, as they are called, include brill, haddock, hake, ling, whiting, and many others. Turbot are also caught.

In each haul there would probably be a vast number of objects which would delight the heart of a naturalist. Dog-fish, too, are sometimes taken, as are conger-eels and horse-mackerel; stones and oysters too come up in the nets, and the latter are the *bêtes-noirs* of the fishing. Sometimes, when the fleet gets over a bed of oysters, a score of nets will be lost in a single night; for when the bag becomes full of oysters, its weight is so great that the utmost power of the fishermen's exertions on the winch is insufficient to lift it from the bottom, and there is nothing to be done but to cut the rope and abandon trawl and net. Upon these occasions the language applied to the admiral is scarcely of a kind for polite ears.

The food of the crews, when once upon the fishing-ground, consists almost wholly of fish. With the exception of soles, each man may select any fish he fancies from the glistening mass upon the deck, and the amount which each consumed at a meal at first astonished William Gale, accustomed as he was to meagre workhouse rations. He soon however, found himself able to keep up with the rest, but the operation of frying seemed sometimes interminable, so many times had the pan to be filled and emptied.

Hard biscuits were eaten with the fish, and the whole washed down with copious draughts of tea without milk. Two or three times a week the men would, as a change, have a meal of salt meat, and on Sundays a duff or pudding of flour and currants was made.

A few days after joining the fleet, the weather changed; the sky became gloomy and threatening. The wind blew hard and a heavy sea got up. Will found that keeping watch at night, which was pleasant enough on a fine star-light night, was a very different thing now. It was no joke looking ahead with the wind blowing fiercely and showers of spray dashing into the eyes; and yet a vigilant watch must be kept, for, if the rockets which ordered the hauling of the trawl were not noticed, some other smack moving rapidly when released from the drag of its net might at any moment come into collision with the smack.

Still more important was it to notice upon which side the trawl was to be lowered, after being emptied, and upon which tack the vessel was to proceed. For a mistake in this respect would be certain to bring the smack across another, in which case the trawl-ropes would become entangled, involving, in a heavy sea, the certain loss of one or the other. Many of the smacks carry dogs, and it is found that these become even better watchers than their masters; for they can be relied on to call the attention of the watch, by sharp barking, to the letting up of the rocket, however distant.

A rocket may seem to be an easy thing to see, but in a large fleet the sternmost smacks may be three or four miles away from the leaders, and in a dark thick night it is exceedingly difficult to make out even a rocket at that distance.

The wind increased to a gale; the trawls were up now, and the fleet lay-to. It may be explained that this operation is performed by bringing a ship nearly into the eye of the wind, and then hauling the foresail across, and belaying the sheet. The aft sail or mizen is then hauled tight, and the tiller lashed amidships. As the fore-sail pays the vessel off from the wind, the after sail brings her up again, and she is thus kept nearly head to sea, and the crew go below and wait till the storm abates.

CHAPTER IV
RUN DOWN

WILLIAM GALE was astonished at the fury of the tempest and the wildness of the sea. Although at the workhouse he had often heard the wind roaring round the walls, there was nothing to show him the force that was being exerted. There were but few trees in the neighbourhood, and William had hardly ever been without the walls except in fine summer weather. He was, therefore, almost bewildered by the force and fury of the gale, and by the noise as it shrieked through the rigging and howled across the water. The occasional flapping of the sails and the rattling of the heavy blocks added to the din, and it seemed to him that the *Kitty*, which, like all fishing-smacks, was very deep in the water, must be completely engulfed by the great waves which swept down upon her.

Several times, indeed, he was obliged to leap down into the cabin to avoid being swept away by the great masses of green water which, pouring over her bows, swept aft, carrying away all before them.

But the Yarmouth smacks are admirable sea boats, and, pounded and belaboured as she was, the *Kitty* always shook off the water that smothered her, and rose again for the next wave. In twenty-four hours the gale abated, the scattered fleet were assembled, each flying its flag, and it was found that three were missing, having either foundered, or been driven away from their consorts.

With the return of fine weather, the fishing began again, and William thoroughly enjoyed his life. The skipper was kind and forbearing; he neither ill-treated the boys himself nor permitted any of the crew to do so, and everything went on regularly and comfortably. There were a few books on board, and of an evening after the trawl was lowered, and before the watch below turned into their bunks, William, who was the best reader on board, would be asked to read aloud for an hour. Sometimes there were songs, and as the *Kitty* was fortunate, and her taking of fish good, the men were all cheerful and good-tempered.

Once every three or four days the collecting steamer came in sight; then there was a general race in the fleet to put the trunks of fish on board her. Each did his best to be in good time, for when the catch had been heavy the steamer was sometimes unable to take the whole of it, in which case the portion left behind would be wholly spoilt before the arrival of another steamer.

The whole of the fleet, therefore, ran down towards the steamer as soon as she was seen; the heavy boats were tossed overboard, and the trunks lowered into them, and two hands jumped in to row them to the steamer. Round her a swarm of boats would soon be collected, each striving to get alongside to deliver the fish.

In calm weather the scene was simply amusing, but when the sea was high it was exciting and even dangerous; indeed, in the course of a year more lives are lost in the process of taking the fish from the smack to the steamer than in vessels foundered by gales.

Sometimes the fleet will be joined by Dutch trading smacks, who exchange fresh bread and meat, tobacco, and spirits, for fish. This traffic is the cause alike of loss to the owners by the fish thus parted with, and of injury to the men by the use of spirits. Fortunately the skipper of the *Kitty*, although not averse to the use of spirits on shore, was a strict man at sea, and saw that no one took more than a single glass of grog of an evening.

Over and over again Will congratulated himself that he had the good fortune to make his first voyage under such a skipper, for he shuddered at the stories Jack told him of the cruelties and barbarities with which apprentices are treated on board some of the smacks. Although, however, there is no doubt many brutal skippers hail from Yarmouth, the fleet from that town bears a good reputation in comparison with that of Grimsby, where the number of apprentices returned as drowned each year is appalling.

FOR NAME AND FAME

One night when the wind was high and the fleet trawling lower down the North Sea than usual, Will, who was on deck, was startled at seeing a great ship bearing down upon the smack. He gave a shout of terror and warning, which was joined in by the crew on deck. One ran for the hatchet to cut the trawl, and thus give steerage-way to the smack. It was too late; in another moment the great ship bore down upon them with a crash, and the *Kitty* sunk beneath the waves.

The bowsprit of the vessel projected across the deck, just at the point where William Gale was standing; and in a moment he caught at the bob-stay, and quickly hauled himself on to the bowsprit. Climbing along this he was soon on board. Two or three sailors were leaning over the bows, peering into the darkness. They had not seen the smack, until too late to avoid it; and the collision which had proved fatal to the *Kitty* had scarcely been felt by the ship. Will was at once taken to the captain, who spoke English; the boy implored him to turn back, but the captain shook his head.

"It would be useless," he said; "the sea is heavy, and in these long boots"—and he pointed to the seaboots up to the thigh which all fishermen wear—"no man could swim for two minutes, nor would there be a chance, if they could, of our finding them on so dark a night. I am very sorry, my lad, but it cannot be helped; it would take half-an-hour to bring the ship about and go back to the spot where the smack sunk, and we might not get within half-a-mile of it. You know that as well as I do."

Will had been long enough at sea to recognize the truth of what the captain said. As he was led forward he burst into tears at the thought of the loss of his kind friend the captain, and the rest of his mates. The sailor who accompanied him patted him on the back, and spoke cheeringly to him in a foreign language, and he was soon between decks with the crew. Several of these could speak English, and Will found that he was on board a Dutch merchantman, bound with troops for Java. The wind got up, and in the morning it was blowing a heavy gale from the east, and the vessel with reefed topsails was running for the straits between Dover and Calais at twelve knots an hour. After breakfast the captain sent for William.

"I am sorry, for your sake, that the state of the weather will prevent our communicating with any ship we may meet. But I promise you that if the gale breaks before we are fairly out from the channel, I will heave to and put you on board a homeward-bound ship."

Such a chance did not occur. For four or five days the gale continued with great severity, and before it ceased, the ship was well down the coast of Spain on her way south. When the captain saw that there was but small chance of his being able to tranship his involuntary passenger, he said to him:

"Look you, my lad. I fear that you will have to make the voyage with me, for we shall not touch at any port until we arrive at our destination. If you like, I will ship you as a hand on board as from the day of the collision. A hand, more or less, will make no difference to the owners, and the money will be useful to you when you leave the ship. Of course, you can return in her if you think fit; but it is likely enough that when we reach Java, we may be sent up to China for a homeward cargo, in which case I will procure you a passage in the first ship sailing for your home."

Will gladly accepted the offer. He was, however, by no means penniless; for upon the morning after his coming on board, the Dutch officers and passengers, hearing what had happened in the night, made a collection among themselves, and presented the boy with a purse containing fifteen pounds.

It was a long voyage, but not an unpleasant one for William; his duties were not very heavy—he had far less to do than had been the case on board the smack. A month on board the *Kitty* had done much towards making a sailor of him, for there are no better seamen in the world than the Yarmouth smacksmen. Going aloft was at first a trial, but he soon learned his duties; and being a strong and active lad, he was quickly able to do efficient work, and speedily gained the good opinion of the Dutch sailors by his good temper and anxiety to please.

FOR NAME AND FAME

They ran some little distance to the south of the Cape before shaping an easterly course, to avoid the bad weather so frequently met with there; and, beyond encountering two or three gales of no exceptional severity, nothing occurred to break the monotony of the voyage, until the coasts of Java were in sight. Upon their arrival in port they found no vessel there about to sail for Europe, and the captain's expectation was fulfilled, as he found orders awaiting him to proceed to China when he had landed the troops and discharged his cargo. Will determined to continue his voyage in her to that place.

Among the ship-boys on board was one between whom and Will Gale a great friendship had been struck up. He was a year or two Will's senior, but scarcely so tall; upon the other hand he was nearly twice his girth. He talked but little, but his broad face was ever alight with a good-tempered grin. He spoke a few words of English, and Will had, when first picked up, been given specially into his charge. Will's superior activity and energy astonished the Dutch lad, whose movements were slow and heavy; while Will, on his part, was surprised at the strength which Hans could exert when he chose.

One day when Will had been plaguing him, and ventured within his reach, the lad had seized and held him out at arm's-length, shaking him as a dog would a rat, till he shouted for mercy.

The two were soon able to get on in a queer mixture of Dutch and English, and when words failed, they would eke out their words by gestures. The vessel had sailed but a few days from Java, when there were signs of a change of weather. Hitherto it had been lovely; now a slight mist seemed to hang over the sea, while overhead it was clear and bright. There was not a breath of wind, and the sails hung listlessly against the masts. Will, who was leaning against the bulwarks chatting to Hans, observed the captain, after looking round at the horizon, go into his cabin; he reappeared in a minute, and spoke to the officer, who immediately shouted an order for all hands to "shorten sail."

"What is that for?" Will said, wonderingly. "There is not a breath of wind."

RUN DOWN

"I egzpect captain haz looked at glass," Hans said; "find him fall; I egzpect we going to have ztorm; very bad ztorms in dese zeas."

Will ran aloft with the sailors, and in ten minutes every inch of canvas, with the exception of a small stay-sail, was stript from the ship; still there was not a breath of wind. The sea was as smooth as glass, save for a slight ground-swell. Although the mist did not seem to thicken, a strange darkness hung over the sky, as if high up a thick fog had gathered. Darker and darker it grew, until there was little more than a pale twilight. The men stood in twos and threes, watching the sea and sky, and talking together in low tones.

"I don't like this, Hans," Will said. "There is something awful about it."

"We have big ztorm," Hans replied, "zyclone they call him."

Scarcely had Hans spoken when the sky above seemed to open with a crash, a roar of thunder louder than ten thousand pieces of artillery pealed around them, while at the same moment a blinding flash of lightning struck the mainmast, shivering it into splinters, and prostrating to the deck five seamen who were standing round its foot. As if a signal had been given by the peal of thunder, a tremendous blast of wind smote the vessel, and, stripped though she was of sails, heaved her over almost to the gunwale.

For a moment the crew were paralysed by the suddenness of the catastrophe, stunned by the terrible thunder, and blinded by the lightning. None seemed capable of moving. Will had instinctively covered his eyes with his hands—it seemed to him for a moment that his sight was gone. Then the voice of the captain was heard shouting:

"Helm hard up; out axes and cut away the wreck at once!"

Those who were least stupefied by the shock sprang in a dazed and stupid way to obey the order. Will drew out his knife, and, feeling rather than seeing what he was doing, tried to assist in cutting away the shrouds of the fallen mast—it had gone a few feet above the deck. Presently he seemed, as he worked, to recover from his stupor, and the power of sight came back to him. Then he saw that the vessel, taken on the broadside by the gale, was lying far over, with several feet of her lee deck under water.

So furious was the wind that he could not show his head over the weather bulwark. The sea was still smooth, as if the water was flattened by the force of the wind. The stay-sail had been blown into ribbons. In order to get the ship's head off the wind, the head of the jib was hauled up a few feet. It happened to be a new and strong one; and, although it bellied and lashed as if it would tear itself into fragments, it still stood. Again the captain gave an order, and the sail was hauled up to its full height. Still further the vessel heaved over, and Will expected every moment that she would capsize; then gradually her head paid off, and slowly she righted and flew before the gale.

"That was a near squeak," Will said.

"What is zqueak?" Hans shouted.

"I mean a close shave," Will replied.

Hans' blue eyes opened wider than usual.

"A zhave!" he repeated. "What are you talking about zhaving?"

"No, no," Will said, laughing, "I mean a narrow escape of being capsized."

Hans nodded. There was no time for talk, for orders were given for getting preventor stays on the foremast. The jib, having done its work, had been hauled down the instant the ship payed off, and a small storm-sail set in its place. The men now had time to attend to those who had been struck by lightning: three of them were found to be dead, but the other two, who were stunned and senseless, still lived, and were lifted and carried below.

Serious as the disaster had been, Will felt that the stroke of lightning had saved the ship. The pressure of the wind upon two masts and hull had nearly sufficed to capsize her; had the main-mast stood, he felt that she must have gone over. The sea got up in a very few minutes, but being now only in light ballast, the vessel rose easily over them. Four men were at the helm, for the waves soon became so high that the ship yawed dangerously on her course.

RUN DOWN

The gale seemed to increase rather than diminish in fury, and the sea, instead of following in regular waves, became a perfect chaos of tossing water such as Will had never before seen. He understood it, however, when half an hour after the outburst of the gale, he heard one of the men, who had just been relieved at the wheel, say that in that time the ship had already run twice round the compass. She was therefore in the very centre of the cyclone, and the strangely tossed sea was accounted for. The motion of the ship was extraordinary; sometimes she was thrown on one side, sometimes on the other. Mountains of water seemed to rise suddenly beside her, and tumbled in great green masses over the bulwarks. So wild and sudden were her movements, that even the oldest sailors were unable to keep their feet, and all clung on to shrouds or belaying-pins.

Will and Hans had lashed themselves by the slack of a rope to the bulwarks close to each other, and there clung on; sometimes half drowned by the waves which poured in above them, sometimes torn from their feet by the rush of green water as the ship plunged head-foremost into a wave or shipped one over her poop.

Presently there was a crash that sounded even above the fury of the gale—the fore topmast had gone at the cap. The axes were again called into requisition, for a blow from the floating spar would have instantly stove in the side. While engaged upon this, the captain called two of the men with axes aft. These were set to work to chop through the shrouds of the mizen, and in a minute later the mast snapped asunder on the level of the deck and went over the side with a crash, carrying away several feet of the bulwark.

This act was necessitated by the loss of the foretopmast, as the pressure of the wind upon the mizen would have brought her head up and laid her broadside to the gale.

The motion of the vessel was now considerably easier, and there was no longer any difficulty in keeping her dead before the wind. She was now describing much larger circles in her course, showing that she was farther removed from the centre of the cyclone.

After five or six hours, the extreme violence of the wind somewhat abated, and it seemed to settle down into a heavy gale.

For two days the vessel ran before it. She had made a good deal of water from the opening of the seams by straining and the pumps were kept going. They were, they found, able to prevent the water from gaining upon them, and all felt that they should weather the tempest, provided that they were not dashed upon any of the islands in which this portion of the ocean abounds.

The crew had had no regular meals since the gale began, for the caboose had been broken up and washed overboard soon after the commencement of the storm, and they had been obliged to be content with biscuits; there was little to be done on deck, and the watch over, they passed their time in their bunks.

In the afternoon of the third day of the tempest, the cry was raised of "Breakers ahead!" Will, with his comrades of the watch below, sprang from their berths and hurried on deck.

Far ahead, as the vessel lifted on the waves, could be seen a gleam of white water. In anticipation of such a danger, a small spar had been erected upon the stump of the mizen and steadied with strong stays. Sail was now hoisted upon this and an effort was made to bring the vessel's head to wind. Watching for a favourable moment between the passage of the heavy seas, the helm was put down and slowly her head came up into the wind. Under such sail the captain had no hope of being able to reach out in the teeth of the gale; but he hoped to be able to claw off the shore until clear of the land which lay to leeward of him.

That hope soon vanished. One of the mates was sent to the top of the foremast, and descended with news that as far as could be seen the line of breakers stretched away, both on her beam and quarter. As the minutes went by, the anxious crew could see but too clearly that the ship was drifting down upon the land, and that she must inevitably be wrecked upon it.

The outlines of the shore could now be seen—a forest of tossing trees, behind which high land could be made out through the driving clouds. Orders were now given to prepare to anchor; but all knew that the chances were slight indeed. The water is, for the most part, deep close alongside the islands of the Eastern

Archipelago; and even were the holding-ground good, hemp and iron would hardly hold the vessel head to the gale and tremendous sea.

When within a quarter of a mile of the breakers the man with the lead proclaimed a depth of ten fathoms. This was better than they had expected. The jib was lowered and her head brought dead to wind. The captain shouted "Cut," and in an instant the stoppers were severed and two heavy anchors dropt into the sea. One had a heavy chain-cable, the other hemp, and these were allowed to run out to the bits. The vessel brought up with less shock than could be expected. A wave or two passed under her and still her cable held.

A gleam of hope began to reign, when a mountainous sea was seen approaching; higher and higher it rose, and just as it reached the ship it curled over and crashed down upon her deck. The cables snapped like pack-thread, and a cry of despair arose from the crew. The captain was calm and collected, and shouted orders for the jib to be again hoisted and the helm put up, so as to run her head-first on to the shore.

As they neared the line of breakers they could see heads of jagged rocks rising among them, while beyond, a belt of smooth water, a quarter of a mile wide, extended to the land. The ship's head was directed towards a point where no rocks appeared above the surface. Everyone held their breath, and, clinging to the bulwarks, awaited the shock.

The vessel lifted on a great wave just as she came to the line of broken water, and, as she settled down, struck with a tremendous crash.

So great was the shock that she broke in two amidships as if she had been made of paper, the portion aft going instantly to pieces, and at once the sea around was covered with fragments of wreck, bales, boxes, and casks. Another great sea followed, filling the now open ship, forcing up the deck, and sweeping everything before it.

William Gale and Hans had gone as far forward as possible. "Come out to the end of the bowsprit," Will said to Hans, and the two lads crawled out together and sat on the end of the spar.

The sea beneath them was white as milk with the foam which poured over the reef, but Will thought that they were beyond the rocks. Every sea which struck the wreck added to the disaster, until a larger one than usual struck it and broke it into fragments. The lads clung to the spar as it fell; it sank deep in the water, but they retained their hold until it came to the surface, and Will looked round. They were safely beyond the edge of the reef. The sea was still rough and broken, but it was quiet compared to that beyond the reef. He saw that the foremast was floating near, and to it several were clinging.

In a quarter of an hour the spar floated to land, the boys felt the bottom with their feet, and soon scrambled ashore. A few minutes later the foremast also drifted up, and several men clinging to fragments of the wreck were also cast ashore. In all, eleven men, including the first mate, were saved.

CHAPTER V
THE CASTAWAYS

AFTER waiting on the shore until all hope that any more of their shipmates survived was at an end, the party, by the mate's orders, detached a sail from a yard that had drifted ashore, and carried it well into the wood, where they were sheltered to some extent from the force of the gale. A stout pole was then cut and lashed between two trees; the sail was thrown over this and pegged down at both sides. A fire was lit with some difficulty; then a quantity of ferns and branches of trees were cut: these made a soft and elastic bed, and the whole party slept heavily until the morning. Then they went back to the shore; it was littered thickly with fragments of wreck, casks, boxes, and other articles: here too were nearly a score of the corpses of their shipmates. The first duty was to dig a long shallow trench in the sand, beyond high water mark, and in this the bodies of their drowned comrades were laid.

The storm was now breaking, glimpses of blue sky were visible overhead, and the wind had greatly abated. The sea upon the reef was, however, as high as ever. Setting to work, they hauled a large number of boxes and bales beyond the reach of the waves. One of the casks contained biscuits, and, knocking in the head, they helped themselves to its contents, and sat down to talk over their position.

"I am not sure," the mate said, "that our poor comrades there"—and he nodded towards the grave—"have not the best of it. The inhabitants of most of these islands are bloodthirsty pirates, who if they find us will either cut our throats at once or keep us as slaves. Our only hope is that we may not be discovered until we have time to build a boat in which to sail away to Singapore or back to Java. Had we been wrecked further south, things would have been more hopeful, for the Papuans are friendly and inoffensive people. These islands here are inhabited by Malays, the most bloodthirsty pirates in the world. However, we must hope that we may not be found before we have finished a boat. My chest is among those which have been washed up, and there are a few tools in it. I always had a fancy for carpentry, and it's hard if in a fortnight we cannot make some sort of craft which will carry us. Indeed, if we content ourselves with a strong framework covered with canvas we may be ready in four or five days."

The men set cheerfully to work under his directions. In his chest was a hatchet, saw, and chisels. With these, young trees of flexible wood were cut down and split; a keel was laid 25 feet in length; cross-pieces 12 feet long were pegged to this by trenails—nails formed of tough and hard wood. The cross-pieces were then bent upwards and fastened to the strips which were to form the gunwale. Strengthening pieces were placed along at distances of 7 or 8 inches apart, and firmly lashed. When the whole was finished, after three days' labour, the framework of a boat 25 feet long, 3 feet deep, and 7 feet in beam stood upon the beach. A barrel of oil had been thrown ashore, and with this the mate intended thoroughly to soak the canvas with which the frame was to be covered. The boat would, he calculated, carry the whole of the men with an ample store of food and water for the voyage.

Upon the morning of the fourth day, as on their way to work they emerged from the wood upon the open beach, the mate gave a low cry and pointed along the shore. There, between the reef and the island, was a large Malay *prahu*. The party instantly fell back among the trees. The Malays were apparently cruising along the reef to see if the late storm had thrown up the wreckage, which might be useful to them; and a loud shout proclaimed their satisfaction as they saw the shore strewn with the remains of the Dutch ship. The *prahu* was rowed to the shore, and fifty or sixty Malays sprang from the bows on to the sand.

Scarcely had they done so when a shout from one of them called the attention of the others to the framework of the boat. There was a minute's loud and excited chatter among them. Then they dashed forward to the wood, the deep footsteps in the sand showing plainly enough the direction from which the builders of the boat had come and gone. The latter, as the Malay boat neared the shore, had retired further into the wood, but from the screen of leaves they were able to see what was going on. As they saw the Malays rush in an excited and yelling throng towards the wood, the little party took to their heels.

"Scatter!" the mate said. "Together, they are sure to overtake us; singly, we may escape."

"Let us keep together, Hans," Will said, as they dashed along through the wild jungle. Torn by thorns, often thrown down by projecting roots and low creepers, they kept on, their pace at times quickening as shouts and screams told them that some of their comrades had fallen into the hands of the Malays. Presently they came upon the little stream which flowed into the sea close to where they had been cast ashore.

"Let us follow this up," Will said; "they can track us through the forest, but the water will set them off our scent."

For a quarter of a mile they followed the course of the stream, stopping breathlessly many times as they heard voices in the wood not far off. Presently Will pointed to a tree rising from a clump of bushes close to the bank.

"Let us get through those bushes," he said. "Be careful, Hans, not to break a twig as you go; we can climb that tree; there are plants with stems like cords winding round it. The top is so thick and bushy that I don't think they can see us there."

Very carefully they parted the bushes that overhung the stream, and entered the thicket; then they made their way with great difficulty to the foot of the tree. It was a very large one, with a trunk fully 15 feet in diameter, rising some forty feet without a branch, then a number of great arms grew out at right angles; these were covered thickly with parasitic vegetation. Round the trunk, like a snake embracing its victim, a great climber had wound itself; its main stem was as thick as a man's arm, and there were dozens of smaller cord-like climbers. Thus the lads had no difficulty in climbing to the point where the branches grew out. Above these was a mass of foliage completely covered by the climbers, whose drooping sprays and clusters gave the tree the appearance of a solid mass of verdure. The boys continued to climb until they were nearly at the top of the tree.

"There!" Will said, wiping away the perspiration which streamed from his face. "If they do not track us through the bushes to the very foot of this tree, I defy them to find us."

For some hours the wood was alive with noises; the Malays were evidently beating every foot of it, and were determined that none of their victims should escape. Several times parties of men came up the stream searching the banks on both sides; but, happily, even their sharp eyes did not detect the spot where the boys had entered the bushes, and gradually the noises ceased, and at night a great glare by the seashore told the lads that their enemies had gathered again there, and were continuing by fire-light the work of breaking open and examining the treasures which the sea had cast up for them.

"What do you zay, Will? Zhall we get down and go furder into wood, or zhall we wait here?"

"I think anyhow we had better wait till to-morrow night," Will answered. "They may search again tomorrow, and might come upon our tracks. If they don't find us they may suppose that they have caught us all, or that we have escaped right into the interior. If they find no traces of us they will likely enough set sail before night."

There was no difficulty in finding a place in which they could sleep, for the cord-like climbers from bough to bough formed natural cradles, in which they lay as securely as if in a hammock on board a ship. In the morning they were woke at daybreak by the cries of the many birds which throng the forests of the Eastern Archipelago. No one approached them during the day, and they doubted not that the Malays were all hard at work on the shore.

That night there was no reflection of a fire on the beach. In the morning they descended from their perches and made their way carefully, and as noiselessly as possible, through the wood, to a point upon the shore a mile distant from the point where they landed. Going to the edge of the trees, they were enabled to take a view along the shore. It was deserted; the Malay *prahu* was gone.

Confident that none of their enemies would have remained behind, they walked boldly along the shore to the spot where the Malays had landed. Every box and barrel had been broken open, and the contents carried away; planks and beams had been split asunder to obtain the copper bolts and fastenings. The framework of the boat had been destroyed, and every portion of canvas and rope carried away. The lads sat down on the shore.

"What shall we do next, Hans?"

Hans shook his head.

"Perhaps some of the others may have got away and may join us here to-day or to-morrow. If any are alive they would be certain to come back here when they thought the Malays had left."

Hans grunted an assent.

"Anyhow, the first thing to do," Will went on, "is to gather up the pieces of biscuits; they have wasted lots in breaking open the barrels, and I am famishing."

Hans rose with alacrity, and they soon were at work collecting pieces of biscuits.

"Let us gather up all the pieces carefully; there are a good lot altogether, and we may want them badly before we have done."

In half an hour they had collected about 30 pounds of biscuits, and having gone to the stream and taken a drink, they made for the spot where their tent had stood. As they expected, they found the canvas was gone. They set to work with their knives, and cutting a number of boughs, erected a shelter sufficient to shield them from the night air. All day they hoped, but in vain, that some of their comrades would return, and listened eagerly to every sound in the forest, but no call or footstep met their ears. They had no means of lighting a fire, the first having been lit by the mate, who, being a smoker, had had a small tin-box of matches in his pocket, This had fitted closely and kept out the water.

"What had we better do if no one comes back?" Will said, as they sat in their little hut.

"Build anoder boat," Hans answered.

"But how are we to do that, Hans? We might make the framework, but we have no canvas to cover it with; besides, even if we had, I have no idea of the direction of Singapore, and I doubt if we could find our way back to Java."

Hans had no further suggestion to offer.

"I suppose we could live in the forest for some time," Will said. "I read a book called *Robinson Crusoe*, and a sailor there lived on a desert island for years; but then he had a gun and all sorts of things. There are plenty of birds, but even if we could make bows and arrows, I suppose we should be months before we could shoot straight enough to hit them."

Several days passed; the lads found plenty of fruit; but the season was advancing, and Will said one day to Hans:

"What on earth are we to do when the fruit and biscuits are all finished?"

Wandering in the woods they found the bodies of the whole of their companions. All were headless, the Malays having carried off these coveted trophies. They did not attempt to bury the bodies, for in such a climate decomposition sets in rapidly, and swarms of insects complete the work. In the grass near the hut they found one treasure—the mate's axe—which had evidently fallen from his belt in his flight, and had been overlooked by the Malays.

"I tell you what, Hans," Will said one day, "fruit is getting scarcer and scarcer, and there are not more than five or six pounds of biscuits left. I vote that we make through the forest into the interior of the island; there must be some villages scattered about. If we enter one boldly they may not kill us. I don't know whether they have any respect for the laws of hospitality, as some savages have; but even if they did kill us, it's better than being starved to death here. It's a chance anyhow. What do you say, Hans?"

"I don't zay noding," Hans answered. "I don't have no obinion at all; if you dink zat is ze best plan, let us do it."

So saying, Hans collected the biscuit, tied it up in his handkerchief, and was ready to start at once.

Will and Hans in search of a shelter.

"There is no hurry, Hans," Will said, laughing; "still, if we are to make a start, we may as well go at once."

Turning their backs upon the sea, they struck into the wood. They had never before gone farther than a mile from the shore. After an hour's walking they found that the character of the forest was changing: the ground rose rapidly, the thick tangled undergrowth disappeared, and they were able to walk briskly forward under the shade of the large trees. The hill became steeper and steeper as they advanced, and Will knew that they were ascending the hill that they had seen from the ship when she was coming towards the shore. Three hours after leaving the coast they were upon its top. The ground was rocky here, and in some places bare of trees. Inland they saw hill rising behind hill, and knew that the island must be a large one.

"Look, Hans, there is smoke curling up at the foot of that hill over there; don't you see it? It is very faint, but it is certainly smoke. There must be a house there, and most likely a village. Come on, we shall get there before the sun sets. I don't think it can be more than a mile and a half away."

Hans as usual assented, and in about half an hour they arrived at a Malay village.

The aspect was curious, each hut being built in a tree. At the point where the lower branches started, a platform was made; the tree above this was cut down and on the platform the hut was erected, access being obtained to it by a ladder. Several of the inhabitants were walking about; these, upon seeing the lads, uttered cries of warning, and instantly flying to the ladders, which were constructed of light bamboo, climbed to the huts and raised the ladders after them. Then at every door men appeared with bent bows and pointed arrows threatening the invaders. Will had cut a green bough, and this he waved as a token of peace, while Hans threw up his hands to show that he was unarmed. Then they bowed several times almost to the ground, held out their arms with outstretched hands, and finally sat down upon the ground.

THE CASTAWAYS

The Malays apparently understood that their visitors came in peace. They held a long conversation among themselves, and at last the ladder of one of the huts, which appeared larger and better finished than the others, was lowered, and four men descended. One of these carried a kriss in his hand, his bow was slung behind his back; the others kept their bows bent in readiness for instant action.

The chief was a tall and well-built man of about forty years of age. He, like his followers, was dressed only in a loin-cloth; he had copper bracelets round his wrists. As he approached, the lads rose and bowed deeply; then Will held out to him the axe, and placing it in his hand, motioned to him that it was a present.

The chief looked pleased at the gift, placed his hands on Will's shoulder and nodded, and performed the same gesture to Hans; then he led them towards his hut and motioned to them to sit down at the foot of the tree.

Curious faces were watching from every hut, and as soon as it was seen that peace was established, the ladders were lowered and a swarm of men, women, and children soon surrounded the visitors. At the chief's order, a woman approached them, bringing a dish of food. This was composed, the boys found, principally of birds cut up and stewed with some sort of vegetable. The dish was by no means bad, and after living for nearly a fortnight upon biscuit and fruit, they much enjoyed it.

Presently women brought bundles of dried fern and spread them at the foot of the tree, and, soon after it was dark, the boys lay down upon them. It was long, however, before they went to sleep; for the din and chatter in the village continued until far into the night. The lads guessed that the reason and manner of their coming was warmly debated, and judged by their reception that the prevailing opinions were favourable, and that the visit from the two white men was considered to be a fortunate omen.

The next day they were again amply supplied with food, and were constantly surrounded by a little group of women and children, to whom their white skins appeared a source of constant wonder. Their movements were entirely unchecked, and they were evidently considered in the light of guests rather than prisoners.

The next night the village retired to rest early. The boys sat talking together for a long time, and then lay down to sleep. Presently Will thought that he heard a noise, and, looking up, saw in the moonlight a number of savages stealthily approaching. They carried with them ladders, and intended, he had no doubt, to surprise the sleeping villagers. They were already close at hand. Will shook Hans, who had already gone off to sleep, and pointed out to him the advancing foes. These were already in the village, and separating, fixed a ladder against each of the huts. So far the boys, who lay in the shadow of the hut, had not been noticed. The Malays, who belonged to a hostile village, began to climb the ladders, when the lads, grasping the heavy sticks which they always carried, and springing to their feet with loud shouts, ran to the ladders before the Malays could recover from their astonishment at the approach of the white-faced men rushing upon them.

Half a dozen of the ladders were upset, the men who had mounted them coming heavily to the ground. Some of these as they rose at once took to their heels; others, drawing their krisses, rushed at their assailants. But the lads were no longer alone. At the first shout, the doors of the huts had opened, and the inhabitants rushed out with their arms; the remaining ladders were instantly overthrown, and a shower of arrows poured upon their assailants.

Will and Hans knocked down the foremost of their assailants, and the whole body, foiled in their attempted surprise, discomfited at the appearance of the strange white-faced men, and exposed to the arrows of the defenders, at once darted away, several of their number having already fallen under the shafts from above. With exulting shouts, the warriors of the village poured down their ladders from the huts and took up the pursuit, and soon no one remained in the village save the white lads and the women and children.

Towards morning the warriors returned, several of them bringing with them gory heads, showing that their pursuit had not been in vain.

The village was now the scene of great rejoicings; huge fires were lighted, and a feast held in honour of the victory. The chief solemnly placed the white men one on each side of him, and made them a speech, in which, by his bowing and placing his hand on their heads, they judged he was thanking them for having preserved their village from massacre. Indeed, it was clear, from the respectful manner of all towards them, that they were regarded in the light of genii who had come specially to protect the village from the assaults of its enemies.

After the feast was over, the chief, after a consultation with the rest, pointed to a tree close to that in which his own hut was situated. The whole village set to work; ladders were fixed against it, and the men, ascending, hacked away with krisses and stone hatchets at the trunk. Hans, seeing their object, made signs to the chief to lend him his axe, and, ascending to the tree, set to work with it, doing in five minutes more work than the whole of the natives employed could have accomplished in an hour. After working for some time, he handed the axe to one of the natives, who continued the work.

The tree was not a large one, the trunk at this point being about 18 inches in diameter. Half an hour's work sufficed to cut it through, and the upper part of the tree fell with a crash. In the meantime the women had brought in from the forest a quantity of bamboos, and with these the men set to work and speedily formed a platform. Upon this a hut was erected, the roof and sides being covered with palm leaves laid closely together, forming a roof impervious to rain. Two large bundles of fern for beds were then taken up, and the chief, ascending solemnly, invited the boys to come up and take possession.

A woman was told off to prepare food for them and attend to their wants, and by nightfall the lads found themselves in a comfortable abode of their own. Pulling up the ladder after the manner of the natives, they sat down to chat over their altered prospects. They were now clearly regarded as adopted into the village community, and need have no further fear as to their personal security or means of living.

"For the time, we are safe," Will said; "but as I don't want to turn Malay and live all my life with no other amusement than keeping my own head on and hunting for those of the enemies of the village, we must think of making our escape somehow, though, at present, I own I don't see how."

CHAPTER VI
THE ATTACK ON THE VILLAGE

A DAY or two later a Malay ran at full speed into the village, and said a few words which caused a perfect hubbub of excitement. The men shouted, the women screamed, and, running up the ladders to their tree abodes, began gathering together the various articles of value in their eyes. The chief came up to the boys, and by signs intimated that a large number of hostile natives belonging to several villages were advancing to attack them, and that they must fly into the interior.

This was very unwelcome news for the lads. Once removed farther from the sea, the tribe might not improbably take up their abode there, as they would fear to return to the neighbourhood of their enemies. This would be fatal to any chance of the lads being taken off by a passing ship.

After a few words together they determined to oppose the movement. Will, in a loud voice and with threatening gestures, intimated that he disapproved of the plan, and that he and his companion would assist them in defending their village. The Malays paused in their preparations. Their faith in their white visitors was very great, and after a few minutes' talk among themselves they intimated to the boys that they would obey their orders. Will at once signed to a few men to stand as guards round the village to warn them of the approaching enemy, and then set the whole of the rest of the population to work cutting sharp-pointed poles, boughs, and thorny bushes. With these a circle was made around the trees upon which the village was built.

Fortunately the hostile Malays had halted in the forest two or three miles away, intending to make their attack by night; and as the news of their coming had arrived at noon, the villagers had, before they ceased work late in the evening, erected a formidable hedge round the village. Some of the women had been set to work manufacturing a number of torches, similar to those used by them for lighting their dwellings, but much larger. They were formed of the stringy bark of a tree dipped in the resinous juice obtained from another. Will had one of these fastened to each of the trees nearest to the hedge. They were fixed to the trunks on the outside, so that their flame would throw a light on the whole circle beyond the hedge, while within all would be shadow and darkness.

It was very late before all preparations were completed. Will then placed a few men as outposts some hundred yards in the forest, in the direction from which the enemy were likely to approach. They were ordered to give the alarm the moment they heard a noise, and were then to run in and enter the circle by a small gap, which had been left in the abbatis for the purpose. Many of the men then took their posts, with their bows and arrows, in the trees near the hedge. The others remained on the ground ready to rush to any point assailed.

For several hours no sounds, save the calls of the night birds and the occasional distant howls of beasts of prey, were heard in the forest; and it was not until within an hour of morning—the hour generally selected by Malays for an attack, as men sleep at that time the heaviest—that a loud yell at one of the outposts told that the enemy were close at hand.

Two or three minutes later the scouts ran in, and the gap through which they had entered was at once filled up with bushes, which had been piled close at hand for the purpose. Aware that their approach was discovered, the enemy abandoned all further concealment, and advanced with wild yells, intending to strike terror into the defenders of the village. As they advanced, the torches were all lighted, and as the assailants came within their circle of light, a shower of arrows from the Malays on the ground and in the trees above was poured into them.

Yells and screams told that the volley had been a successful one; but, discharging their arrows in turn, the Malays, with demoniac yells, rushed against the village. The advance, however, was arrested suddenly when they arrived at the abbatis. From behind its shelter so deadly a rain of arrows was poured in that they soon shrank back, and bounded away beyond the circle of light, while taunting shouts rose from its defenders.

For a time they contented themselves by distant shouting, and then with a wild yell charged forward again. Several dropped from the fire of arrows from those in the trees and behind the abbatis; but, discharging their arrows in return, the assailants kept on until they again reached the impediment. Here they strove furiously to break through, hacking with their krisses and endeavouring to pull up the stakes with their hands; but the defenders in the shade behind sent their arrows so fast and thick that the assailants again shrank back and darted away to shelter.

Throughout the night there was no renewal of the attack, and in the morning not a foe was visible. Two or three scouts went out to reconnoitre, but no sooner did they enter the forest than one of them was shot down and the rest sent flying back.

"I believe the scoundrels are going to try to starve us out," Will said. "Let us speak to the chief and ask how much provisions they have got."

After much pantomime Will succeeded in conveying his meaning to the chief, and the latter at once ordered all the inhabitants to produce their stock of food. This was unexpectedly large, and Will thought that there was sufficient for a fortnight's consumption. He now made signs of drinking, but the reply to this was disheartening in the extreme. A few gourds full of water were brought forward, and two or three of the close-woven baskets in which water is often carried in this country: there was, in fact, scarce enough to last the defenders for a day.

The stream from which the village drew its supply of water was about a couple of hundred yards away; consequently the villagers fetched up their water as they needed it, and no one thought of keeping a store. Will looked in dismay at the smallness of the supply.

"If they really intend to starve us out, Hans, we are done for. No doubt they reckon on our water falling short. They would know that it was not likely that there would be a supply here."

The natives were not slow to recognize the weak point of their defence. One or two of the men, taking water baskets, were about to go to the stream, but Will made signs to the chief that they must not do this.

The only hope was that the enemies would draw off; but if they saw that water was already short, they would be encouraged to continue to beleaguer the place. Will was unable to explain his reasons to the chief, but the latter, seeing how great was the advantage that they had already gained by following the counsel of their white visitors in the matter of the hedge, acquiesced at once in their wishes.

Will then ascended to one of the huts, and carefully reconnoitred the whole ground. There was, he saw, at the end farthest from the stream, a slight dip in the land extending into the forest. Beckoning the chief to join him, he made signs that at night the warriors should issue silently from the village at this point, and make noiselessly through the wood; they would then take a wide circuit till they came upon the stream, and would then, working up it, fall upon the enemy in the rear.

The chief was dubious, but Will made an imperative gesture, and the chief in a humble manner agreed to do as he was ordered. The day passed slowly, and before nightfall the supply of water was entirely finished. Once or twice scouts had gone out to see if the enemy were still round the village, but returned each time with the news that they were there.

The last time, just before nightfall, Will directed two or three of them to take water-buckets, and to go in the direction of the stream; signing to them, however, to return the moment they saw signs of the enemy. They were soon back; and, as Will had expected, the sight of the water-buckets showed the enemy that the garrison of the village were badly supplied in that respect, and taunting shouts arose from the woods asking them why they did not go down to drink.

THE ATTACK ON THE VILLAGE

Will felt certain that the Malays would now draw the greater part of their number down to the side of the stream, and that there would therefore be the more chance of the garrison making their way out at the other end of the village.

Three hours after it was dark the chief mustered all his men; they were about five-and-forty in all. Will signed that each should take with him a water-basket or large gourd, so that, in case they failed in defeating the enemy and breaking up the blockade, they might at least be able to bring a supply of water into the village. Will then, with much difficulty, explained to the chief that the old men, boys, and women remaining in the village were, the moment they heard the sound of the attack upon the enemy's rear, to shout and yell their loudest, and to shoot arrows in the direction of the enemy.

A few sticks had already been pulled up at the point of the hedge through which Will intended to make a sally, and the band now passed noiselessly out. The chief himself led the way, the white boys following behind him. Lying upon their stomachs, they crawled noiselessly along down the little depression, and in ten minutes were well in the wood without having met with an enemy, although they had several times heard voices among the trees near them. They now rose to their feet, and, making a wide detour, came down, after a quarter of an hour's walk, upon the stream. Here the gourds and baskets were filled; and then, keeping along by the waterside, they continued their march.

Presently they saw a number of fires, round which many Malays were sitting. They crept noiselessly up until within a few yards, and then with a yell burst upon the enemy. Numbers were cut down at once, and the rest, appalled by this attack on their rear, and supposing that the inhabitants of some other village must have arrived to the assistance of those they were besieging, at once fled in all directions. Those remaining in the village had seconded the attack by wild shouts, so loud and continuous that their besiegers had no reason to suppose that their number had been weakened.

63

For a few minutes the pursuit was kept up; then the chief recalled his followers with a shout. The water-baskets, many of which had been thrown down in the attack, were refilled, and the party made their way up to the village, where they were received with shouts of triumph.

The panic of the Malays had been in no slight degree caused by the appearance of the two boys, who had purposely stripped to the waist, and had shouted at the top of their voices, as, waving the krisses which they had borrowed, they fell upon the foe.

The idea that white devils were leagued with the enemies against them had excited the superstitious fear of the Malays to the utmost, and when in the morning scouts again sallied from the village, they found that the enemy had entirely gone, the fact that they had not even returned to carry off the effects which had been abandoned in the first panic showing that they had continued their flight, without stopping, to their distant villages.

The chief, like an able politician, took advantage of the impression which his white visitors had created, and the same day sent off messengers to the villages which had combined in the attack against them, saying that the white men, his guests, were very angry; and that unless peace was made and a solemn promise given that there should be no renewal of the late attempts, they were going to lay a dreadful spell upon the villages. Women and children would be seized by disease and the right arms of the warriors wither up.

This terrible threat carried consternation into the Malay villages. The women burst into prolonged wailings, and the bravest of the men trembled. The messenger said that the white men had consented to abstain from using their magical powers until the following day, and that the only chance to propitiate them was for deputations from the villages to come in early the next morning with promises of peace and offerings for the offended white men.

It was not for some time afterwards that the lads learned enough of the language to understand what had been done, but they guessed (from the exultation of the chief and the signs which he made that their late enemies would shortly come in, in an attitude of humiliation) that he had in some way succeeded in establishing a scare among them.

On the following morning deputations consisting of six warriors, and women bearing trays with fruit, birds, and other offerings, arrived at the village. The men were unarmed. At their approach the chief made signs to the boys to take a seat at the foot of the principal tree; and then, accompanied by his leading warriors, led the deputation with much ceremony before them. The women placed their trays at their feet, and the men addressed them in long speeches and with many signs of submission. The boys played their part well. As soon as they saw what was required of them, they signified with an air of much dignity that they accepted the offerings, and then went through the ceremony of shaking hands solemnly with each of the warriors. Then they made a speech, in which with much gesticulation they signified to the visitors that a terrible fate would befall them should they again venture to meddle with the village.

Much awed and impressed, the Malays withdrew. The boys made a selection from the baskets of fruit for their own eating, and then signified to the chief that he should divide the rest among the inhabitants of the village. When this was done, the boys ascended to their tree and passed the day there quietly, the villagers indulging in feasting, singing, and rejoicing over their victory.

"The worst of all this is," Will said to Hans, "that the more they reverence us, and the more useful they find us, the more anxious they will be to keep us always with them. However, there is one comfort; we are safe as long as we choose to remain here, and that is more than we could have hoped for when we first landed from the wreck. It is curious that the Malays, who have no hesitation in attacking English ships and murdering their crews, have yet a sort of superstitious dread of us. But I suppose it is something the same way as it was in England in the days of the persecution of old women as witches: they believed that, if left to themselves, they could cast deadly spells, and yet they had no hesitation in putting them to death. I suppose that it is something of the same feeling here."

CHAPTER VII
THE FIGHT WITH THE PRAHUS

VERY frequently, in the days that followed, William Gale and his friend Hans talked over the possibility of effecting an escape, but the difficulties appeared almost invincible. The various villages which, so far as the boys could understand, were scattered at some distance apart, had little dealings with each other, and indeed were frequently engaged in feuds. The particular people with whom they lived had nothing whatever to do with the sea. They used—at least so the boys understood by their signs—to fish at one time; but they had been robbed of their boats and maltreated by some of the cruising tribes who lived in villages on the coast or on creeks and rivers.

The possibility of escape seemed small indeed. To escape they must get on board a ship, and to do this they must first go out to sea, and this could only be done in a boat of their own or in one of the piratical *prahus*. The latter course could not be thought of, for the coast pirates were bloodthirsty in the extreme; and even could they change their residence to one of the sea-side villages, and gain the friendship of the inhabitants, they would be no nearer to their end. For as these go out to attack and not to trade with European ships, there would be no chance of escaping in that way.

Upon the other hand, they might build a boat of their own; but they considered it improbable that the Malays would allow them to depart, for they evidently regarded their presence as a prodigy, and revered them as having miraculously arrived at the moment when a great danger threatened the village; but, even should they be allowed to build a boat and depart, they knew not whither to go. They knew nothing of navigation, and were ignorant of the geography of the Archipelago, and the chances of their striking upon the one or two spots where alone they could land with safety were so small that it would be madness to undertake the voyage.

For six months they lived quietly in the Malay village. The people instructed them in the use of their blow-guns, in which they are wonderfully skilful, being able to bring down a bird sitting on a lofty bough of a tree with almost an unerring accuracy. They also taught them to shoot with the bow and arrow, and they found that the natives used the roots of various kinds of plants for food. The time did not pass unpleasantly, and had they known that it would last but a few months only, they would have enjoyed it much.

At last, after much deliberation, they determined that they would, as a first step towards escape, construct a little boat under pretence of wanting to fish. Accordingly, one day when out with the chief and two or three of his men in the direction of the sea, they pointed there and signified that they wished to go there, for they had picked up a good many Malay words. The chief shook his head, but they insisted in so authoritative a manner that he gave way and followed them.

When they reached the shore they made signs that they wanted to construct a boat. Again the chief shook his head vehemently, and enforced his meaning by pointing along shore and going through the action first of rowing, then of fighting, intimating that they would certainly be killed, if they ventured out, by the fierce coast tribes. The boys nodded to show that they understood what he wished to say; but pointing to the water a few yards from shore, went through the action of fishing; then, burdening themselves with imaginary fish, they pointed to the village and showed that they would supply it with food.

The Malays talked for some time among themselves. They had so vast a respect for the white men that they did not like to thwart their wishes. The thought too of a supply of fish, of which they had been long deprived owing to their feuds with some of the coast villages, also operated strongly in favour of their yielding an assent; and at last the chief made signs that he agreed, and, pointing to the village, intimated that assistance should be given in building a boat.

The next day, accordingly, ten or twelve men came down to the shore with them. A tree was felled, the ends were pointed, and the whole formed roughly into the shape of a canoe; fires were lighted on the top, and by dint of flame and axe a hollow was dug out. The operation lasted three days, the men having brought provisions with them so as to avoid making the journey—two and a half hours long—to and from the village each day. The boat when finished was but a rough construction, and would have excited the mockery of any of the coast villagers, as they are expert boat-builders; still, it was amply sufficient for the purpose for which it was intended, namely, for fishing inside the line of reefs.

It was heavy and paddled slowly, and the lads had a strong suspicion that the Malays had purposely made it more clumsy and unseaworthy than need be in order that they should have no temptation to attempt a distant journey in it. There was no difficulty about lines, the Malays being skilled in making string and ropes from the fibres of trees. The hooks were more difficult; but, upon searching very carefully along the shore, the lads found some fragments of one of the ship boats, and in these were several copper nails, which, hammered and bent, would serve their purpose well. The lines were ready on the day the canoe was finished, and as soon as she was launched the chief and one of the other Malays and the boys took their seats in her.

The natives paddled her out nearly to the edge of the reef; four lines, baited with pieces of raw birds' flesh, were thrown overboard. A few minutes passed rather anxiously for the lads, who were most desirous that the fishing should be successful so as to afford them an excuse for frequently pursuing it. Then there was a bite, and Hans, who held the line, found that it taxed his strength to haul in the fish which tugged and strained upon it. When it was got into the boat it proved to be some fourteen pounds in weight.

THE FIGHT WITH THE PRAHUS

By this time two of the other baits had been taken, and in less than an hour they had caught upwards of thirty fish, most of them of considerable size.

The natives were delighted; and, paddling to shore, the burden was distributed among the whole party, with the exception of the chief and the two whites. Before starting, a young tree was cut down and chopped into lengths of a few feet each, and on these rollers the canoe was hauled high up the beach. Then the party set out for the village, where their arrival with so large a supply of food occasioned great rejoicing.

After this the boys went down regularly every day to fish. At first three or four of the natives always accompanied them, under pretence of carrying back the fish, but really, as they thought, to keep a watch over them. To lessen their hosts' suspicions, sometimes one or other stayed in the village. As time went on the suspicion of the Malays abated. The number of the guard was lessened, and finally, as the men disliked so long a tramp, some of the boys were told off to accompany the white men and assist in bringing back their fish. They were in the habit of starting soon after daybreak, and of not returning till late in the evening, accounting for their long absence by pointing to the sun.

The fishing was always performed immediately they reached the coast. When they had caught as many as they and the boys could carry, these were placed in a large covered basket, which was sunk in the water close to the shore to keep the fish in good condition until they started. Then they would paddle about within the reef; or, during the extreme heat of the day, lie in the boat, shaded by bunches of palm leaves.

The Malay boys, who were set on shore after the fishing, were left alone, and amused themselves by bathing, or passed the time asleep under the trees.

After the first day or two it had struck the boys that it was dangerous to leave the canoe high on the sand, as it would be observed even at a distance by a passing *prahu*. Consequently, a deep trench had been dug from the sea, far enough up to allow the canoe, when floating in it, to lie below the level of the beach. Before leaving her she was each day roughly covered with sea-weed, and might therefore escape observation by any craft passing at a short distance from the shore.

In their expeditions along the reef, the boys discovered a passage through it. It was of about double the width of a ship, and of amply sufficient depth to allow a vessel of any size to cross. At all other points, for a distance of a mile or two either way, which was the extent of their excursions, the reef came very near to the surface, its jagged points for the most part showing above it.

Several months passed, and still no sail which promised a hope of deliverance had shown over the surface of the sea. Scarce a day passed without their seeing the Malay *prahus* passing up and down the coast, but these always kept some distance out, and caused no uneasiness to the fishermen. They had during this time completed the hollowing out of the boat, until her sides were extremely thin, and she was so light that she could be paddled at a high rate of speed.

They were both now expert with the paddle, and felt that if in a light wind a vessel should be seen off the coast, they would be enabled to row out and reach her. It might be, they knew, months or even years before such a ship could be seen. Still, as there were many vessels trading among the islands, at any moment an occurrence might arise.

One afternoon they had been dozing under their leafy shade, when Will, who first awoke, sat up and uttered a cry. Almost abreast of them, and but a quarter of a mile outside the reef, was a large brig. The wind was light, and with every stitch of canvas set, she was making but slow progress through the water.

Hans leaped up, echoed the cry, and, seizing their paddles, they rowed with all their strength away to the opening through the reef, passed through, and headed for the ship. They now saw what they had not at first observed. At a distance of some three miles astern were five large *prahus* with their sails set, and the banks of oars rising and falling rapidly. The brig was chased by the pirates. The boys rested on their paddles for a moment.

THE FIGHT WITH THE PRAHUS

"They are more than a match for her, I am afraid," Will said. "What do you say, Hans, shall we go on or not?"

Hans made no reply. He was never quick at coming to a decision.

"We had better go," Will went on. "We can see whether they mean to fight or not."

The boys were naked to the waist, for the thorns of the forest had long since torn in pieces the shirts which they had on when they landed from the wreck, and their skins were bronzed to a deep copper colour. Still they differed in hue from the natives of the island, and the men on board the brig regarded them with some surprise as they approached it.

"Throw us a rope!" Will shouted, as they neared her.

There was a cry of surprise from the crew at being addressed in English, but a rope was thrown and the boys soon sprang on board. They saw at once that the ship was an English one.

"Hallo! Where do you spring from?" asked the captain.

"We were shipwrecked here ten months ago," Will said, "and have been living with the natives."

"At any other time I should have been glad to see you," the captain said; "but just at present, if you will take my advice, you will get into your canoe and row on shore again. As you see," and he pointed to the *prahus*, "we are chased; and although I mean to fight to the last, for there is no mercy to be expected from these bloodthirsty scoundrels, I fear the chances are small."

Will looked round and saw that the six cannons which the brig carried—for vessels trading in the Eastern Archipelago are always armed—had already been loosened, ready for action, and that a group of men were at work mounting a long gun which had just been raised from the hold. Knowing the number of men that the *prahus* carried, Will felt that the chance of a successful resistance was slight.

There were about eighteen men on deck, a number larger than the brig would carry in other seas, but necessary in so dangerous a trading ground as this. The *prahus*, however, would each carry from eighty to one hundred men, and these attacking at once from opposite sides would be likely to bear down all opposition. Suddenly an idea occurred to him.

"Look, sir, there is a passage through the reef there, with plenty of water and width enough for your ship. I can take her through. There is no other passage for some distance. If you take her inside and lay her across the channel the *prahus* can only attack on one side, and you can place all your guns and strength there."

The captain at once saw the advantage of this scheme.

"Capital!" he exclaimed. "Take the helm at once, my lad. Ease off the sheets, men."

They were now nearly opposite the entrance, and the light wind was blowing towards the shore. The captain ordered all hands to reduce sail, only keeping on enough to give the vessel steerageway. Two boats were lowered and an anchor and cable passed into each, and, as the brig passed through the opening, the rest of the sail was lowered.

The boats rowed to the reef, one on either side. The anchors were firmly fixed into the rock, and one being taken from the head and the other from the stern, the crews set to work at the capstan and speedily had the vessel safely moored, broadside on, across the entrance to the reef.

The Malay boats were now about a mile astern. They had ceased rowing when they saw the vessel headed for the land, supposing that the captain was about to run on shore. When, to their astonishment they saw her pass the reef with safety, they again set to at their work. The guns were now all brought over to the side facing the entrance and were loaded to the muzzle with bullets. A number of shots belonging to the long gun were placed by the bulwarks in readiness to hurl down into the *prahus* should they get alongside.

The sailors, though determined to fight till the last, had, when the boys came on board, been making their preparations with the silence of despair. They were now in high spirits, for they felt that they could beat off any attempt of the enemy to attack them. When the Malays were abreast of the ship, they ceased rowing and drew close together, and evidently held a consultation.

The brig at once opened fire with her long gun, and the first shot hulled one of the *prahus* close to the water's edge.

"That's right, Tom," the captain said, "stick to the same craft: if you can sink her there is one the less."

Several more shots were fired, with such effect that the Malays were observed jumping overboard in great numbers and swimming towards the other boats, their own being in a sinking condition. The other four *prahus* at once turned their heads towards shore, and rowed with full speed towards the ship.

They knew that the entrance, of whose existence they had been previously unaware, was an exceedingly narrow one; and, as they neared the shore, could see by the line of breaking surf that it could at most be wide enough for one to pass at a time. Accordingly, one drew ahead, and discharging the cannon which it carried in its bow, rowed at full speed for the entrance, another following so close behind that its bow almost touched the stern.

"Train the guns to bear on the centre of the channel," the captain said; "let the three bow-guns take the first boat, the other three the second. Do you, Tom, work away at the two behind."

The *prahus* came along at a great rate, the sweeps churning up the water into foam. The leading boat dashed through the channel, the sweeps grating on the rocks on either side; her bow was but two yards distant from the side of the ship when the captain gave the word. The three cannon poured their contents into her, sweeping her crowded decks and tearing out her bottom. Great as was her speed, she sank below the water just as her bow touched the side of the ship. Ten seconds later the command was again given, and a broadside as destructive was poured into the second boat. The damage done was somewhat less, and her bow reached the side of the ship.

A dozen Malays sprang on board as their boat sank under their feet; but the sailors were ready, and with musket, pistol, and cutlass fell upon them, and either cut down or drove them overboard. The sea around was covered with swimmers, but the ship was too high out of the water for them to attempt to board her, and the Malays at once struck out for the shore, the sailors keeping up the musketry fire upon them until out of range. The other two boats had not followed: the mate had plumped a shot from the long gun full into the bow of the first; and, seeing the destruction which had fallen upon their leaders, both turned their heads and made for sea, the mate continuing his fire until they were out of range, one shot carrying away the greater part of the oars on one side of the boat previously struck.

When at a distance of upwards of a mile, they ceased rowing and for some time lay close together. The men of the injured boat were observed to be stopping the yawning hole in her bows a few inches above the water level; the other started off at full speed up the coast. It was now evening, and there was scarcely a breath of wind. The men crowded round the lads and thanked them warmly for having been the means of saving them from destruction.

"I am afraid you are not out of danger yet," Will said, as the captain shook him by the hand. "No doubt that boat has gone off with the news, and before morning you will have half a dozen fresh enemies coming down inside the reef to attack you."

"If we had but a breath of wind we might do," the captain said.

"I fear you will have none before morning; then it generally blows fresh for two or three hours. I don't know how far it is to the village, which is the headquarters of the pirates. As far as I could make out from the Malays with whom we have been living, it is about six hours' walking, but the boats will row twice as fast as a man would walk through the forest. In that case you may be attacked at two or three o'clock in the morning, and you won't get the breeze till after sunrise."

"Are there any other channels through the reef?" the captain asked.

"I do not know," Will replied. "We have never explored it very far either way; but as I should think from the action of the Malays that they did not know of this, they might not know of any other, did it exist."

"Then," the captain said, "I will warp the brig out through the channel again, and anchor her, stem and stern, across it outside. They will find it as hard to attack us there as they did before. Then, when the breeze comes, we will slip our cable and run for it. She is a fast sailer, and can, I think, get away from the pirates even with their sails and oars; besides, by shifting the long gun and two of the others to her stern we can give it them so hot that even if they are the fastest we may sicken them."

"I do not know, sir," Will said. "They would be likely to hang about you until the breeze drops, and then to attack you on all sides at once. If we could but keep them from coming through the channel in pursuit we should be safe."

"Ah! But how on earth are we to do that?" the captain asked.

William Gale was silent for a minute or two.

"Have you plenty of powder on board the ship, sir?"

"Plenty—we use it for barter."

"It seems to me,"—Will went on—"that if, before sailing, you could sink a couple of barrels of powder in the channel, with a fuse to explode them a few minutes after we had left, the Malays would be so astonished at the explosion that they would not venture to pass through."

"Your idea is a capital one," the captain said warmly; "but how about a fuse which would burn under water? What do you think, Tom; could it be managed?"

"I should think so, sir," the mate answered. "Suppose we take one of those empty 30-gallon beer casks, and fill that up with powder—it will hold ten or twelve of the little barrels; and then we might bung it up and make a hole in its head. Over the hole we might fix a wine-bottle with the bottom knocked out, and so fastened with tow and oakum that the water won't get in. Then we might shove down, through the mouth of the bottle and through the hole below it into the powder, a long strip of paper dipped in saltpetre to make touch-paper of it. I don't know as a regular fuse would do, as it might go out for want of air; but there would be plenty to keep touch-paper alight. We could sling three or four 18-pounder shots under the bottom of the cask to make it sink upright. Just before we slip our cables, we might lower it down with the boats, lighting the fuse the last thing, and sticking in the cork. If we don't put too much saltpetre it might burn for some minutes before it reached the powder."

"It's worth trying, at any rate," the captain said, "but I fear it would not burn long enough. I think that, instead of a bottle, we might jam a piece of iron tube six or eight feet long, into the head of the cask, and cut a bung to fit it. In that way we could get a good length of fuse."

This plan was carried out. A large cask was filled with powder, and an iron tube three inches in diameter and six feet long, fitted into it, and made water-tight. A long strip of paper, after being dipped in water in which gunpowder had been dissolved, was then dried, rolled tight, and lowered down the tube until it touched the powder. A bung was cut to fit the top of the tube, a piece of wash-leather being placed over it to ensure its being perfectly water-tight; the top of the fuse was then cut level with the pipe. Several bits of iron were lashed to the lower end of the cask to make it sink upright, and the cask was steadily lowered into a boat lying alongside the ship, in readiness for use.

The sailors entered into the preparations with the glee of schoolboys, but the machine was not ready until long after the ship had been towed out again through the channel and moored broadside to it just outside.

CHAPTER VIII
THE TORPEDO

IT was about two o'clock in the morning when the watch awoke the crew with the news that they could hear the distant sound of oars coming along the shore. All took their places in silence. After a time the rowing ceased and all was quiet again. Half an hour passed and then there was a slight sound close alongside, and in the channel they could dimly make out a small boat which was rapidly rowed away into the darkness again; several musket shots being fired after it.

"They have sent on ahead to find if we were lying in the same berth," the captain said. "I expect they will be puzzled when they hear that we are outside and that the entrance is guarded. I should not be surprised if they did not attack before morning. They had such a lesson yesterday, that I don't think they will try to force the channel in our teeth again; but will play the waiting game, sure that they will secure us sooner or later."

So it turned out. The hours passed slowly on, but no sound was heard. Then, in the dim morning light, a pirate fleet of eight *prahus* was seen lying at a distance of half a mile within the reef. As the day broke, the breeze sprang up, the sails were hoisted, and the captain prepared to slip his cables. A similar preparation could, through the glasses, be observed on board the Malay fleet.

"That will do very well," the captain said. "Those fellows will be along in about eight or ten minutes after we have started, and the fuse, according to the experiments we made as to its rate of burning, will last about seven. Now, quick, lads, into the boat. Tom, you take charge of the sinking."

In another minute the boat was rowed to the channel and the cask lowered over the side. It was held there for a minute while the mate struck a light and applied it to the touch-paper. Then he pressed the bung firmly into the top of the tube, the lashings of the cask were cut, and the boat rowed back to the ship. The anchors were already on board, and the brig was getting way on her as the boat rowed alongside. The men jumped on board, and the boat was suffered to tow behind, while all hands set the whole of the sails. The vessel was soon running briskly before the land-breeze.

The pirate fleet was instantly in motion. Every eye in the ship was directed towards them.

"They will be there in less than ten minutes from the moment I lowered the cask," the mate said, looking at his watch.

"Not much," the captain said, "they are rowing fast now, but the trees keep off the wind and their sails do not help them. They were a minute or two behind us in starting."

It was just eight minutes from the time when the cask had been lowered, that the first of the Malay boats rowed out through the channel.

"I hope nothing has gone wrong," the mate growled.

"I am not afraid of that, though we may be wrong a minute or two as to the length of the fuse."

Another boat followed the first; the third was in mid-channel, when suddenly she seemed to rise bodily in the air, and then to fall into pieces. A mighty column of water, a hundred feet high, rose into the air, mingled with fragments of wood and human bodies. A deep, low report was heard, and the brig shook as if she had come into collision with some floating body.

Although they were nearly a mile away, the yell of astonishment and fright of the Malays reached the ship. The *prahus* still inside the reef were seen to turn round and row away along the coast at the top of their speed; while those which had passed the channel, after rowing wildly for some distance, lay on their oars, the crews apparently stupefied at what had taken place. The craft which had been injured the day before, still lay seaward on watch, but now turned her head and rowed towards the shore to join her consorts.

The *Sea Belle* left the coast. The Malays attempted no pursuit, but, so long as they could be seen, remained inactive near the scene of the sudden and, to them, inexplicable catastrophe which had befallen their consort. Once fairly freed from all fear of pursuit, the captain invited the two lads into his cabin, and there heard from them an account of all the adventures through which they had passed. When they had finished, he questioned them as to their plans. Hans said that he intended to take the first ship bound for Holland.

"And you?" he asked Will.

"I have no particular plan," Will said. "I am in no hurry to return to England, having no relatives there. After being so long absent—for it is now a year since I sailed from Yarmouth—I should not care to return and take up my apprenticeship as a fisherman."

"Will you ship regularly on board the *Sea Belle*?" the captain asked.

"Thank you, sir, I think I would rather not decide upon anything until we get to Calcutta. I have £30 in money, £15 of which were given me on board the Dutch ship, and the rest I received as wages for the voyage from England to Java. I carried the money in a belt round my waist, and have kept it ever since. So I need not be in any great hurry to settle upon what I shall do; but certainly, after a regular sea life, I should not like to go back to being a fisherman. I am now past sixteen, and in another three years shall be able to earn more wages."

"I should have taken you for at least two years older," the captain said; "you are as big and strong as many lads of eighteen."

"I have done a good lot of hard work in the last two years," Will said; "for on board the Dutch ship, although, of course, I was only rated as a boy, I used to do man's work aloft."

Other people would have been deceived as well as the captain. Hard work and exposure to the air had done much to age the boy. He had been tall and slight for his age when he left the workhouse, and while he had not ceased growing in height, he had widened out considerably; and, had he asserted himself to be eighteen years of age, few would have questioned the statement.

The *Sea Belle* for some time kept south, touching at some of the islands where a trade was done with the Papuans; then her head was turned north, and after an eventful voyage, she reached Calcutta, where the captain had been ordered to fill up with cotton or grain for England.

The captain at once landed, and proceeded to the office of the agent of the firm who owned the *Sea Belle*. He was shown into that gentleman's private room, where at the time two gentlemen were seated, chatting. The agent was personally acquainted with the captain, and asked him to sit down and smoke a cigar.

"This is Captain Mayhew of the *Sea Belle*," he said to his friends. "He has been trading for the last three months down among the islands. These gentlemen, Captain Mayhew, are Major Harrison and Captain Edwards, who have just arrived from China with their regiment in the *Euphrates*. Has your voyage been a pleasant one, captain?"

"Pleasant enough, sir, on the whole; but we were attacked by the Malay pirates, and I should certainly not be here to tell the tale at present had it not been for the quickness and shrewdness of a lad who had been shipwrecked on the coast."

"How is that, Mayhew? Tell us all about it."

Captain Mayhew related the whole story of the fight with the pirates, saying that, unquestionably, had it not been for Will's pointing out the passage through the reef in the first place, and his idea of burying a submarine mine in the second, the *Sea Belle* would have fallen into the hands of the pirates.

"But where did the boy spring from? How on earth came he to be there?"

Captain Mayhew then related the story of William Gale's adventures as he had them from his own lips.

"He must be a cool and plucky young fellow, indeed," Major Harrison exclaimed. "I should like to see him. What style and type is he, captain? A rough sort of chap?"

"By no means," the captain answered. "He is surprisingly well-mannered. Had I met him elsewhere, and in gentleman's clothes, I do not think that I should have suspected that he was not what he appeared. His features, too, somehow or other, strike one as being those of a gentleman, which is all the more singular when, as a fact, he told me he had been brought up in a workhouse."

"In a workhouse!" Major Harrison repeated. "Then I suppose his parents were farm labourers."

"No," the captain answered; "he was left at the door on a stormy night by a tramp who was found drowned next morning in a ditch near. He had, when found, a gold trinket of some kind round his neck; and he tells me that, from that and other circumstances, it was generally supposed by the workhouse authorities that he did not belong to the tramp, but that he had been stolen by her, and that he belonged at least to a respectable family."

"All this is very interesting," Captain Edwards said. "I should like much to see the boy. Will you come and dine with us this evening on board the *Euphrates*—Mr. Reynolds here is coming—and have the boy sent on board, say at nine o'clock, when we can have him in and have a chat with him?"

Captain Mayhew readily agreed. William was even then waiting outside for him, having landed with him; and the captain, when he entered the office, had told him to walk about for an hour and amuse himself with the sights of Calcutta and then return and wait for him. He said nothing about his being close at hand, as he did not wish the officers to see him in the rough outfit which had been furnished him on board ship, intending to surprise them by his appearance in decent clothes. Accordingly, on leaving Mr. Reynolds' office he took him to one of the numerous shops in the town where clothes of any kind can be procured.

"Now, Will," he said, "I want you to get a suit of shore-going clothes. You can get your sea outfit tomorrow at your leisure; but I want you to show up well at the mess this evening, and a suit of good clothes will always be useful to you."

Captain Mayhew had intended to pay for the outfit himself, but this Will would not hear of, and Captain Mayhew was the less reluctant to let the lad have his own way, as he had in the course of the interview with the agent agreed that the lad's services deserved a handsome recognition from the firm, and that the sum of one hundred guineas should be given to him at once. The agent felt no doubt that the firm would thoroughly approve of the payment. Twenty pounds were to be given to Hans for his share of the services; but the two suggestions which had saved the *Sea Belle* had both originated with Will.

By Captain Mayhew's advice Will purchased a suit of dark-coloured tweed, a black tie, and some white shirts and collars. At other shops he bought some boots and a panama straw-hat. Having completed their purchases, they walked for some hours about Calcutta, Will being delighted with the variety of the native costumes and the newness and singularity of everything which met his eye.

On their return to the ghaut, as the landing-stage is called, they found their various purchases already stowed in the *Sea Belle's* boat, which had about an hour before come to shore to fetch them off. At seven o'clock Captain Mayhew went off to the *Euphrates*, leaving orders that the boat was to bring Will over at nine. At that hour the lad was dressed in his new clothes, which fortunately fitted him well.

"By jingo, Will," the first mate said, as he entered the cabin, "you look a tip-topper, and no mistake."

The mate was right; the lad with his sun-burnt face, quiet manner, and easy carriage, looked thoroughly at home in his attire.

"I don't know who your parents were, but I would bet a month's pay that the old tramp you were telling us of had nothing to do with it; for you look every inch a gentleman from head to foot."

Will found, on gaining the deck of the *Euphrates*, that orders had been left by the officer in command that he was to be shown into the saloon cabin upon his giving his name to the sergeant, who came up at the sentry's call. He was at once conducted below.

For a moment he felt almost bewildered as he entered; the size of the cabin, the handsomeness of its fittings, the well-laid table decked with fragrant flowers, so far surpassed anything he had ever seen or thought of. He was conducted to the head of the table, where Major Harrison, with Mr. Reynolds on one hand and Captain Mayhew on the other, sat, near the colonel commanding the regiment.

Captain Mayhew, who had already told the outline of the story, smiled quietly to himself at the expression of surprise which crossed the faces of the major and Mr. Reynolds, as well as of the other officers sitting near, at the appearance of the lad he introduced to them. The colonel ordered a chair to be placed next to himself, and told the servant to fill a glass of wine for Will, and entered into conversation with him.

"I think, gentlemen," he said, after a minute or two, seeing that the lad did not touch the wine that was poured out for him, "it will be pleasanter on deck; for it is terribly hot here, and I see that most of you have finished your wine." An adjournment was at once made to the deck. Here cigars were lighted, and the colonel and senior officers taking their places in some of the easy-chairs which were still about, the rest gathered round to hear the story, which Major Harrison had promised them would be an interesting one.

Captain Mayhew first gave his account of the fight between the *Sea Belle* and the pirates, beginning at the point when, as he was hotly chased and despairing of making a successful defence, the canoe with the two lads in it came out to him. Then Will was called upon to explain how he came to be there at that moment. He told briefly how the fishing-smack was sunk, how he had saved himself by clinging to the bob-stay of the Dutch Indiaman, and how he had sailed in this vessel to Java, and was on his way in her to China, when wrecked in the cyclone. Here his audience insisted upon his giving them full details; and he accordingly told them the manner in which he and a few of the crew had escaped; how, when they were building a boat, they had been attacked by Malays, and all—except another lad and himself, who were hiding in a tree— were massacred by the pirates; how they had gone inland to a village, where, having aided the natives when attacked by a hostile tribe, they had been most kindly received; how they had finally obtained a canoe and spent their time in fishing in hopes of seeing a passing sail, until the *Sea Belle*, chased by the Malay pirates, had appeared off the shore.

There was a genuine murmur of approval from those thickly clustered round as the lad finished his story, and the colonel warmly expressed his approval of his conduct under such exciting circumstances.

"What are you going to do now?" he asked.

"I have not made up my mind, sir," the lad said. "I expect that I shall ship in some vessel sailing for England shortly."

"Major Harrison," the colonel said, "will you and Captain Mayhew come with me to my cabin? I should like to have a few minutes' private chat with you," he went on, putting his hand on Will's shoulder. A minute or two later the three gentlemen and Will were seated in the private cabin.

"Look here, my boy," the colonel said; "I have heard from Major Harrison what you had told Captain Mayhew concerning your birth; and certainly your appearance and manner go far to sustain the belief that the tramp who left you was not your mother, and that your parents were of gentle birth. I do not say that a man's birth makes much difference to him; still, it does go for something, and in nine cases out of ten the difference both in face and figure is unmistakable. Unless I am very wrong, your father was a gentleman. However, that is not to the point: it is your quickness and activity, your coolness in danger, and the adventures which you have gone through which interest us in you. Now I think it is a pity that a lad who has shown that there is so much in him should remain a sailor before the mast. You have not been so long at sea as to become wedded to it, and to be unable to turn your hands to anything else. Now, what do you say to enlisting? In the ranks are men of all sorts—gentlemen, honest men, and blackguards. The steady respectable man is sure to rise. You can, the captain tells me, read and write well. There is a chance of active service at present, and when there is active service, a man who distinguishes himself gets rapid promotion. The regiment land to-morrow and go straight through by train to the North. There is trouble in Afghanistan, and an ultimatum has just been sent to the Ameer that if he does not comply with our terms, it will be war, and we hope to be there in time for the beginning of it. I can only say that, if you like to join, Major Harrison and myself will keep our eyes upon you, and if you deserve it you may be sure of rapid promotion. You have greatly interested me in your story, and I should be very glad to give a helping hand to so deserving a young fellow. It is not usual, certainly, for a regiment to take recruits in India, but I don't suppose that there can be any objection to it."

"Thank you very much," Will said, when the colonel ceased. "I am greatly obliged to you for your kindness. I have never thought about the army, but I am sure that I cannot possibly do better than accept your kind offer. The only thing, sir, is about my age."

"Tut, tut!" the colonel interrupted. "I don't want to know anything about your age. When you go up for attestment you will say that you are under nineteen, which will be strictly true. I will give a hint, and no further questions will be asked. Neither I nor anyone else know that you are not past eighteen, and in time of war no one is particular as to the age of recruits as long as they are fit to do their duty. You must work hard to pick up enough knowledge of drill to enable you to take your place in the ranks. There is neither parade work nor difficult manoeuvring in the face of an enemy, and you can finish up afterwards. Are you quite agreed?"

"Quite, sir," Will said joyously, "and am indeed obliged to you."

"Come on board then to-morrow at eight o'clock, and ask for Sergeant Ringwood."

William Gale left the cabin with a new prospect of life before him. He had of late rather shrunk from the thought of again taking his place as a ship-boy; and the prospect of adventures, to say nothing of the advancement which might befall him through the interest taken in him by the colonel, was delightful to him.

The last words the colonel had said when he left the cabin were: "Say nothing about the workhouse, and as little as possible of anything which happened before you were wrecked on the island, in the barrack-room."

When William and Captain Mayhew had left the cabin, Colonel Shepherd sent for Sergeant Ringwood.

"Sergeant," he said, "a young fellow will come on board to-morrow at eight o'clock to join the regiment as a recruit. Take him at once to the surgeon and get him passed. I know we shall be able to give him but little drill before we get to the frontier, but do all you can for him and I will make it up to you. He is a smart young fellow, and I have a good deal of interest in him. He was on his way to China and was wrecked among the Malays, and has gone through a good deal. Finding himself here with nothing to do, and with a prospect of active service on the frontier, he has decided to enlist; and, as he is a gallant young fellow, I do not wish to balk his fancy."

The sergeant saluted and took his leave, impressed with the idea—although the colonel had not said so—that the new recruit was a young gentleman who had joined the service simply for the sake of taking part in the war.

The next morning Will took leave of his friend Hans, who had the previous day shipped on board a Dutch ship homeward bound, and who was a few hours later to shift his berth to her, after he had been on shore to fit himself out in clothes. Hans was much affected at saying good-bye to his companion, and the two promised to correspond with each other. On bidding farewell to his friend the captain of the *Sea Belle*, the latter informed Will that Mr. Reynolds had, on behalf of the owners of the *Sea Belle*, paid £100 to his account into the Bank of Hindustan, and that this or any portion of it would be paid to his order, as the captain had furnished the agent with a slip of paper upon which Will had at his request signed his name. This had, with the money, been deposited at the bank, so that his signature might be recognized and honoured.

THE TORPEDO

On reaching the *Euphrates*, Will was at once taken charge of by Sergeant Ringwood, who took him before the doctor, to whom the colonel had already spoken. The medical examination was satisfactory, the doctor remarking:

"You are rather slight yet, but you will fill out in time."

The age was asked, and given as under nineteen, and eighteen was inscribed against him in the books. Then he was taken before the colonel and attested, and was from that moment a member of the regiment. A uniform was served out to him, and the usual articles of kit. The sergeant saw that his belts were put on properly and his knapsack packed; and half an hour afterwards he fell in, with his musket on his shoulder, among the troops paraded on the deck of the *Euphrates* prior to embarkation.

So quickly had it all been managed that Will could hardly believe that he was awake, as, feeling strangely hampered by his belts and accoutrements, he descended the accommodation ladder and took his place with his new comrades on board one of the great native boats and rowed to the shore.

The regiment was marched direct to the railway station, where the heavy baggage had been sent on the previous day. The men took their places in the long train which stood in readiness, and half an hour later steamed north from Calcutta.

Hitherto none of his comrades had spoken to Will. In the bustle of landing all had enough to do to look to themselves, and it was not until he found himself with eight comrades and a corporal in the railway carriage that he was addressed.

"Well, young 'un," one said, "what's yer name, and where do you come from? Calcutta isn't much of a place for recruiting."

"I was on my way to China," Will replied, "and got wrecked among the Malays; then I got picked up by a vessel, and we had some hot fighting. Then I was landed at Calcutta, and seeing nothing much to do and hearing that there was a chance of a fight with the Afghans, I thought the best thing to do was to enlist. My name is William Gale."

"I wasn't quite sure that you were an Englishman; you are pretty nigh as dark as them copper-coloured niggers here."

"So would you be," Will laughed, "if you had been living, as I have, for ten months among savages without even a shirt to your back."

"Tell us all about it," the soldier said. "This is a bit of luck, mates, our having someone who can tell us a tale when we have got such a long journey before us."

Will made his story as full as he could, and it lasted a long time. When it was finished, the men expressed their opinion that he was a good sort; and Will having handed over to the corporal a sovereign to be expended on drinks by the way, as his footing in the regiment, he became quite a popular character, and soon felt at home in his new position.

CHAPTER IX
THE ADVANCE INTO AFGHANISTAN

THERE was but little talking in the middle of the day in the train, for the heat was excessive. All the men had taken off their coats and sat in their shirt-sleeves. But they were, nevertheless, bathed in perspiration. Late at night the train arrived at Allahabad. Here there was a stop till morning. The men alighted from the train, and lay down on their folded blankets, with their knapsacks for pillows, on the platform or in the waiting-rooms. A plentiful supply of water had been prepared for their use at the station, and outside were several water carriers, and many of the men stripped off their shirts and had water poured over their heads and bodies.

Will Gale was among these, and, greatly refreshed, he enjoyed some fruit and cakes which he purchased from native vendors; and then, lying down on a bench in the station, was soon asleep. Four days' travelling brought them to the end of the railway. They were ferried across the Attock, and there their real work began.

Although it was now late in September the heat was still intense. Tents were struck an hour before day-break, and by eleven o'clock each day the column was at its halting-place. It was, however, hours before the tents and baggage arrived. Many of the draft cattle were very poor, forage was scarce, and the arrangements far from good. The consequence was that great numbers of the oxen broke down and died, and many of the troops were often obliged to sleep in the air owing to the non-arrival of their tents. The defects of the transport were aggravated as the time went on, and the Norfolk Rangers fared much better than some of the troops which followed them.

The regiment was destined to operate in the Khuram valley under the command of General Roberts. The advanced column of this division consisted of the 7th company of Bengal Sappers, the

23d Bengal Pioneers, a battery of horse artillery, one of Royal Artillery, and two mountain batteries, a squadron of the 10th Hussars, and the 12th Bengal Cavalry. The first brigade of infantry comprised the 2d battalion of the 8th Foot, the 29th Bengal Native Infantry, and the 5th Punjaub Infantry. The second brigade consisted of the 72d Highlanders, the 21st Native Infantry, the 2d Punjaub Infantry, and the 5th Goorkhas. The place of assembly was Kohat. The Norfolk Rangers were to act as a reserve.

It was on the 2d of October that the Rangers arrived at Kohat, heartily glad that their march across the sandy plains of the Punjaub was at an end. The other regiments comprising the force poured in rapidly, and on the 9th the general arrived and assumed the command. The next day the Punjaub regiments were sent forward to Thull. It was not until the middle of November that the European regiments followed them, and the six weeks were by the Rangers for the most part employed in drill; for, after their voyage and journey up the country, their commanding officer considered it necessary to work them hard to get them to the highest state of discipline.

William Gale was worked exceptionally hard, as he had in that short time to learn the manual and platoon exercises, and to pick up enough of drill to enable him to take his place in the ranks. Fortunately he carried himself well and required far less drilling than the majority of the recruits. By the time that the regiment moved forward he was able to take his place in his company, and had mastered all the movements which were likely to be necessary in the campaign.

The road between Kohat and Thull runs in a valley between mountains, those on the right being inhabited by the Waziries, a fierce and independent tribe. The regiment which had first marched had exercised every precaution against an attack. The convoys of stores and provisions sent forward had always been accompanied by strong escorts, and orders were issued that officers going forward on duty should not travel without protection. The Waziries, however, contrary to expectation, remained quiet, probably waiting to see the turn which matters took; for had we suffered a repulse they would assuredly have taken part at once against us, and would have aided in massacring fugitives and robbing baggage-waggons.

The march to Thull occupied five days, which were very pleasant ones to William Gale. His heavy work at drill was now over: he was no longer considered a recruit, but ranked as a soldier. The marches were not long, and for many hours in the afternoon the high hills threw the valley in shade; and the soldiers, after pitching their tents, were able to stroll about or to lie under the trees in which the valley abounded. The regiment reached Thull on the 18th of November, and on the morning of the 21st the column advanced.

The river, whose bed was 500 yards wide, was fortunately now low, being reduced to a stream of 40 yards wide by 3 deep. A trestle-bridge had been thrown across it for the use of the infantry. The river was distant a mile and a half from the town. No opposition was expected; but as a small Afghan garrison was stationed in a fort at Kapizang, a short distance beyond the river, an attempt was to be made to capture it. The 29th Punjaub Infantry first crossed the river at the bridge. The 10th Huzzars forded the river and extended in skirmishing order to cut off the retreat of the garrison. When they reached the fort, however, which was a square inclosure with round towers at the corners, it was found that the garrison, who had doubtless received warning from spies in Thull, had abandoned the place in the night.

The cavalry were now sent forward to reconnoitre, the infantry following, and the advanced force halted at Ahmed-I-shama for the night. Not a single habitation was passed during the nine miles march. The road was generally a mere track, 6 feet wide, passing through tangled brakes of dwarf palms, intersected by stony gullies except when it ran along the steep bank of the river.

The following day the rest of the first brigade marched up to Ahmed-I-shama, while the advanced force under Colonel Gordon moved on to Hazir-pir. The Rangers were with the first brigade, but not with the advanced party. This was composed wholly of native troops, consisting of the Pioneer regiments and the Sappers and Miners; these had hard work, for the road, which was fifteen miles in length, was scarcely passable for wheeled carriages, and the guns could not be taken along until the boulders and blocks of stone which strewed the way were removed or blasted into pieces.

On the 23d the Rangers, with the Horse Artillery battery and two native regiments, marched towards Hazir-pir; but the difficulties of the road were so great that they had to camp for the night four miles short of that place. General Roberts and the headquarters went forward the same day.

As the general passed along the road, the head-men of all the villages near came and paid their respects, and the villagers lined the roads as the troops passed, offering fowls, eggs, milk, and dried fruit for sale. As William Gale had brought a supply of money with him, he was able to indulge in all those luxuries; and, indeed, as the men had had few opportunities of spending money at Thull, all were well supplied with cash. The halt at Hazir-pir was then a very pleasant one. Supplies of grass, fuel, and provisions were brought in in considerable quantities there; but much difficulty arose in settling the terms of purchase, as coin was almost unknown in the valley, and therefore there was no established price; one native being ready to sell for a few coppers, articles for which another demanded as many pieces of silver. On the hills around a considerable number of sheep were seen grazing, but the natives did not care about selling these, which indeed belonged for the most part, not to the Turis, the tribe which inhabit the valley, but to nomad Ghilzais, who, like the Swiss shepherds, move about with their charges among the mountains wherever fodder is to be obtained. Khuram valley itself is bare and monotonous. With the exception of fruit-trees planted round the villages, scarce a tree is to be found; but each village is marked by a huge chunar or oriental plane, beneath which the villagers rest during the noonday heat.

But if the valley itself was bare and desolate, the scenery around was lovely. The great range of mountains known as the Safaid-Koh bound the valley on the east and north. This range averages 14,000 feet high, from which spurs run out at right angles, enclosing narrower valleys with broiling torrents rushing through boulders.

The slopes of these valleys are covered with luxuriant vegetation till the limit of trees is reached at a height of about 11,000 feet, above which in winter the snow lies thick, while in summer it furnishes the finest pasture to the Ghilzai flocks and herds.

The valley lands and the lower slopes of the hills are laid out in terraces, and irrigated rice-fields extend near the rivers. Valley and hill are alike covered with stones and boulders, Afghanistan being probably the most stony country in the world.

On the 24th the headquarters, with the cavalry and two regiments, moved forward ten miles and encamped at the south end of the Darwazi Pass, the road leading to open broad valleys covered with dwarf palms and wholly uncultivated. On the 25th the advanced force crossed the pass, which was a gentle slope and offered no great difficulty, and at night encamped at the Khuram fort, which had been evacuated by the enemy. The buildings, which would have been useful for the troops, had, however, been wrecked by the Turis, who have a deadly hate for the Afghans, their masters, and who were also animated in their work of destruction by a desire to obtain wood, which is exceedingly scarce there.

At Khuram there are two forts, the one 120 yards and the other 100 yards square. Inside these were quarters for the governor, and huts for the garrison and officers, and in the smaller forts were stables for the cavalry forces. This place was made the head-quarters of the forces in the Khuram valley. The general now rode on with two squadrons of the 12th Bengal Cavalry to reconnoitre in the direction of the Peiwar-Khotal, towards which the enemy were supposed to be retreating, and where they were expected to make a stand. As they approached the village of Peiwar, two villages were seen in flames, and news was brought in that three Afghan regiments, with twelve guns, had lately passed through.

The natives reported that they were encumbered by their guns, and that forced labour was procured for the purpose of removing them. Later on a rumour came that the twelve guns were stuck in the ravine at the foot of the Khotal or pass.

With but a small force of cavalry at his command, the general could do nothing, and so returned to Khuram and determined to hurry up the troops faster than he had intended, so as to capture the guns reported—as was afterwards proved falsely—to have been left behind by the Afghans. The sick and all superfluous baggage were left behind at Khuram, and on the 28th the troops moved at daybreak, the two brigades marching in parallel columns.

The cold was now severe at night, although it was hot in the daytime. It had been intended to halt at Halid-Kitta, four miles from the Khotal; but the intelligence arriving that the Ameer's troops had abandoned their guns and were in disorderly retreat, decided the general to push forward at once to the Peiwar-Khotal, seven miles further, instead of waiting and giving the enemy time to strengthen their position. A mile from the foot of the actual ascent of the Khotal lies the village of Turrai, two miles and a half beyond Peiwar. Turrai is situated in a valley, the ground at whose entrance is very much broken up by the shoulders and spurs of the hill. The left column—the 5th and 29th Punjaub in advance, with the 2d battalion of the 8th, and the 23d Pioneers, the Rangers, and two guns of the No. 1 mountain battery in support—were sent to the left with instructions to turn a ridge forming the south boundary of the valley, and to seize the village of Turrai. They were also to follow up closely any body of retreating Afghan troops that they might come across. The light brigade were to march up the regular road to the Peiwar, thus supporting the attack of the left brigade.

The left brigade followed out its orders, except that the regiment in support did not go round the southern side of the spur, but kept to the north. No enemy was seen on the south side of the spur, so, when a track leading across to Turrai was reached, the troops moved down towards the village, the regiments in support advancing at the foot of the open on the north side. The mountain path that the advanced troops were now filing down did not lead directly to the village, but fell into the valley ahead of it at a point where it widens out into what was known as the "punch-bowl valley" at the foot of the Peiwar-Khotal.

THE ADVANCE INTO AFGHANISTAN

As soon as the head of the column reached this spot, they came in sight of the Afghans, who showed themselves in great numbers on the crest of the mountain far above their heads. As the troops had no orders to attack so formidable a position, they fell back towards Turrai, which was about a quarter of a mile to the rear. At the sight of this movement, the Afghans swarmed down a spur of the hill and commenced an attack on the regiments that were moving towards the village. The 29th Punjaubees climbed the hill, and a sharp skirmish ensued, the two mounted guns coming into action.

While this was going on, the main body of the troops arrived at Turrai. The advanced troops were recalled and the 5th Ghoorkas were advanced to cover the movement. As it was now seen that the story of the abandonment of the guns was false, orders were given to pile arms in the village and to encamp there. This step was an imprudent one, as the Afghans speedily showed. While our men were sitting or lying upon the ground waiting for the baggage to arrive, the Afghans brought up a mountain-gun from the main ridge, about three-quarters of a mile distant, to the point of the spur overlooking the village of Turrai, and opened fire at 1700 yards range.

The astonishment of the troops when the first shell fell among them was great. Every one jumped to his feet and seized his rifle, and the guns of the Royal Horse Artillery were brought at once into action. It was four o'clock in the afternoon when the Afghans opened fire. Had they waited for a few hours, brought up another gun or two, and made a night attack immediately after opening fire, it is morally certain that the imprudence of camping in such a position would have been punished by a disaster which might have vied with that of Isandula. Huddled together in a small village surrounded by scrub, and impeded as the troops would have been by the baggage animals and native followers rushing in terror in all directions, our men would have been taken at an immense disadvantage. Fortunate was it that the enemy opened fire before the darkness set in. The troops were at once ordered to fall back a mile and a half and to pitch on fresh ground.

There was much confusion in the retreat, as the road in the rear was crowded with the baggage animals. The spot chosen for the camp was a rough one, for the ground was covered with scrub and a scattered growth of hill oak and thorny bushes, and was broken by the remains of some ancient terraces, but as the jungle and broken ground extended for three and a half miles, there was nothing for it but to take up the best position possible under the circumstances. The troops bivouacked on the ridge of a ravine with steep banks which formed a line of defence in front of the camp, while the view in every other direction was obscured by trees. The regiments passed a wretched night on the rough ground. Most of them were unable to find their baggage, which was wandering in the scrub in the dark, and the greater part of the troops lay down on the bare ground and went supperless to sleep after their fatiguing march of twenty-one miles.

In the morning both men and cattle were greatly exhausted by their long marches and almost sleepless nights, and General Roberts determined to wait for a day or two to reconnoitre the formidable position of the enemy before undertaking its attack. The camp was shifted to a more secure site, the brushwood and trees were cleared away, the tents pitched, and the troops were again comfortable.

A reconnaissance was made by Colonel Perking, commanding the Royal Engineers, with two companies of the Pioneers. He ascertained that a deep ravine lay between the ridge on which they were encamped and the Khotal itself, and that it was impossible to direct an attack on that side. Major Collett also, with two companies of the 23d, proceeded to reconnoitre the route known as the Spingawi or Cow Pass. This, instead of going straight up the hill in front, wound round its foot to the right of the valley.

Ascending the mountain at a point some three or four miles to the east of the Peiwar-Khotal, the reconnaissance reached the summit of a ridge about five miles distant from the camp and overlooking the Spingawi-Khotal. It was ascertained that the road up the pass seemed easy and practicable for all arms, that the top of the pass appeared to be on the same ridge as the Peiwar-Khotal, and that a force working from it towards the Peiwar would pass over a series of dominating positions. It did not appear to Major Collett that the enemy held the Peiwar-Khotal in force, although there was a gun on a commanding knoll on the south, and there seemed to be one at the top of the pass. The road from the village of Peiwar to the top of the Spingawi Pass seemed perfectly easy for troops of all arms.

The next two days were spent in clearing the camp, and so far as possible improving its military position; but it was still surrounded by thick oak jungle, which would have afforded cover for an enemy making a sudden attack. A further reconnaissance was made of the Spingawi Pass, and as the examination confirmed Major Collett's report, it was determined to attack by it. Orders were issued on the 1st of December for a march that night. The regiments which were to form the main attack by the Spingawi plateau route were the 29th Punjaub Infantry and the 5th Ghoorkas, commanded by Colonel Gordon in advance; these were to be followed by the mountain battery, a wing of the 72d Highlanders, a company of the Rangers, the 2d Punjaubees, and the 23d Pioneers, under Brigadier-general Thelwell. Four guns on elephants were to proceed with the column. The 5th Punjaub Infantry, the 8th Regiment, two guns Royal Horse Artillery, three guns Royal Artillery, and the 5th Bengal Cavalry, the whole under the command of Brigadier-general Cobbe, were to make an attack on the Peiwar-Khotal direct.

The rest of the force was to remain to guard the camp, and in order to convince the enemy that a front attack upon the Peiwar-Khotal was intended, a party of pioneers with an engineer officer, and a covering party of the 8th Regiment, were to construct a battery near the village of Turrai. Frequent reconnoitring parties had also been sent out in this direction, and so well was the secret of the general's intention to attack by the Spingawi Khotal kept that everyone in camp who had not been let into the secret was confident that the Peiwar-Khotal would be stormed on the morrow. The enemy, although those in camp were ignorant of the fact, were reinforced on the 1st by four regiments of infantry with a mountain battery, and on their side were meditating an attack upon the British camp.

The regiments which had freshly arrived were, however, fatigued by their long march, and the assault on our camp was postponed until the next day, and the chance of its coming off was therefore lost forever. To William Gale's great satisfaction, a company of the Rangers, that to which he had been posted, was the one selected by the colonel to accompany the column marching up the pass. He did not indeed know that this was the route by which they were to advance, but he was pleased at not being left behind with the regiment in charge of the camp.

"Well, young 'un," a corporal said to him that evening, "we are going to be under fire at last, and a nice climb we shall have of it; it puts one out of breath to look at that steep road running up the hill, and when it comes to fighting one's way up it, with cannon and Afghans on the top, we shall find it hard work."

"I expect," William answered, "that we sha'n't go up it at any extraordinary pace; if we skirmish up, as I expect we shall, from rock to rock, we shall have plenty of time to get our wind at each halt. We are not to take our knapsacks, so we shall fight light, and we have not much extra weight to carry. What with the heat and what with the long marches, I should think I must have lost a stone in weight since we landed in Calcutta."

"I don't think you have lost weight at all," the corporal said; "it seems to me that you have grown and widened out in the two months; and only yesterday, when I was sizing the company, I had to move you two men higher; for a young 'un you stand the fatigues well."

"I am all right," Will said, "except that I have got some frightful blisters on my feet. I was not going to say anything about it, because I should have been kept in hospital and left behind at Khuram, but I have hardly known how to march the last few days. I don't think I could possibly have managed it if I had not adopted the native dodge of wearing putties, which I have greased well on the inside, and wear instead of stockings."

THE ADVANCE INTO AFGHANISTAN

Putties, it may be said, are slips of woollen cloth about two and a half yards long and three inches wide, with a tape sewn into one end. They are wound round and round the leg, from the ankle to below the knee, and secured by the end being tied with the tape. Nearly every one, officers and men, wore them through the campaign. For a long march there could be no doubt that these bandages, wound round the foot instead of stockings, are very preferable, as they obviate the liability to foot-sores. Even with well-made boots all pedestrians may at times suffer from sore feet, but the liability is immensely increased when, as in the case of the British soldier, the boots are coarse, roughly sewn, and frequently ill-fitted.

CHAPTER X
THE PEIWAR-KHOTAL

AT ten o'clock at night on the 1st of December, the troops detailed for the attack mustered in the camp. The assembly took place without sound of bugle, and even the necessary words of command were given in a low tone. Through the still night air the Afghans on the hills, little more than two miles away, would have heard the stir. It was a very dark night, although the stars shone clear.

"Where can we be going?" William Gale asked the soldier next to him. "We are going right away from the pass instead of towards it."

"So we are!" the soldier replied. "I am blest if I know what we are up to, and it's so precious dark that I can scarcely see the file before me. I hope we ain't going to fight in the dark, anyhow. What would be the good of being a marksman when you cannot see the end of your own rifle, let alone the man you are firing at?"

"Oh, we can't be going to attack in the dark!" Will said. "I expect we have got a long march before us, and are going to work round somehow and take them in rear."

"Well, I hope whoever is acting as guide can see better in the darkness than I can, else we are safe to lose our way, and may find ourselves anywhere in the morning. Confound it!" The exclamation was elicited by the speaker stumbling over a boulder and nearly going on to his head.

"Silence in the ranks there!" an officer said close by.

Each regiment was followed by its ammunition mules and hospital doolies, the latter being covered stretchers or palkies carried by natives; besides these were dandies or chairs slung upon mules. This greatly added to the difficulty of a night march; for, even in the daytime the presence of baggage animals in a column upon a narrow road greatly hinders the troops, and at night the delays occasioned by them are naturally very much greater. For the first three and a half miles the column marched away from the enemy upon the Khotal, and the surprise of the soldiers increased at every step they took.

At the end of that time they arrived at the village of Peiwar. Here they turned to the left, and after crossing several ravines and stony water-courses, arrived on a cultivated terrace and kept along this till they reached a very stiff nullah twenty feet deep. The night was bitterly cold, the bank of the nullah was extremely slippery, and the boulders in the watercourse below coated with ice; the difficulty of getting the loaded animals across in the darkness was therefore very great. The passage of the various water-courses caused great delays, and it was difficult to keep the column together in the dark. At each passage the rear was immensely delayed while the leading troops were passing, and these again had to be halted while those behind them struggled over the difficulties.

The men suffered much from cold, as the pace was so slow that they could not warm themselves, and the mounted officers specially suffered in their hands and feet. At midnight the ravine leading up to the Spingawi Pass was reached; but so dark was it that the 2d Punjaubees, separated by a few yards from the regiment in front of them, marched straight on instead of turning up it; and the 22d Pioneers and the four artillery guns carried on elephants, being behind them, naturally went astray also.

Brigadier-general Thelwall, who commanded the column, was at the head of his brigade, and was for some time unaware of the absence of two of his regiments; but, after halting and finding that they did not come up, sent back a mounted officer, who, after a two-mile ride, came up with the missing troops and guided them back to the point where they had left the route.

From the foot of the ravine to the top of the pass is six miles in distance; and, dark as it was in the open, it was still more so in the ravine shadowed by the steep hills on either side. As the ascent continued the road became worse, the boulders being larger, and the holes and dried-up pools deeper. The darkness and the prevailing white colour of the stones prevented the difference of level being observed, and many of the men had heavy falls, as the steep sides of these pools were often from two to four feet deep.

After marching for a mile and a half up the ravine, the report of a rifle was heard in the ranks of the 29th Punjaubees, who were leading the column, followed instantly by another discharge. Colonel Gordon, commanding the regiment, halted, and he and the general tried in vain to discover who had fired. No one could or would identify them, and this seemed clearly to prove that the rifles had been fired as a signal to the enemy, for they had not been loaded before the column started.

The Punjaubee regiments contained many hill tribesmen men—closely connected by ties of blood and religion with the enemy whom they were marching to attack. A non-commissioned officer and several of the men who were just about the spot where the guns had been fired were placed under arrest and sent back. It was afterwards found that two of their rifles had been discharged, and the men who fired and their noncommissioned officer were tried by court-martial for treachery, and were hung.

After these men had been sent back, the 5th Ghoorkas, the company of Rangers, and two companies of the 72d, passed the 23d Punjaubees and took their places at the head of the column. In the course of the march a good many other men of the 23d left the column in the dark and made their way back to camp. It turned out afterwards that the Afghan sentries at the top of the pass heard the reports and woke up the commander of the post, who, hearing no further cause of alarm, took no action in the matter.

Had the traitors waited until the column was within a mile of the top of the pass, the Afghans would assuredly have taken the alarm; but, firing at a distance of four and a half miles, they failed in the desired effect. The advance was resumed up the bed of the stream for another mile and a half. About three in the morning the main water-course was quitted, the road now entering a ravine to the left, up which three miles further on was the summit of the pass. The column continued its weary way up the ravine, slowly stumbling along in the dark.

THE PEIWAR-KHOTAL

One incident occurred in this part of the road showing the necessity in night marching for the regiments to keep close to each other. In one place a fir-covered island lay in the middle of the ravine, the torrent's bed lying on either side of it. When the two companies of the 72d Highlanders, who had been following close to that of the Rangers, came to the spot, they were surprised to find that the troops in front had suddenly vanished. No explanation could be given as to the cause of this disappearance, so the company were halted until the mystery was solved. The leading regiment had taken the passage to the right of the island, while the 72d had gone to the left, the separation of the roads being unnoticed in the dark. Had the roads diverged instead of reuniting, much inconvenience might have been caused by the delay in collecting the separated portions of the force.

At last the foot of the Khotal was reached, where the track left the ravine and turned up the spur. The two guides, natives of the country, who had led the head of the column to this point, refused to go any further; and as the column was now at the point where the fighting might begin, they were allowed to depart. It was about six o'clock when the Ghoorkas began to climb the spur. The morning had broken, but it was still dark, and the path was almost invisible in the shadow of the trees.

The Ghoorkas, their rifles loaded now, made their way quietly up the hill. Presently the challenge of the sentry was heard, followed by two shots. It was a relief to the men, after ten hours of weary stumbling along in the cold and darkness, to know that they were at length face to face with their foe. Cold and fatigue were at once forgotten, and with eyes strained through the darkness, and rifles ready for use, every man pressed forward. Fifty yards up the hill, behind the sentry who had fired, was the first stockade of the enemy, formed by several large trees, which had been felled so as to completely block up the road, presenting an obstacle of about eight feet high to the attacking force. The Afghan pickets lining the stockade poured a volley into the Ghoorkas, who, led by Major Fitzhugh and Captain Cook, made a rush at the place.

For a few minutes there was a fierce fight at the trees; but as fresh assailants momentarily poured up, the obstruction was scaled, and the Afghans retired on a second stockade eighty yards back. Here another stand was made, but the spur being a little wider, the Ghoorkas were able to work round, and, taking the defence in flank, soon drove the Afghans back. Beyond this point the ground was clear of trees, and the road ran in short zigzags up the steep hill to the breast-work which lined the edge of the top zigzag.

A mountain gun at this point swept the approach to the position, while the hill at its back was now covered with Afghans, who opened a heavy fire upon the troops as in the dim morning light they issued from the trees. By the time that the Ghoorkas and the Rangers had cleared the second stockade, the wing of the 72d Highlanders, ascending by the right flank, had made their way up to the front, and the whole now advanced together. As quickly as possible they pushed up the hill under the heavy fire of the enemy. The latter fought well, and a number of them were killed before retiring. At the defence erected at the top of the zigzag so obstinately did the Afghans in front hold their ground that their comrades behind were enabled to remove their mountain gun.

To the right of the enemy's position was a knoll, and the 72d at once took possession of this, and two mountain guns were brought up to their assistance. The Afghans were seen in great numbers in the broken ground ahead. The Ghoorkas and the little body of Rangers pushed on against them. Presently the enemy gathered and made a rush down upon them, and a desperate hand-to-hand fight took place for a few minutes. The men were scattered among the trees and each fought for himself. William Gale had just reloaded his rifle when he saw Captain Herbert, who commanded his company, fall to the ground, and three Afghans spring forward to finish him. With a bound Will reached the side of the officer. Two of the Afghans had already discharged their pieces, the third levelled and fired. So close was he that the flash almost burnt the soldier's face, and he felt a sharp pain as if a hot iron had passed across his cheek. In an instant he shot his assailant dead, and then with bayonet stood at bay as the other two Afghans rushed upon him. They had drawn their tulwars and slashed fiercely at him; but he kept them off with his bayonet until a Ghoorka, running up, cut down one of them with his kookerie, a heavy sword-like knife which the Ghoorkas carry, and which they always employ in preference to the bayonet in fighting at close quarters. The remaining Afghan at once took to flight.

The 29th Punjaubees had now come into action, and the Afghans, disheartened at the loss of their position, fell back and withdrew into the woods which cover the plateau. At half-past seven o'clock the whole force, except the elephant guns, had reached the plateau; and General Roberts was able to flash the news of the successful capture of the enemy's first position to Brigadier-general Cobbe, who was in command of the force which was to operate direct against the Peiwar-Khotal. A rest was given the troops after their long march, and at half-past nine they again fell in for the attack upon the pine-covered slopes in the direction of the Peiwar-Khotal. How strong were the enemy who might be lurking there they knew not. But it was certain that he would fight obstinately, and in so dense a forest much of the advantage gained by drill and discipline is lost.

A change was made in the order of the advance. The troops who had before led the advance and had done the fighting were now placed in the rear, and the 23d Pioneers led the way, followed by the 2d and 29th Punjaubees. The column crossed the plateau without opposition, and began the ascent towards the enemy's position in the woods. Considerable caution was needed, as no one had any knowledge of the country and all were ignorant of the position and numbers of the enemy, who might, for aught they knew, be massing in great numbers for an attack upon the front or one of the flanks. The line of skirmishers entered the pine-wood near the rocky hillside, and a rolling fire of musketry soon told that they were engaged from end to end of the line. It was slow work, for fallen trees, rocks, and bushes everywhere hampered the advance. Still the skirmishing line, reinforced from behind, pushed forward steadily, and presently cleared the Afghans off the hillside.

Captain Herbert saved.

THE PEIWAR-KHOTAL

When the troops reached the top they found a valley in front of them, and from the woods on the opposite side so heavy a musketry fire was kept up that it was evident the Afghans intended to make a desperate stand here. The valley, or rather ravine, was a narrow one: fifty yards wide at its foot, and scarce three times as much from brow to brow. The enemy, hidden among the trees, could not be made out except by their continual fire. They did not content themselves, however, with the mere defence of their side of the hill, but from time to time large numbers charged down and tried to force their way up that held by the British.

Each time, however, when they attempted this, the Punjaubees drove them back with slaughter. It was clear that the Afghans were in great numbers, for their line extended for a mile and a half along the hillside. Major Anderson of the 23d Pioneers, after repulsing one of these attacks, led four companies to the assault of the Afghan position, and drove the enemy back for some little distance; but Major Anderson fell and the party retired.

Colonel Curry, who commanded the regiment, again led the men forward, and for a time a hand-to-hand fight took place. For two hours the rifle contest continued without cessation. The storm of bullets was tremendous, but no very great execution was done on either side, both parties lying behind the shelter of trees. So far no advantage had been gained by the British, and General Roberts felt that, with the force under his command, it would be rash to attempt to carry so strong a position held by a greatly superior force. In the meantime the attack upon the Peiwar-Khotal from the valley had commenced. Before daylight Brigadier-general Cobbe, with the 5th Punjaub Infantry and the 8th Regiment, left camp, his object being to co-operate with the flank attack. The 8th Regiment moved directly towards the pass, while the 5th Punjaubees climbed one of the principal spurs between the Peiwar and Spingawi Khotals.

The ascent was extremely difficult, and it took the troops six hours to reach the summit. During the last portion of the ascent they came under the fire of the enemy. When near the summit Major Macqueen of the 5th Punjaubees saw, through an opening in the pine-wood, the Afghan camp, with their baggage animals, which were placed for shelter in the glade behind the Peiwar-Khotal. Two mountain guns were at once brought up and a fire opened upon the Afghan camp. In a few minutes the tents caught fire, the animals stampeded in all directions, and the enemy in front, seized with a panic, began rapidly to retreat. The Afghan troops facing General Roberts' column, when they found their comrades on their right retreating, began to draw off, and the fire sensibly diminished.

The movement was accelerated by the four elephant guns, which had at length come up, opening fire into the pinewood forest. As the fire slackened, a reconnaissance of the hill was made by General Roberts and his staff; but the result showed that the mountain was so covered with pines and brushwood that it formed an almost impenetrable barrier to the advance of troops, for the growth was so thick that it was impossible to say in which direction any movement should be made. The experience gained in the last six hours of hard fighting had shown how difficult it was to keep command over troops scattered along a front of half a mile long in the forest where nothing could be seen beyond a radius of a few yards.

The general therefore determined to desist from the attempt to force his way direct to the top of the Peiwar-Khotal, and to march to his left, and so, by menacing the Afghan line of retreat, to hasten the movement towards the rear which had evidently begun. The men were therefore brought back to the plateau to the east of the ravine.

Here they were halted for a time, and the contents of their haversacks furnished them with a meal. At two o'clock they again drew up on the Spingawi plateau. The 2d Punjaub Infantry being left on the hill to oppose the Afghans should they again advance in that direction, the rest of the column entered the defile leading into the Hurriab valley, far in the rear of the Peiwar-Khotal.

As soon as the enemy, who were still opposing the 2d Punjaub Infantry, saw the head of the column enter the defile, they were seized with a panic lest their retreat should be cut off, and began to retreat with the greatest haste, as they had to make their way across two mountain ridges before they could pass the spot towards which our troops were moving. The advance of the column, however, was necessarily slow, as the woods and side valleys had to be carefully examined lest a flank attack should be made upon them.

In two hours the head of the column emerged from the forest on to the open slopes above the highest cultivated point in the Hurriab valley. It was now four o'clock. The short December day was drawing to a close; no enemy were in sight, for their line of retreat was hidden in the bed of the stream a couple of miles further on, and no one knew where they were to be found. The troops were much exhausted with the want of rest and with their heavy work, for they had now been marching and fighting for eighteen hours, and they were glad to receive the order to bivouac, although they had no tents or food, and the cold, as might be expected on a winter day at an elevation of over 9000 feet above the sea, began to be very severe.

A number of the nearest trees were felled by the pioneers, and huge fires were soon alight. There was still some uneasiness, as no one knew where the force under General Cobbe was, or whether the attack on the Peiwar-Khotal had been successful or not.

While the 5th Punjaub Infantry had been mounting the spur half-way between the Peiwar and the Spingawi Khotal, the 8th Regiment had moved directly upon the pass. The Afghans, who had expected an attack, had remained under arms until three in the morning, when, hearing no sounds in our camp, they had been dismissed to rest.

Three guns of the Royal Artillery and two of the Royal Horse Artillery took up their post 800 yards in front of our camp, where their fire at the crest of the pass would assist the advance of the 8th. These, after two hours' march, found themselves at seven in the morning on the last spur, which is separated from the Peiwar-Khotal by a deep ravine. When it became daylight a few minutes later, the enemy caught sight of our artillery in the valley, and at once opened fire. Although they had six field-pieces at the top of the hill, only three had been placed in position to command the valley and the ascent, and the mountain battery which had arrived the afternoon before was not brought to the front.

The three field-pieces and the mountain gun on the spur kept up a continuous fire on our battery of five guns. These were, however, almost beyond their range, and but little damage was done. On our side the fire was chiefly directed against the mountain gun at the end of the spur, and at any bodies of men who showed themselves.

The artillery duel went on for four hours, and in the meantime the infantry were engaged sharply with the Afghans. These had taken up their position in the woods on the other side of the ravine, and kept up a continuous fire upon the 8th. The distance, however, was too great for much execution on either side, especially as both parties were sheltered in the woods.

About ten o'clock the Afghans were seen gathering in strength, as if to come down across the road leading up to the Khotal to attack the 8th in the rear. A squadron of the 18th Bengal Cavalry charged up the valley, and the enemy retired up the hill again; and, seeing that they could not cross the road without the chance of being cut up by the cavalry, they did not try to repeat the experiment.

At eleven o'clock Brigadier-general Cobbe was wounded in the leg, and Colonel Barry-Drew succeeded him in the command, receiving the orders which had been given to General Cobbe that the Khotal was not to be attacked till there was some evidence that the flank attack had shaken the enemy's defence in front.

At twelve o'clock, the guns with the 2d Punjaub Infantry alarmed the Afghans by their fire upon the camp, and although the Afghan guns in front kept up their fire, the musketry fire decreased considerably. Seeing this, Colonel Drew ordered the artillery to be brought up nearer. When, after advancing 300 yards, they came to a ravine crossing the road, the Afghans, who had come down the hill to meet them, opened a heavy fire; and the road being narrow, only the leading gun could come into action. However, the two companies of the 8th, which were acting as an escort to the guns, advanced in skirmishing order, and drove the Afghans up the hill. The panic among the Afghans on the plateau having now spread to the troops at the Khotal, their fire entirely ceased, and the 8th Regiment descended the defile, and began to climb the path to the Khotal. Not a hostile shot was fired, and at half-past two they reached the enemy's camp, which they found deserted.

CHAPTER XI
A PRISONER

THE panic which had seized the Afghans when they found their retreat menaced had been thorough and complete, and when the 8th Regiment entered the camp, they found that the tents were standing; food had been left ready cooked, and every possession had been abandoned. In the artillery camp the gunners had left their silver-mounted brass helmets and caps, as well as their guns and carriages. A body of friendly Turis had accompanied the column making a demonstration on its flank, and these, arriving upon the spot, plundered the Afghan camp of everything of the smallest value.

No one knew what had become of the main body under General Roberts.

The Bengal Cavalry scouted for some distance in advance, but found no signs of the enemy. Strong pickets were set in case the Afghans should rally and return. The tents were brought up from the camp below, fires were lit, and the 8th encamped for the night. In the morning communication was established between the two camps, and it having been ascertained that the enemy had fled in the greatest disorder towards the Shatur-gardan Pass leading down to Cabul, there was no prospect of further fighting. The Afghans had abandoned all their guns, and even thrown away a great quantity of muskets, in their rapid retreats. Great stores of flour and other provisions were discovered in the various villages and were divided among the troops.

The winter was now setting in, and the Shatur-gardan Pass might any moment be closed by deep snow; there was therefore no prospect of a renewal of hostilities before the spring. Preparations were made for hutting a regiment on the top of the Khotal. The rest of the force were to winter at Khuram. General Roberts, with

112

an escort of cavalry, rode to the Shatur-gardan Pass, and assured himself that the whole of the Afghan army had fled beyond this point.

The troops were for some time kept hard at work lowering the captured guns and ammunition down to the valley. A portion of the troops advanced as far as Alikheyl, the principal town of the plateau. The Jajis, the inhabitants of the country, had hitherto been extremely hostile; but, cowed by the defeat of the Afghans, they submitted without resistance.

On the 12th all the preparations for the return were complete. It was known that there was another pass from Alikheyl into the Khuram valley by the south: this had never been explored by any European, but General Roberts determined to return by it with a portion of his force, as the pass might be found valuable in future operations. The force detailed for the march through the Sappir defile was composed of the 8th Ghoorkas, a wing of the 72d Highlanders, a company of the Norfolk Rangers, the 23d Punjaub Pioneers, and a mountain battery.

The country through which the march was to be made was inhabited by the Mongals, a turbulent robber tribe. The column marched at nine in the morning, and after their down march arrived at the village of Sappir at mid-day. The road lay down the Hurriab river till the Khuram river was reached, and then along the right bank, passing through the village of Kermana, after which it turned up a narrow road for two miles, till an open plateau was reached, at the farther end of which stood the village of Sappir. It was reported here that the Mongals intended to defend a defile and hill pass two miles farther on. The 23d Pioneers were therefore pushed on to occupy the pass and bivouac there; the remainder of the troops camped in the village.

No signs of the enemy were seen either by the 23d Pioneers or in the vicinity of the camp. The troops were to march at three in the morning and the tents were struck an hour after midnight. The track up the pass was excessively steep and very difficult for the camels. The cold was bitter, and in places where water had crossed the road there were slippery surfaces of ice, which hindered the camels considerably, and it was past eight o'clock before the rear-guard arrived at the top of the pass. From a commanding position overlooking the defile and surrounding waste of rugged and barren mountains, not an enemy could be seen, and it was hoped that the report of the intended attack was a false one. The troops now began to descend the defile, which was known as the Manjiar Pass. Troublesome as the ascent had been, the descent was infinitely more so; and it was with difficulty that the camels could be made to go down the deep and slippery roads.

The gorge was five miles in length. The track for the first part ran through a deep ravine of perpendicular walls, which narrowed in places to a few yards, overhanging the path until they seemed to meet and form a tunnel, through which it ran. Had an attack been made on the column as it struggled with its difficulties through this portion of the pass, the result would have been disastrous; for it would have been impossible to place troops on the heights to cover the advance. Here and there side ravines broke into the road, in any of which ambushes might have been laid.

It was not, however, until the difficult part of the road had been passed, and a comparatively open valley reached, that any of the natives were seen. Then a few men were observed on the heights, but as they were supposed to be shepherds no notice was taken of them. Believing that all danger of attack was now over, the general ordered all the troops, with the exception of the baggage guard, which was composed of the 3d Ghoorkas, and a few of the 72d Highlanders and Norfolk Rangers, to march forward to the camp, which was to be pitched at a village called Keraiah in the open valley. This, as the result proved, was a very rash move. Before the head of the column had extricated itself from the ravine, numbers of the country people were seen collecting in small detached parties; by degrees they closed in, and were soon within fifty yards of the convoy.

Captain Goad, in charge of the baggage, was close to a small guard of 72d Highlanders, when suddenly a volley was fired by the Mongals. Captain Goad fell, his thigh-bone broken by a bullet. Sergeant Green, with three privates of the 72d, picked him up, and having placed him under cover of a rock, turned to defend themselves. They were but four men against a large number, but they stood steady; and, firing with careful aim, and picking off their man each time, they kept the enemy at bay until help arrived. Simultaneously all along the line of the baggage column the Mongals attacked.

From the heights on both sides a fire was kept up while the more daring swept down in parties upon the rear-guard of Ghoorkas commanded by Captain Powell. The baggage-guard all behaved with great steadiness, defending the path on both sides, while the baggage animals continued their way along it.

William Gale was on duty with the party, and was, like the rest, busy with his rifle; a sergeant next to him was hit in the leg, and Will, laying down his rifle, stopped one of the camels, and assisted the wounded man to mount it. The attack of the Mongals became more furious as they saw their anticipated prey escaping them in spite of all their efforts; but their attempts to close were in vain, and the convoy made its way down to the village with the loss of one killed, and two officers and eight men wounded. Captain Powell and Captain Goad both died from the effects of their injuries.

The enemy's loss must have been considerable, as the fire of the troop was steady and accurate, and the distance small. After a halt for a day or two, the column marched to Khuram, where it encamped.

Captain Herbert had reported to the colonel the manner in which Private Gale had defended him when wounded and attacked by three Afghans; the incident, too, had been observed by many of his comrades, and as a reward the young soldier was promoted to the rank of corporal; and the colonel told him that, had not similar acts of bravery been performed in the hand-to-hand action on the Spingawi-Khotal, he would have been mentioned for the Victoria Cross.

The mountain tops were now deep in snow, but in the valley the temperature was very agreeable, and the troops enjoyed their rest much. This was not, however, to be of long duration. From the lower end of the Khuram valley, runs off another valley known as the "Khost." This was an entirely unknown country to the Europeans, but it was said to be extremely hostile. Parties had come down and carried off cattle; and at any time a formidable raid might have taken place, and our line of communication been entirely cut.

The country was ruled by an Afghan governor, who sent in to say that he was willing to hand it over to us. There was, therefore, no expectation that there would be any resistance; and the expedition was designed rather to overawe the country and to obtain information as to its extent and capabilities, than with any idea of permanent occupation. The column consisted of a squadron of the 10th Hussars, the 5th Bengal Cavalry, the 21st and 28th Punjaub Infantry, two mountain batteries, a wing of the 72d Highlanders, and two companies of the Norfolk Rangers. This force marched from Hazir-pir, and halted for the night at Jaji-Midan at the head of the valley leading to the Darwiza Pass, through which the track runs into the Khost valley.

At eight o'clock next morning the troops moved forward. The ground was difficult, for the road ran between terraced fields on the side of the ravine, and obliged men and animals to pass in single file. It was not therefore until twelve o'clock that the rear-guard moved out of the camp. Beyond this point the road up the pass was not difficult; from the summit a wide view was obtained. At the end of the valley, six miles distant, the plain of the Khost country was seen. It was seen that, owing to the slow progress the troops were making, the baggage-train, consisting of 1000 camels, would not be able to reach the proposed camping-ground at the lower end of the valley before dark; the general, therefore, ordered it to halt at the top of the pass, where the ground was open. The 21st Punjaubees and a mountain battery were to stay there for its protection, and bring it on next day. The mules with the regimental baggage went on with the troops.

The column met with no opposition. It halted near the village of Bakh, half a mile from the foot of the hills, where the valley widened into a plain six miles long and four broad. The force encamped here on the 4th, to allow the convoy to come up. The following morning the column marched to the other end of the valley, and the next day the Afghan governor of Matun, the chief place of the Khost, rode in to welcome the general.

On the 6th of January the force marched to Matun. They found that this fort was a square-walled enclosure 100 yards each side, with circular corner bastions. There was a central square inclosure with round towers at its angles. As the fort was approached, its garrison, which consisted of 100 local militia, were formed up in two lines at a mosque outside the fort. The general, with his staff, rode in, and a long interview took place between him and the governor. The troops encamped outside; in the evening information came in from the villages in the plain that large numbers of the Mongals, who inhabited the hills, were meditating an attack. Strong pickets were posted, and the night passed quietly. In the morning large numbers of tribesmen flocked down into the villages and gradually surrounded the camp. At one o'clock the troops fell in. The cavalry were sent out against the enemy in the northwest direction, followed by the 28th Punjaubees and No. 2 mounted battery. The Mongals at once fell back to the hills. The squadron of the 10th Hussars were dismounted, and ordered to skirmish up a small knoll to the west. From this they drove the enemy, who gathered again on a spur opposite.

Here they were charged by the 5th Punjaub Cavalry, and fell back higher up the ridge. The mountain guns and infantry now arrived and speedily drove them over the crest. General Roberts with his staff rode out to watch the skirmish; and, soon after he had left, the enemy, who occupied the village to the northeast, showed in force. Two of the mountain guns opened upon them. On the south they now approached, under the cover of the old Afghan cavalry lines, to within half a mile before being perceived, and also occupied a walled village there. The other two guns in camp shelled the village, and soon drove the enemy out.

When the general returned to camp at half-past two, he found the attack driven off in all directions, and ordered the 21st Punjaubees, the 72d Highlanders, and the Norfolk Rangers to follow up the enemy to the east and southeast with the mountain guns, and to burn the villages which had sheltered the enemy. The first village was found deserted; at another, a quarter of a mile behind, the enemy made a stand, but were shelled out, and the plain beyond the Matun river was soon covered with fugitives. Major Stewart, with forty men of the 5th Punjaub Cavalry who accompanied the column, charged 400 of them and cut down many, until checked by the heavy fire of matchlock men from the high bank.

No more fighting took place. The combination of tribes which had attacked the camp were estimated at 6000 men. Eighty prisoners were taken. These, two nights afterwards, took advantage of a night alarm to attempt to escape, and attacked the guard. The attempt, however, was frustrated, but only after several of the prisoners had been shot down. Some days passed quietly. Reconnaissances were made up the valley. While waiting here, the news of the capture of Candahar by General Stewart arrived. Parties of engineers surveyed the country, and all passed off quietly.

On the 25th a portion of the force marched back to Hazir-pir. On the 26th of January the general determined to withdraw this force altogether, as no advantage was gained by its retention, and the garrison would be constantly exposed to the attacks of the natives, who were already threatening it. The fort was handed over to Sultan Jan, a man of good family, who was appointed to govern the Khost temporarily. He had under him the guard of the former governor, and some fresh natives, being in all 100 men. The head-men of the villages were called together, and these promised to obey his rule. Some of the chiefs of the Mongals and other neighbouring tribes came in; sheep were given to them, and they were told that, so long as they desisted from interference in the valley, no steps would be taken against them.

The troops, however, had only made one day's march when a messenger arrived from Sultan Jan, saying that immediately the troops had marched, the Mongals had come down to attack the fort. A strong party were therefore marched back at once. After destroying the stores and setting fire to the fort, they drew off the governor and marched back to camp, the Mongals, although in great force, not venturing to offer any resistance. On the return of the force to the Khuram valley, a wing of the Norfolk Rangers was sent up to reinforce the troops stationed on the top of the Peiwar-Khotal, as the Jajis and Mongals had been gathering in large numbers, and threatening an attack on that post.

William Gale was with his company stationed at Alikheyl. The enemy abstained from any open attack, but they often harassed the sentries. One night Will was corporal in charge of a picket of eight men posted at a hut half a mile from the village. The object of the picket was to prevent any sudden attack being made upon the company, who were in a small village a quarter of a mile in the rear where a large quantity of grain was stored. Two men were posted as sentries some hundred yards in advance of the hut. Will had visited the sentry to the right, and, finding all was well here, moved across to the left.

"Is everything quiet?" he asked the sentry.

"I don't know, corporal. Two or three times I have thought that I heard noises, and twice I have challenged."

"What sort of noise?"

"Once it seemed to be a crack like a dried stick when some one treads on it. The other time it was as if a stone had been dislodged."

"I will wait with you," Will said. "Two pairs of ears are better than one."

Again there was a slight sound heard.

"I don't like to fire," Will said. "The alarm would spread and the whole camp get under arms. There is something moving, I am convinced, but it may be only a stray bullock. I will go forward and see if I can make it out, and do you stand ready to fire if I am attacked. After doing so, fall back on the picket at once. If the enemy are in force, hold the hut to the last. In ten minutes you will have help from the village behind."

Holding his rifle advanced, in readiness to fire, William Gale made his way forward cautiously towards the spot whence the noise seemed to proceed. When he was some forty yards in advance of the sentry, a number of figures rose suddenly from some bushes and fired.

Will fired, and saw the man at whom he aimed go down; but at the same instant three or four guns were discharged, and he fell to the ground, shot through the leg. There was a rush of men towards him. A tulwar was waved and fell with a crushing blow on his shoulder, and he became insensible. When he recovered consciousness he was being carried along, a man holding his arms and another his legs. The pain was excruciating, and he fainted again, after hearing, during his brief period of consciousness, a sharp fusilade of musketry, which told him that his comrades were defending the hut against the enemy. When again he came to his senses it was daylight. He was lying in a small room, and an old woman was applying bandages to the sword-cut on his shoulder. Although he did not know it, he was ten miles from the spot where the attack had been made. Among those who had taken part in it was the head of a small Jaji village lying behind the hills.

This chief was a crafty old savage, who had been desirous of remaining neutral in the strife. The determination of his people to join in the attack by the tribes had forced him to consent to their so doing.

Before starting he had, however, made them swear that any wounded men who fell into their hands should not, in accordance with the Afghan custom, be instantly despatched, but should be brought back to the village. His intention was to have some hostages. If the English repulsed the attack and in the spring again advanced, he would be able to prove his good-will to the cause by handing the soldiers whom he had protected over to them.

Upon the other hand, should the British fall back and the Afghans advance in the spring, he could hand the prisoners over to them, or send them down to Cabul as a proof that his people had fought against the British. He had himself accompanied his men, and seeing after Will had fallen that he was still living, had at once ordered two of his men to carry him off to the village.

The attack upon the guard-house proved unsuccessful; the six soldiers defended themselves until the company from the village behind came up to the rescue. Several other attacks at various points took place. But the British were on the alert, and the hillsmen, finding that their enemies were not to be taken by surprise, scattered again to the village. The ball had fortunately passed through William Gale's leg without either breaking a bone or cutting an artery; but the wound in the shoulder was more serious, and the effect of the strain upon it in carrying him brought on violent inflammation; fever set in with delirium, and for weeks the lad lay between life and death.

The old woman who nursed him was, like most of her country people, skilled in the treatment of wounds. The bandages were kept bathed with water, snow was constantly applied to his head, and a decoction of herbs given him to drink. His good constitution was in his favour, and at last he recovered his senses, to find himself convalescent, but as weak as an infant. In April the snow melted, and the chief, having by this time found that the English were not likely to advance beyond Alikheyl, thought that it would best benefit his interest to send his prisoner down to Cabul.

The Ameer was reported to be about to conclude peace with the British, and the chief thought that he was more likely to receive a reward from him for the care he had bestowed upon the prisoner than from the English. Moreover, it would have been difficult to send him into the English camp through the hostile villages, while no unfavourable comment would be incited by his sending his prisoner down to Cabul.

Will Gale was far too weak to perform the journey on foot; he was therefore placed on a camel. The chief himself and four of his head-men accompanied him as an escort, and a week after the pass was open, they started up the valley to the Shatur-gardan, and thence descended into the Logan valley below on the way to Cabul.

121

CHAPTER XII
THE ADVANCE UP THE KHYBER

NOTHING has yet been said of the doings of the other columns—that under General Browne advancing by the Khyber Pass upon Tellalabad, that under General Stewart by the Bolan Pass upon Candahar. General Browne's force had been gathered at the frontier line at the mouth of the pass, awaiting the reply of the Ameer to the British ultimatum. None having been received up to the night of the 20th of November, the advance took place in the morning at the same hour at which General Roberts advanced from Thull in the Khurum valley.

The principal defence of the Khyber Pass was the fort Ali-Musjid. This fort stands on a most commanding position on a rock jutting out from the hillside far into the valley, which its guns commanded. It was flanked by batteries erected on the hillsides, and was a most formidable position to capture. It was situated about six miles up the valley.

The force under General Browne was divided into four brigades. The first, under General Macpherson, consisted of the 4th battalion of the Rifle Brigade, the 20th Bengal Infantry, the 4th Ghoorkas, and a mountain battery. These were ordered to take a mountain road, and, led by a native guide, to make a long circuit, and so to come down into the pass at a village lying a mile or two beyond Ali-Musjid.

The second brigade, under Colonel Tytler, consisting of the 1st battalion of the 17th Foot, the infantry of the Guides, the 1st Sikhs, and a mountain battery, were also to take to the hills, and, working along on their crests, to come down upon the batteries which the Afghans had erected on the hillside opposite to Ali-Musjid.

THE ADVANCE UP THE KHYBER

The third brigade, consisting of the 81st Regiment, the 14th Sikhs, and the 24th Native Infantry, and the fourth brigade, composed of the 51st Regiment, 6th Native Infantry, and the 45th Sikhs, were to advance straight up the valley; with them was a mountain battery, a battery of Horse Artillery, one of Royal Artillery, and a battery of 40-pounders drawn by elephants.

These brigades marched forward until they reached some rising ground in the valley, whence they could see Ali-Musjid at a distance of a mile and a half in front of them. The enemy at once opened fire. The gunners in the fort had been practising for some weeks, and had got the range with great accuracy, and their shot and shell fell thick along the slope. The column was therefore marched back behind its crest and there halted; and the men were allowed to fall out and eat their dinners, as it was desired that the flanking columns of Macpherson and Tytler, which had very much further to go, should reach the positions assigned to them before the attack began.

The artillery, however, took up their position on the crest, and opened fire on the fort. The effect of the light guns was but slight, but the 40-pounders produced considerable effect on the face of the fort. After a halt for some time the troops were ordered to advance. The 45th Sikhs were first thrown out upon the hillside, and, working their way along on the right of the valley, opened a heavy musketry fire against the Afghans in the batteries there. Presently the 51st and 6th Native Infantry joined them; while the 81st, the 24th, and 14th Sikhs worked along on the left.

The scene was one of the most picturesque ever witnessed in warfare. From the fortress standing on the perpendicular rock in the centre of the valley, the flashes of the great guns came fast and steadily, while the edges of the rock and fort were fringed with tiny puffs of musketry. From the rising ground in the valley the smoke of the British guns rose up in the still air, as, steadily and fast, they replied to the fire of the fort. Both sides of the steep hill slopes were lined with British infantry, the quick flash of the rifles spurting out from every rock and bush; while continuous lines of light smoke

123

rose from the Afghan entrenchments which faced them. Gradually the British skirmishers advanced until they were close to the Afghan entrenchments on the hillsides abreast of the fort.

So far there was no sign that Macpherson's brigade had reached the post assigned to it high up on the hill, or that Tytler had worked round to the village in the enemy's rear. Some attacks which were made upon the Afghans were repulsed with loss. Major Birch and Lieutenant Fitzgerald were killed and Captain Maclean wounded, and between thirty and forty of the rank and file were killed or wounded. As the fort and its defences could not have been carried by direct attack without immense loss of life, it was determined to cease operations until morning in order to give the flanking columns time to reach the positions assigned to them; a wing of a regiment from each brigade was ordered to remain on the hillside facing the Afghan entrenchments; the rest of the troops fell back a short distance and lay down as they were for the night.

In the meantime the brigades of Macpherson and Tytler had encountered enormous difficulties on the line of march. The roads they had taken were mere tracks, and there were many places where it was almost impossible to get the mountain guns along. From daybreak until late at night the troops laboured unceasingly. They knew by the dull roar echoed and re-echoed among the mountains that their comrades below were engaged; and the thought that a failure might ensue, owing to their absence from the contest, nerved them to continued exertions.

Late at night, however, Macpherson with his brigade arrived on the top of the hill facing Ali-Musjid, and Tytler with his column came down into the Khyber valley in rear of the fort. But, though unopposed, their march had not been unnoticed, and late in the evening the news reached the Afghans that the British were marching down into the valley behind them. A wild panic instantly seized them. Clothes, ammunition, guns, everything that could impede their flight, were thrown away, and the garrison of Ali-Musjid and the Afghans in the hillside entrenchments fled, a herd of frightened fugitives, up the valley.

Hasty as was their retreat, they were not in time. Tytler with his column debouched into the valley before they had passed the spot where the mountain path descended into it, and large numbers were taken prisoners. As at the Peiwar-Khotal, the Afghans proved themselves capable of defending a strong position valiantly, but were converted into a mob of panic-stricken fugitives by their line of retreat being threatened.

A European army under like circumstances would have fallen back in good order. Their force was amply sufficient to have swept aside the little column which barred their retreat, and they would have occupied a fresh position farther to the rear and renewed the conflict. Not so the Afghans. The capture of Ali-Musjid brought with it the entire demoralization of the Afghan army, which a few hours before had been fully confident in its power to repulse any attack which might be made upon it.

The British continued their advance, passed through the Khyber Pass, and entered the broad valley near whose head stands the town of Jellalabad. Beyond a few shots fired at them by tribesmen high up on the mountainside, they experienced no opposition whatever, and a week after the fight in the Khyber entered Jellalabad and encamped around it. Further than this it was not intended to go for the present. Winter was now close at hand. Between Jellalabad and Cabul were a series of most difficult passes; an army advancing up them would have immense difficulty to encounter, and might find itself cut off from India by the snows.

In the Jellalabad valley the weather is mild, large stores of provisions were obtainable, and here it was determined to remain through the winter, and to recommence the campaign in the spring with the advantage of the Khyber Pass, one of the keys of Afghanistan, being in our hands. But a day or two after reaching Jellalabad, having defeated and dispersed one of the two Afghan armies, the news arrived of the capture of the Peiwar-Khotal, the second key of Afghanistan, and the utter rout of the army defending it. Thus, in little more than a week after the commencement of the campaign, Sheer-Ali, the Ameer, saw the entire overthrow of the army which he had for so many years been occupied in organizing and training.

The positions which he had deemed impregnable had both been taken after a single day's fighting, and his capital lay virtually at the mercy of his conquerors. In one short week his hopes and plans had been scattered to the winds. Sheer-Ali was not wholly to be blamed. He had for many years received an annual present of money and arms from the British government; but upon the other hand he saw Russia marching with giant steps towards his northern frontier, and contrasting the energy and enterprise of the great northern power with the inactivity which he may have supposed to prevail among the men who governed England, he became more and more anxious, and asked the English definitely to state whether he could rely upon them for assistance should he be attacked by the Russians.

He received a reply from the Duke of Argyle, the British minister for India, of a doubtful nature, couched in terms which seem to have aroused his resentment. From this moment there can be no doubt that the Ameer's course was decided upon. He was between the hammer and the anvil, and as he could obtain no guarantee of assistance from England, he determined to throw himself into the arms of Russia.

Letters were exchanged between him and General Kaufmann, the Russian viceroy in Turkestan, and the latter gave him the warmest promises of support if he would ally himself with Russia.

Although he had for years declined to accept a British resident at Cabul or to allow Englishmen to enter the country, he now, believing in the power and willingness of Russia to help, received the visit of a Russian general and staff at Cabul.

Unfortunately for the Ameer, the government of England had now changed hands, and the ministry at once sent to Sheer-Ali to demand that he should receive a British resident. It was late in the year, and the Ameer, acting no doubt on the advice of his Russian friends, sought to gain time by evasive answers. The British government, who saw through the ruse, ordered the envoy to advance with a strong escort. This obliged the Ameer to come to a final decision, and the die was cast by the escort being stopped by force on its arrival at Ali-Musjid.

There is no doubt that the Ameer and his friends calculated that it was already too late in the season for the English to gather a sufficient force on the frontier to force the passes held by the Afghan army before the snows. The promptness of action of the English government, the valour of their troops, and the unusually late setting in of the winter combined to overthrow the Ameer's plans. Had the campaign been delayed till the spring there can be little doubt that the British in their advance would have found themselves opposed, if not by a Russian army, at least by an army led and officered by Russians, with Russian engineers and artillerymen. The promptness of their advance, and the capture of the passes and the dispersion of the Afghan armies within a week of the opening of the campaign, altogether altered this position.

Sheer-Ali found himself a king without an army. The plains of Cabul were thronged with the panic-stricken fugitives from the Khyber and Peiwar, and Sheer-Ali started at night from his capital with his Russian friends and made for the north, sending letter after letter ahead of him to General Kaufmann imploring the promised aid of Russia. The rapid course of events, however, had entirely disconcerted the Russian plans.

In the spring a Russian army might have advanced and co-operated with that of the Ameer, but the winter had set in, the distance was immense, and the Russians unprepared for instant action. The appeals of the unfortunate prince were responded to with vague generalities. He was no longer a powerful ally, but a broken instrument; and heart-broken with disappointment and failure, the unfortunate Sheer-Ali was seized by fever and died in an obscure village almost alone and wholly uncared for. His son Yakoob Khan, who had in his youth proved himself a brave and able soldier, but who, having incurred his father's displeasure, had been for years confined as a prisoner at Herat, was now liberated and took his place as his father's successor. He saw at once that with a broken and disorganized army he could not hope to resist the advance of the three British armies which, coming from Jellalabad, from the heights of the Shatur-Gardan, and from Candahar, would simultaneously advance upon his capital as soon as the snows melted.

He therefore opened negotiations, and early in May himself descended from Cabul and had an interview with General Browne at Gundamuk, when the preliminaries of peace were arranged and signed. The terms insisted upon by the British were not onerous. Yakoob was recognized as the Ameer of Afghanistan; the annual subsidy paid to his father was to be continued. The Khyber Pass and the Khurum valley as far as the Peiwar-Khotal were to remain in the hands of the British, and a British minister was to be stationed at Cabul. When peace had been signed the greater portion of the British army retired to India, and the Khurum column, leaving two or three regiments in that valley, also fell back.

While the first and second divisions had been gaining victories in the Khyber and Khurum valleys, the column under General Stewart had met with difficulties of another kind.

Between the Indus and the foot of the range of mountains through which the Bolan Pass leads to the lofty plateau land above, a great waste of sand stretches. In the wet season this tract of country is overflowed by the Indus; in the dry season it is a parched and bare desert with its wells few and far apart. There were great difficulties met with in crossing this inhospitable plain, and the losses among the baggage animals were great; but the labours up to this point were as nothing to those which had to be undergone on the way up the Bolan Pass.

This pass, whose ascent occupies three days, is in fact the mere bed of a stream, covered deeply with boulders and stones of all sizes, in which the baggage and artillery horses sank fetlock deep. The difficulties encountered were enormous, and vast numbers of camels, horses, and bullocks died by the way. Even with a double complement of horses, it was almost impossible to drag the guns up the deep shingly pass, and great delays were experienced before the force intended for operations against Candahar were assembled at Quettah. So far the advance had taken place through British territory, as Quettah has long been occupied by us.

When the advance began, it was rapid. No opposition was experienced by the way until the column arrived within a few hours' march of Candahar, and then the enemy's attack was feeble and easily repulsed. On the 9th of January General Stewart entered the city.

Candahar, though not the capital, is the chief town of Afghanistan; it stands in a slightly undulating plain, and was at one time a city of great importance and wealth. Its position is the most important in Afghanistan. It bars the road to an enemy advancing from the north through Herat, and threatens the flank and rear of one advancing against India through Cabul.

The country around is extremely fertile, and were irrigation properly used and a railway constructed to India, Candahar and the surrounding country would again become one of the gardens of the world. The authorities of the city made their submission as the column approached it, and the army settled down to quiet occupation, broken only by isolated attacks upon individual soldiers by fanatical Ghazis.

When peace was concluded, one of the conditions distinctly insisted upon by the British general and agreed to by the Ameer was that Candahar should remain in our possession. The alleged advantage thus gained, and the territory thus acquired, were afterwards abandoned by the British government succeeding that which had so vigorously carried out the war. The occupation of Candahar by the British had been insisted on at first, on the ground that if Russia should make an advance against India, the British nation would have ample cause to rue the cession of Candahar, for it was declared that with this city strongly fortified and surrounded by outlying works, 10,000 British troops there could arrest the progress of an invading army however large, until England had had full time to put forth all her strength and to assemble an army amply sufficient to secure the safety of the most valuable of our possessions—the empire of India.

FOR NAME AND FAME

It was said that whatever allies Russia might have prepared for herself by intrigues among the princes of India, these would not think of moving so long as they knew that the fortress of Candahar remained as a British bulwark against an invading force. It was represented that so long as this place held out, England would be able to devote her whole force towards repelling the foreign invader, instead of being obliged simultaneously to oppose him and to put down a formidable rising in India itself. It was, however, not the universal opinion that the best policy of England was to occupy this territory by an armed force, and subsequent events, with the change of government in England, led to a different determination.

CHAPTER XIII
THE MASSACRE AT CABUL

AT each village through which William Gale and his escort passed, the inhabitants turned out and hooted and yelled at the prisoner, and it was with the greatest difficulty that the chief protected him from personal violence. William himself was scarce conscious of what was passing. The swinging action of the camel added to his great weakness, and he would not have been able to keep his seat on its back had not his captors fastened him with ropes to the saddle. Although the snow had only just melted on the Shatur-Gardan Pass, in the valleys below, the heat of the sun was already great, and often as it poured down upon him he lapsed into a state of semiconsciousness and drowsily fancied that he was again in his canoe tossing on the tiny waves in the shelter of the reef.

On the sixth day after the start, a shout from his guard aroused him as they emerged from a steep ascent amongst some hills. Before him an undulating ground dotted with villages stretched for three or four miles. At the foot of some steep hills to the left of a wide valley was a large walled town which he knew to be Cabul.

On the hillside above it was a strong building, half fort, half palace. This was the Bala-Hissar, the abode of the Ameer, and the fortress of Cabul. In addition to the king's residence it contained barracks, storehouses, magazines, and many residences. Towards this the cavalcade made its way.

They halted two miles from the town, and the chief sent his son forward to the Ameer to inform him that he had brought in an English prisoner, and to request that an escort might be sent out lest he should be killed by the people on approaching the town. An hour after the man had left, a troop of cavalry sallied out from the

131

gate of the Bala-Hissar and rode rapidly to the spot where the party had halted. Surrounding the camel on which William Gale was mounted, they conducted it to the fortress.

When he was lifted down from his camel, Will was unable to stand. Fever had set in again, and he was conveyed to an apartment in a house near the royal residence. The Ameer was already negotiating with the British, and orders were consequently given that the prisoner should receive every attention. The king's own doctor was ordered to attend him, and two attendants were told off to take charge of him. The old chief received a recompense for the care which he had taken of the prisoner, which fully answered to his expectations, and he returned home well satisfied with the success of his policy.

For weeks Will lay between life and death, and he was a mere skeleton when, two months after his arrival, he was able for the first time to sit up at the window and look across the valley. Very gradually he recovered strength. He was well supplied with food, and especially enjoyed the delicious fruits for which Cabul is celebrated. His attendants were an old man and his son, the latter a lad of some fifteen years of age. The father did his duty because ordered to do so, but his scowling face often showed the hatred which he felt of the Kaffir. The lad, however, took kindly to his patient. He it was who for hours together would, while Will was at his worst, sit by his bedside constantly changing the wet cloths wrapped round his head, and sometimes squeezing a few drops of the refreshing juice of some fruit between his parched lips; and as his patient turned the corner and became slowly convalescent, his pleasure over the life he had saved by his care was very great.

Like most soldiers in the expeditionary force, Will had picked up a few words of Afghan, and had greatly increased his stock during the time he lay in the hut in the mountains. Alone now all day with the boy, with nothing to do but to look out on the town below and the wide valley beyond, he made rapid progress, and was, by the time he was strong enough to walk alone across the

William Gale in the hands of the Afghans.

room, able to hold some sort of conversation with his friend; for so he had come to regard his devoted attendant. One morning the boy came into the room in a state of great excitement.

"English officers are coming," he said, "with soldiers!"

"But I thought it was peace!" Will exclaimed, delighted. "You told me peace had been signed at Gundamuk two months ago."

"Yes, it is peace," the boy said; "the officers are coming in friendship to be here with the Ameer."

Will was greatly moved at the news. When he had heard, six weeks before, that peace was signed, he had begun to hope that some day or other he should again be able to return to India, but the news that some of his countrymen were close at hand almost overcame him. The next day, which was the 24th of July—although Will had lost all account of time—he saw vast numbers of people out on the plain, and presently far away he beheld a large body of horsemen. These, the lad told him, were the Ameer and his body-guard, accompanied by the English officers.

Cannon were fired in salute, and the garrison of the Bala-Hissar stood to their arms, and presently Will saw a cavalcade riding up from the gate of the fortress. First came some Afghan cavalry, then rode a tall and stately man whom the boy told him was the Ameer. But Will had no eyes for him; all his thoughts were centered on the white officer who rode beside him, Major Sir Lewis Cavagnari, the English envoy. Behind, among the chiefs of the Ameer's suite, rode two or three other English officers, and then came a detachment of some twenty-five cavalry and fifty infantry of the Guides, a frontier force consisting of picked men.

As they passed near his window Will stood up with his hand to his forehead in salute. Major Cavagnari looked up in surprise and spoke to the Ameer. The latter said a few words in reply, and then the cavalcade rode on to the palace. Ten minutes later two of the Ameer's attendants entered and told Will to follow them.

THE MASSACRE AT CABUL

He had that morning, for the first time since his arrival in Cabul, put on his uniform. He was still very weak, but, leaning one hand upon his attendant's shoulder, he followed the messengers. He was conducted to a large room in the palace, where the Ameer and his adviser and the British officers were sitting.

"Well, my lad," Major Cavagnari said kindly, "I hear you have had a bad time of it. The Ameer tells me that you were taken prisoner near Ali-Kheyl, that you were badly wounded, and that after the snow melted you were brought down here. He says he gave orders that everything should be done for you, but that you have been very ill ever since."

"I have been treated very kindly, sir," Will said, "and I am now getting round. I owe my life chiefly to the care and attention of the lad here, who has watched over me like a brother."

Will's words were translated to the Ameer, who expressed his satisfaction, and ordered a purse of money to be given to the boy in testimony of his approval of the care he had taken of his patient. As Major Cavagnari saw that the young soldier was almost too weak to stand, he at once told him to retire to his room, adding kindly:

"I will ask the Ameer to assign you quarters in the same house with us; we will soon bring you round and make you strong and well again."

The same evening Will was carried over—for the fatigue he had undergone had been almost too much for him—to the large house assigned to Major Cavagnari, his officers, and escort. It was built of wood, surrounded by a court-yard and wall. A room was assigned to Will on the same floor as that occupied by the officers. The Afghan lad had received orders to accompany his patient and remain with him as long as he stayed in Cabul.

Will's progress towards recovery was now rapid. He had no longer any cause for anxiety. He was carefully attended to by Dr. Kelly, the surgeon of the Guides, who had accompanied the mission as medical officer. The escort was commanded by Lieut. Hamilton, and Sir Lewis Cavagnari was accompanied by Mr. William Jenkyns of the Indian Civil Service as his secretary. The care of Dr. Kelly and the influence of quinine and tonics quickly added to Will's strength, but his best medicine was the sound of English voices and the kindness which was shown to him.

In a fortnight he was able to get about as usual, and the doctor said that in another month he would be as strong as ever. For two or three weeks after Major Cavagnari's arrival in Cabul, all went well; and it appeared as if the forebodings of those who had predicted trouble and danger to the little body who had gone up, as it were, into the lion's den, were likely to be falsified. That the mission was not without danger the authorities and Major Cavagnari himself were well aware; but it was important that the provision in the treaty of Gundamuk by which England secured the right of maintaining a resident at Cabul should be put into operation; besides, the Ameer had himself given the invitation to Major Cavagnari, and had pressed the point warmly, giving the most solemn promises of protection. At any rate, for the first two weeks, the soldiers of the escort moved freely in the city without molestation or insult, and it appeared as if the population of Cabul were content with the terms of peace, which indeed imposed no burdens whatever upon them, and was supposed to have inflicted no humiliation on their national pride.

On the 5th of August several regiments marched in from Herat. These troops, which were considered the flower of the Afghan army, had, in consequence of the distance of Herat from the seat of war, taken no part whatever in the struggle. Upon the very day after their arrival they scattered through the town, and were loud in their expression of hostility to the terms of peace. Had they been there, they said, the Kaffirs would have been easily defeated. Why should peace have been made at the very first reverse, and before the best fighting men had come to the front?

That evening Will Gale's young attendant came to him in his room looking very serious.

"What is the matter, Yossouf?"

The lad shook his head. "Trouble is coming," he said. "The Heratee men are stirring up the people, and the Budmashes are threatening that they will kill the English."

"But the Ameer has promised his protection," Will said; "he has sworn a solemn oath to stand by them."

"Yakoob Khan is weak," the boy said; "he was a great warrior once, but he has been in prison for many years and he is no longer firm and strong. Some of the men round him are bad advisers. Yakoob Khan is no better than a reed to lean upon."

The next day there were riots in the town. The Heratee men taunted the people of Cabul with cowardice, and the excitement spread in the city. The soldiers of the escort could no longer stroll quietly through the bazaars, but were hooted at and abused, although of the same religion and race as the people around them— for the Guide regiments were recruited from Pathans and other border tribes. Day after day the position became more threatening. The men of the escort were ordered no longer to go down into the town, where their presence was the occasion of tumults.

A native officer of one of our cavalry regiments who was spending his furlough at a village near Cabul came into the Bala-Hissar and told Major Cavagnari that he feared, from rumours that reached him, that the Heratee regiments would break into mutiny and attack the embassy. The officer, who was a man of immense courage and coolness, replied quietly:

"If they do, they can but kill the three or four of us here, and our deaths will be revenged."

He, however, made representations to the Ameer as to the threatening behaviour of the Heratee troops; but Yakoob assured him that he could rely thoroughly upon his protection, and that even should the Heratee troops break out in mutiny, he would at once suppress the movement with the Cabul regiments. Yossouf became daily more anxious. Going into the town to buy fruits and other necessaries, he heard more of what was going on than could the members of the embassy.

"Things are very bad," he said over and over again. "It would be better for you all to go away. Why does your officer stop here to be killed?"

"It is his duty to stay at his post," Will said. "He has been sent here by the commander-in-chief. He is like a soldier on outpost duty, he cannot desert his post because he sees danger approaching; but I wish with all my heart that an order would come for his recall, not only because of the danger, but because I am longing to be back again with my regiment; and although I am strong enough to ride down to the Punjaub now, I cannot go except with Sir Lewis and his escort. Although it is peace, a single Englishman could not travel down to Jellalabad through the passes."

Will had from the first week after the arrival of the mission fallen into the position of an orderly-room sergeant. His duties were little more than nominal, but he acted as assistant to Mr. Jenkyns, and made copies and duplicates of reports and other documents which were from time to time sent down to Jellalabad. Being the only Englishman there, with the exception of the four officers, these greatly relaxed the usual distance prevailing between an officer and a corporal, and treated him as a civilian clerk when in office, and with a pleasant cordiality at other times. Except, indeed, that he messed alone and kept in his own room of an evening, he might have been one of the party. Each day he reported to Sir Lewis the rumours which Yossouf had gathered in the town. In his reports to headquarters, Major Cavagnari stated that trouble had arisen from the conduct of the Heratee troops, but he scarcely made enough of the real danger which threatened the little party. Had he done so, the embassy would probably have been recalled.

"What have you got there, Yossouf?" Will asked one day, when his follower returned with a larger bundle than usual.

"I have brought the uniform of an Afghan soldier," the boy replied, "which I have purchased from the bazaar; it is for you. I am sure that soon you will be attacked. The English are brave, but there are only four of them. Their soldiers will fight, but what can they do against an army? When the time comes, you must dress yourself in these clothes and I will try to conceal you."

"But I cannot do that, Yossouf," Will said. "It is very good of you to try and aid me to escape; but I am a soldier, and must share the fortunes of my officers, whatever they may be. If they fight, I shall fight. If they are killed, I must be killed, too. I cannot run away and hide myself when the danger comes."

The lad hung his head.

"Then Yossouf will die, too," he said quietly; "he will not leave his white friend."

"No, no, Yossouf," Will said warmly; "you have nothing to do with the business. Why should you involve yourself in our fate? You can do me no good by sacrificing your life."

Yossouf shook his head.

"If," he said presently, "the time comes, and you see that it is of no use any longer to fight, and that all is lost, would you try to escape then?"

"Yes," Will said, "certainly I would. When all hope of further resistance is gone, and fighting is useless, my duty would be at an end, and if I could manage to escape then, I should be justified in trying to save my life."

Yossouf looked relieved. "Very well," he said, "then at the last I will try and save you."

"Still, Yossouf," Will said, " we must hope that it is not coming to that. The Ameer has sworn to protect us, and he can do so. The Bala-Hissar is strong, and he can easily hold it with one or two of his Cabul regiments against the Heratee men. He has three or four of these regiments here. He cannot be so false to his oath as to allow his guests to be massacred."

Yossouf made a gesture which expressed his utter disbelief in the Ameer, and then again went about his duties. On the 2d of September, on his return from the town, he reported that there was great excitement among the people, and that he believed that the night would not pass off without trouble. Major Cavagnari, to whom Will reported the news, sent in a message to the Ameer, whose palace was within two or three hundred yards, and begged him to take measures to secure the Bala-Hissar against any attack by the Heratees.

FOR NAME AND FAME

The members of the escort available for the defence of the residency were but about fifty men. Most of the cavalry were away; some were down the pass with despatches, the rest were stationed a short distance off in the plain, as forage was difficult to obtain in the fort. The Ameer returned a curt message to Major Cavagnari, saying that there was no cause for uneasiness. The latter, however, doubled the sentries at the gate of the little inclosure.

Just as the officers were about to retire to rest, Yossouf, who had a short time before gone out again, telling Will that he would bring back news of what was going on, ran in.

"The Heratees are coming!" he said. "The gates of the fort have been left open. The Cabul men are all in their barracks. They are pouring in at the gates; do you not hear them?"

William Gale ran to the window, and could hear a loud and confused noise of yelling and shouting. He ran in to the envoy's room and warned him that the Heratees were at hand. Without the loss of a moment's time, Lieutenant Hamilton got his men under arms, and posted them at the upper windows of the house, where their fire would command the approaches to the gate. Quickly as this was done, the Afghans were close at hand by the time that each man was at his post, and instantly opened a scattering fire at the residency, shouting to the soldiers to come out and join them, and to bring out the Kaffir officers to be killed. The Pathans were, however, true to their salt, and in reply opened a steady fire upon the mass of the enemy. With wild yells the Afghans rushed at the gate, but so steadily and rapidly did the defenders shoot from the upper windows and loopholes cut in the gate that the assailants were forced to fall back.

"That's right, my lads," Major Cavagnari said cheerfully to his men; "we can hold the place for some time, and the Ameer will bring the Cabul regiments down in no time and sweep away these rascals."

The Afghans, now some thousands strong, assisted by all the Budmashes and turbulent portion of the population of Cabul, surrounded the house on all sides, and kept up a heavy and incessant fire, which was coolly and steadily returned by the Guides. After an hour's fighting there was a sudden roar above the rattle of musketry, followed by another and another. Simultaneously came the crash of shells. One burst in the house, the other tore through the gate. Still there was no sign of the Cabul regiments.

Eight or ten guns were brought to play on the little garrison. The gate was broken down, and nearly half the force of the house were already killed or wounded by the musketry and shell fire. Still they continued the defence. Over and over again the Afghans swarmed up close to the gate, only to fall back again before the steady fire of the Snider rifles of the Guides. Major Cavagnari went from room to room encouraging the men, while the other officers and Will Gale, taking rifles which had fallen from the hands of men no longer able to use them, set an example of cool and steady firing to their men.

For four hours the unequal contest continued; then a cry arose from the men that the house was on fire.

It was but too true. A shell had exploded in the lower part of the house and had ignited the woodwork, and the fire had already obtained so firm a hold that it was impossible to extinguish it. A few of the men continued their fire from the windows to the last, while the rest carried their wounded comrades out into the court-yard. As the flames shot out from the lower windows the yells of the Afghans rose higher and higher, and a fearful storm of lead and iron swept down upon the little band, who were now plainly visible in the light of the flames. Even now the enemy did not dare, although numbering hundreds to one, to come too close upon them, though they flocked up close to the gate.

"Now, lads!" Major Cavagnari exclaimed. "Let us rush out and die fighting hand to hand; better that than to be shot down defenceless here."

Thus saying, he led the way, and charged out upon the crowded foe. There were but Lieutenant Hamilton and eight men to follow him; all the rest had fallen. Dr. Kelly had been shot in the house while dressing the wound of one of the soldiers. Mr. Jenkyns had fallen outside. Will Gale had twice been wounded, but was still on his feet, and, grasping his musket, he rushed forward with his comrades. A figure sprang out just as he reached the gate, and with a sudden rush carried him along for some paces. Then he stumbled over a fragment of the wall, and fell just at the corner of the gate, which had swung inward when burst open by the enemy's shell. Confused and bewildered, he struggled to regain his feet.

"Keep quiet, master!" Yossouf's voice said in his ear. "It is your only chance of safety."

So saying, he dragged Will into the narrow space between the gate and the wall; then, as he rose to his feet, he wrapped round him a loose Afghan cloak, and pressed a black sheepskin cap far down over his face. In a minute there was the sound of a fierce struggle without. The shots of the revolvers of the two English officers rang out in quick succession, mingled with the loud report of the Afghan muskets. The savage yells rose high and triumphant. The last of the gallant band who had for hours defended the embassy had fallen. Then there was a rush through the gate as the Afghans swarmed into the court-yard, till the space around the burning house was well-nigh full.

Unperceived, Will Gale and Yossouf stepped from behind the gate and joined the throng, and at once made their way into the stables, where several of the Budmashes were already engaged in their work of plunder. Yossouf caught up three or four horse-rugs and made them into a loose bundle, and signed to Will to do the same. The young soldier did so, and lifted them on his shoulder so as to partly hide his face. Then he followed Yossouf into the court-yard again.

Already there was a stream of men with saddles, rugs, muskets, and other plunder, making their way out, while others were still thronging in. Joining the former, Will and his guide were soon outside the inclosure. At any other time his disguise would have been noticed at once, but in the crowd his legs were hidden, and all were too intent upon plunder and too excited at their success to notice him.

Once outside the wall, he was comparatively safe; the light thrown over the court-yard by the blazing house made the darkness beyond all the more complete. Keeping carefully in shadow, Yossouf led him along to a clump of bushes in a garden a hundred yards from the house. Stooping here, he pulled out a bundle.

"Here," he said, "is the uniform. Put it on quickly!"

It was but the work of a minute for Will to attire himself in the uniform of the Afghan soldier. He had still retained the musket which he had in his hand when Yossouf had leapt upon him, and as he now went on with his guide he had no fear whatever of being detected. He still carried the bundle of rugs on his shoulder. As they walked round towards the lower gate of the Bala-Hissar, they met numbers of villagers and townspeople thronging in. These had waited to hear the issue of the attack before leaving their homes; but now that the arrival of the plunderers from the residency and the cessation of the fire told of the successful termination of the assault, they flocked up to join in the rejoicings over the annihilation of the Kaffirs.

CHAPTER XIV
THE ADVANCE UPON CABUL

THROUGHOUT the long hours of the night of the 2d of September, while the roll of musketry and the roar of cannon had gone on without a moment's pause just outside the walls of his palace, Yakoob Khan had made no movement whatever to protect his guests or fulfil his own solemn promises. Silent and sullen he had sat in his council-chamber.

The disgrace of a broken promise is not one which weighs heavily upon an Afghan's mind, and it is not probable that the thought of his tarnished honour troubled him in the slightest degree; but he knew that the massacre which was being perpetrated at his door would be avenged, and that the English troops which had so easily beaten the army which his father had spent so many years in preparing would be set in movement against Cabul the moment the news reached India. He cannot but have dreaded the consequences. But he apparently feared even more to incur the hostility of the Heratee regiment by interfering to save their victims.

Again and again during the night his wisest councillors besought him to call upon the loyal Cabullee regiments to act against the Heratees, but in vain. It is doubtful whether Yakoob was previously informed of the intended massacre, but there is strong reason to believe that he was so; the proofs, however, were not clear and definite. His conduct cost him his throne, and condemned him to remain to the end of his life a dishonoured pensioner and semi-prisoner in India.

Many eager questions were asked of Will and his companion as they made their way down to the gate of the Bala-Hissar. Yossouf took upon himself to answer them, and they passed through the gate without the slightest suspicion.

144

"Which way now?"

"I think it will be safest to go into the city. We might lie hid for a few days in some deserted hut, but sooner or later our presence there would excite comment. It will be best, I think, to go into the city. In the quarters of the Parsee merchants there are assuredly some who would give you shelter. Domajee, who was the contractor for the supply of the mission, would, I should think, be best to go to. There is little danger, for none will suspect your presence there; his servants are all Hindoos."

"That is the best place, Yossouf. I have been down several times to Domajee, and he is certainly devoted to the English; we can but try him."

The first dawn of morning was breaking when Will and his faithful friend arrived at the door of the Parsee trader in the Hindoo quarter of Cabul. The doors were fastened and barred, for it was impossible to say whether the attack upon the mission which had been heard going on all night might not be followed by a fanatic outbreak against the Hindoo and Parsee traders in the Hindoo quarter; therefore there was little sleep that night. Yossouf knocked gently at the door.

"Who is there?" a voice at once inquired from within.

"I come on urgent business with Domajee," Yossouf replied; "open quickly, there are but two of us here."

There was a slight pause, and then the door was opened, and closed immediately the two visitors had entered. A light was burning in the large ante-room as they entered it, and several Hindoos who had been lying wrapped up in cloths on the floor rose to their feet to inspect the new-comers. A moment later the trader himself came down the stairs from an apartment above.

"What is it?" he asked. He did not pause for an answer. The light from the lamp he carried fell upon Will's face, now white as a sheet from loss of blood. With the one word, "Follow," the Parsee turned on his heel and led the way upstairs.

"Has the mission been captured?" he asked, as they entered an empty room.

"Yes," Will replied, "and I believe that I am the only survivor."

145

The fatigue of climbing the stairs completed the work caused by prolonged excitement and loss of blood; and as he spoke he tottered and would have fallen had not Yossouf seized him, and with the assistance of the Parsee laid him on a couch.

In a few words Yossouf informed the trader of what had happened, and satisfied him that no suspicion could arise of the presence of one of the British in his house. As the residency had been burnt down, and the bodies of those who had fallen within it consumed, no one would suspect that one of the five Englishmen there had effected his escape, and it would be supposed that Will's body, like that of Dr. Kelly, had been consumed in the flames.

The Parsee was sure that Cabul would soon be reoccupied by the British, and, putting aside his loyalty to them, he felt that his concealment of an English survivor of the massacre would be greatly to his advantage, and would secure for him the custom of the English upon their arrival at the town. He first descended the stairs, and warned his Hindoo followers on no account whatever to breathe a word of the entry of strangers there. Then he again returned to the room, where Yossouf was sprinkling water on Will's face, and was endeavouring to recover him to consciousness.

"There is blood on the couch," the trader said; "he is wounded, and is suffering from its loss. See! The sleeve of his coat is soaked with blood, but I see no mark on the cloth."

"No," Yossouf replied; "he has put on that uniform since the fight."

"Go down-stairs," the trader said; "my wife and daughter will see to him."

As soon as Yossouf left the room, Domajee's wife and daughter entered with many exclamations of surprise and alarm. They were at once silenced by the trader, who bid them cut off the wounded man's uniform and stanch his wounds. Will had been hit in two places. One ball had passed through the left arm, fortunately without injuring the bone; the other had struck him in the side, had run round his ribs and gone out behind, inflicting an ugly-looking but not serious wound—its course being marked by a blue line on the flesh behind the two holes of entry and exit. The wounds were washed and bound up, some cordial was poured between his lips, and ere long he opened his eyes and looked round in bewilderment.

"You are safe and among friends," the Parsee said. "Drink a little more of the cordial, and then go off quietly to sleep. You need have no fear of being discovered, and your friends will be here ere long."

Four of the Hindoo servants now, at the order of the trader, came upstairs, and, lifting the couch, carried Will to a cool and airy chamber in the upper story of the house. Here a soft bed of rugs and mattresses was prepared, and Will was soon in a quiet sleep, with Yossouf watching by his side.

It was but twenty-four hours after the massacre that a well-mounted native from Cabul brought the news over the Shatur-Gardan Pass into the Khurum valley; thence it was telegraphed to Simla, and in a few hours all India rang with it. Not an instant was lost in making preparations for avenging the murder of the British mission. On the same day orders were sent to Brigadier-General Massy, at that time commanding the field force in the Khurum valley, to move the 23d Punjab Pioneers, the 5th Ghoorkas, and a mountain battery to the crest of the Shatur-Gardan Pass, and to intrench themselves there.

A day or two later the 72d Highlanders and the 5th Punjaub Infantry ascended the Peiwar-Khotal to Ali-Kheyl, to secure the road between the Khotal and the pass. The 72d then moved forward and joined the 23d Pioneers and 5th Ghoorkas on the Shatur-Gardan, and on the 13th General Baker arrived there and took the command; but some time was needed before the advance could commence. As is usual with the British, the great transport train which had with such pains been collected and organized for the war, had been dispersed immediately peace was signed, and the whole work had now to be recommenced.

Vast numbers of animals had been used up during the campaign, and there was the greatest difficulty in obtaining the minimum number which was required before the troops could move. At last General Roberts managed to collect in the Punjaub

2000 mules and 700 camels and bullocks. The tribes in the Khurum valley, too, who had been kindly treated and were well satisfied with the change of masters, furnished many animals for the transport of stores as far as the Shatur-Gardan.

The news had thrown the Gilgis and other tribes among the mountains beyond the Peiwar-Khotal into a state of ferment, and several determined attacks were made by them upon convoys on their way up to the head of the pass. These, however, were always successfully repulsed by the baggage guards, with considerable loss to the assailants, and on the 26th September, three weeks from the date of the massacre, General Roberts joined the troops at Ali-Kheyl and moved forward to the Shatur-Gardan.

During this time two or three letters had been received from the Ameer, who wrote to General Roberts deprecating any advance of the British troops, and saying that he was trying to restore order, to put down the mutinous Heratee troops, and to punish them for their conduct.

As, however, the details which had been received of the massacre showed that the Ameer had behaved in a most suspicious if not in a most treacherous manner at the time of the massacre, and that, if he possessed any authority whatever over the troops, he had not attempted to exercise it, no attention was paid to his letters.

The advanced party of the invading force moved down from the Shatur-Gardan Pass. It consisted of the 12th and 14th Bengal Cavalry, two guns of the Royal Horse Artillery, two companies of the 72d Highlanders, and the 5th Punjaub Native Infantry. The road was found to be extremely steep and difficult, and much labour was necessary before it could be made practicable for guns and wheeled carriages. No enemy was encountered, and the little force encamped at night in the Logan valley, over which the cavalry skirmished far ahead, but found no foes awaiting them.

On the following day they made another march forward, the brigades of Generals Baker and Macpherson descending from the pass into the valley. The advance force halted at Zerghun-Shah, and soon after they had done so, some of the cavalry rode in with the surprising news that the Ameer was close at hand.

THE ADVANCE UPON CABUL

Half an hour later Yakoob Khan, attended by some of his principal nobles, rode into camp. He was received with the honour due to his rank, but personally General Roberts greeted him with great coldness. The Ameer stated that he came into camp because he could not control the soldiery of Cabul, and that therefore he had left the place and come in to show his friendship for the English.

Whatever may have been the motives for his coming, they were never fully explained; circumstances which afterwards occurred strongly confirmed the suspicion that he meditated treachery. He was treated honourably; but the guard of honour which was assigned to him was in fact a guard over him, and from that time he was virtually a prisoner.

General Roberts declined altogether to discuss with him the events of the massacre of Cabul, saying that this was a matter which could not now be entered into, but would be fully investigated on the arrival at the Afghan capital. The following day the brigades of Generals Baker and Macpherson joined the advance at Zerghun-Shah.

The amount of transport available was only sufficient for half the baggage of the army, and it was necessary, therefore, to move forward in two divisions, the one advancing a day's march, and then halting while the animals went back to bring up the baggage of the second division on the following day.

A proclamation was now issued by the general and sent forward among the people of the valley, saying that the object of the expedition was only to punish those concerned in the massacre at Cabul, and that all loyal subjects of the Ameer would be well treated. On the 3d of October Macpherson's brigade, with the cavalry, reached Suffed-Sang. Here they halted while the baggage animals went back to bring up General Baker's brigade.

The attitude of the people of the valley had now become very threatening. Great numbers of hill-tribemen had come down, and on this day an attack was made upon the rear-guard, but was beaten off with loss. That the natives were bitterly hostile was undoubted, but they were for the most part waiting to see the result of the approaching fight. The Heratee and Cabul regiments were confident that they would defeat the approaching column. They had a great advantage in numbers, had been drilled in European fashion, were armed with Enfields, and had an enormous park of artillery at their disposal. They were able to choose their own fighting ground, and had selected a spot which gave them an immense advantage. They were therefore confident of victory.

Had the British troops been beaten, the inhabitants of the Logan valley were prepared to rise to a man. The Ghilzais and other hill-tribes would have swept down upon the line of retreat, and few if any of the British force would have returned to tell the tale.

The next day Baker's division had the post of honour, and made a short march to Chaurasia. Beyond this village the enemy had taken up their position. Three miles beyond the village the valley ends, a mass of hills shutting it in, with only a narrow defile leading through them to the plain of Cabul beyond.

Upon both sides of the defile the enemy had placed guns in position and lined the whole circle of the hills commanding the approach to it. Mountaineers from their birth, they believed that although the British infantry might possess a superiority in the plain, they could be no match for them on the steep hillside; and they no doubt thought that no attempt would be made to storm so strong a position, but that the British column would march straight up the valley into the defile, where they would be helplessly slaughtered by the guns and matchlock men on the heights. Judging from their own tactics, they had reason for the belief that their position was an impregnable one.

In their hill fights the Afghans never come to close quarters. Posted behind rocks and huge boulders, the opposing sides keep up a distant musketry duel, lasting sometimes for days, until one side or the other becomes disheartened with its losses or has exhausted its ammunition. Then it falls back, and the other claims the victory. The idea that English soldiers would, under a heavy fire from their concealed force, steadily climb up the broken mountain-side and come to close quarters, probably never entered into their calculations.

THE ADVANCE UPON CABUL

At daybreak on the 6th a working party were sent forward to improve the road towards the defile. But they had scarcely started when the cavalry patrol in advance rode in and announced that the enemy were in great strength on the hills, and had guns in position to command the road.

General Roberts had now a choice of two courses—he could either attack the whole Afghan force with the one division at hand, or he could wait until joined by Macpherson's brigade next morning. The feat of carrying such a position in face of an immensely superior force with only half of his little command was a very serious one; but, upon the other hand, every hour added to the number of hillmen who swarmed upon the flanks of the army just beyond musket range. A delay of twenty-four hours would bring the whole fighting force of the tribesmen into the valley, and while attacking the enemy's position in the front, he would be liable to an assault upon his rear by them.

Confident in the valour of his soldiers, he chose the first alternative, and at eleven o'clock his little force marched out from the camp to attack the Afghan army.

By this time the enemy's position had been reconnoitred, and it was found to be too strong for a direct attack. It was therefore resolved to ascend the hills on both flanks and so to drive their defenders back beyond the defile. This in any case would have been the best mode of assault, but against semi-savage enemies, flank attacks are peculiarly effective. Having prepared for an assault in one direction, they are disconcerted and disheartened by finding themselves attacked in a different manner, and the fear of a flank being turned and the line of retreat thereby menaced will generally suffice to cause a rapid retreat.

General Baker himself took the command of the left attack. His force consisted of four guns of No. 2 Mountain Battery, two Gatling guns, the 7th company of Sappers and Miners, a wing of the 72d Highlanders, six companies of the 5th Ghoorkas, 200 men of the 5th Punjab Infantry, and 450 of the 23d Pioneers. This was the main column of attack. The right column, under the command of Major White of the 72d Highlanders, consisted of a wing of that regiment, 100 men of the 23d Pioneers, three guns of the Royal Artillery, and two squadrons of cavalry. This attack was intended only as a feint, and to distract the attention of the Afghans from the main attack. A strong reserve was left in Charasia to guard the baggage and to overhaul the tribesmen.

As General Baker's column reached the foot of the hills, the 23d, who led the advance, thrown out in skirmishing line, began to climb the ascent. The enemy were armed with Sniders and Enfields, and their fire was rapid and continuous; fortunately it was by no means accurate, and our losses were small.

The Afghans in their hill fighting are accustomed to fire very slowly and deliberately, taking steady aim with their guns resting on the rocks, and so fighting they are excellent shots. It is probable, however, that the steady advance of our men towards them flurried and disconcerted them, and that they thought more of firing quickly than of taking a correct aim. The 72d pressing up the hill were assisted by the fire of the mountain guns and Gatlings, and by that of the Punjaubees in their rear. Gradually the upper slopes of the hills were gained, and the British troops, pressing forward, drove the Afghans back along the crest. Several times they made obstinate stands, holding their ground until the 72d were close to them.

These, however, would not be denied. The massacre of the mission at Cabul had infuriated the soldiers, and each man was animated with a stern determination to avenge our murdered countrymen. For an hour and a half the fight continued, and then the Afghans abandoned the ridge and fled in confusion. They rallied upon some low hills 600 yards from the rear, but the mountain guns and Gatlings opened upon them, and the whole line advancing to the attack, the enemy fell back. Major White's column had been doing excellent service on the right. Although the attack had been intended only as a feint, it was pushed forward so vigorously that it met with a success equal to that which had attended the main column on the left. The enemy were driven off the hills on the right of the defile. Twenty guns were captured, and the direct road cleared of the enemy.

THE ADVANCE UPON CABUL

Unfortunately our cavalry was in the rear. The road through the pass was difficult, and before they could get through into the plain on the other side, the masses of Afghans had fallen back into the strong villages scattered over it, and could not be attacked by cavalry alone. The enemy had from 9000 to 10,000 men upon the ridge, including thirteen regiments of regular troops. They left 300 dead upon the field, and besides these carried off large numbers of killed and wounded during the fight. Upon our side only 20 were killed and 67 wounded.

Had General Roberts had his whole force with him, he could, after capturing the hills, have at once pushed forward and have attacked the enemy on the plain, and the Afghans, disheartened and panic-stricken, would have been completely crushed. With so small a force in hand, and the possibility of a serious attack by the tribes on his rear, General Roberts did not think it prudent to advance farther, and the regiments which had taken the principal part in the massacre of Cabul marched away unmolested.

Enormously superior as they still were in numbers, they had no thought of further resistance. The capture of positions which they deemed impregnable by a force so inferior in number to their own had utterly disheartened them, and the Heratee regiments, which but the day before had been so proudly confident of their ability to exterminate the Kaffirs, were now utterly demoralized and panic-stricken. In the night the whole of the Afghan troops scattered and fled. Our cavalry, under General Massy, swept along the plain of Cabul, and, skirting the town, kept on as far as the Ameer's great intrenched camp at Sherpur, three miles further along the valley. Here 75 guns were captured.

In the morning Macpherson arrived. General Roberts now advanced with his whole force of infantry and found that he had no longer a foe before him. The Afghan army had disappeared. There was no longer any occasion for haste, and the column halted until all the baggage had been brought up through the difficult defile. The total defeat of the Afghan army had overawed the tribesmen, and these at once retired to their hills again.

The villagers, however, were bitterly hostile, and seized every opportunity of firing at small bodies of troops on cavalry patrols. This continued for some time, and General Roberts at last was obliged to punish it with severity, and in such cases all found with arms in their hands were at once shot. On the 11th of October, Sir Frederick Roberts and his staff, with a cavalry escort, rode into the Bala-Hissar, and the next morning the British troops marched into the fort. The gates of Cabul stood open, and a column was marched through the town and formal possession taken of it.

During the first five weeks which elapsed after the massacre of the mission, William Gale remained almost prostrate in the house of the friendly Parsee trader. He had barely recovered his strength after his prolonged illness when the attack was made, and the events of that night, and the great loss of blood which he had suffered, had reduced his strength to that of an infant. Under the care of the Parsee and his family, however, he slowly but steadily regained strength. For the first month but little news reached him from without; then a report came that the British had assembled in considerable force on the crest of the Shatur-Gardan, and were going to move on Cabul from that direction. Then day by day the tidings came in of the advance of the force.

It was reported generally that the Ameer had gone out to meet them, with the intention of leaving them when the decisive moment arrived and taking command of the tribesmen, who would fall upon and annihilate them. On the 6th the town was unusually quiet, and Will heard that the Afghan army had moved out to occupy the hills commanding the approach through the defile, and that with the aid of the tribesmen the British army was to be exterminated there.

CHAPTER XV
THE FIGHTING ROUND CABUL

ALL day long, on the 6th of October, William Gale sat at an open window in the upper story of the Parsee's house facing west, and listened to the distant roar of the battle, while all Cabul was in a state of wild excitement in the sure anticipation of victory. Will felt equally confident as to the result of the battle. He knew that, well led, a British force could be trusted to carry any position held by the Afghans, and he felt sure that even should he fail to carry it by direct attack, the English general would sooner or later succeed in turning it by flank movements.

About two o'clock in the afternoon William noticed a change in the character of the sounds in the town. In the Hindoo quarter all had been quiet, for the inhabitants greatly feared that, in a burst of fanaticism following a victory achieved over the British, the Afghans might sack the Hindoo quarter and murder its inhabitants. Yossouf, however, had been all the morning out in the town, and had from time to time brought in a report of the rumours current there.

At first it was said that the British were being utterly routed, that they were being exterminated by the Afghan fire, that the hill-tribes were sweeping down upon their rear, and that not a man would escape. Presently the reports became more contradictory. The firing was still heard, but it was no longer one continuous roll. Some said that the British were annihilated; others that, repulsed in their attack, they had fallen back to their camp; but soon after two o'clock Yossouf rushed up to William's room with the news that the Afghans had been driven from the heights, and that the British were in possession of these and of the defile through them. Yossouf had throughout the morning been swayed by conflicting emotions and wishes. At one moment he hoped that his countrymen

155

might conquer; then the fear that after victory the Hindoo quarter might be sacked and his English friend discovered and killed, overpowered his feeling of patriotism.

It must be remembered that Afghanistan has for centuries been rather a geographical expression than a country. Its population is composed of a great number of tribes without any common feelings or interest, and often engaged in desperate wars and conflicts with each other. The two leading tribes, the Ghilzais and Duranees, had long struggled for ascendency in the cultivated portion of the country. For a long period the Ghilzais had had the supremacy, but the Duranees were now lords of the country.

The mountain tribes for the most part held themselves entirely independent, and although in time they gave a nominal allegiance to the Ameer of Cabul, yet, as had been shown in the Khurum valley, they hated their native masters with an animosity far exceeding that which they felt towards the British. That throughout the war the tribesmen were ready when they saw an opportunity to attack English convoys and small columns is true, but they were animated by a love of plunder rather than of country; and over a considerable area of Afghanistan, notably at Candahar, the people in general would have infinitely preferred the mild and just rule of the English to the military tyranny of Cabul.

Thus Yossouf had grown up without understanding the meaning of the feeling which we call patriotism. He had, it is true, been taught to hate the unbelievers, but this feeling had disappeared on his acquaintance with Will Gale, and he now ranked the safety and happiness of his friend far before any national consideration.

How weak is the feeling of patriotism among the Afghans is shown by the fact that most of the British frontier troops consist of Afghan hillmen, who are always ready, when called upon, to fight desperately against their countrymen and co-religionists. Examples of treachery, such as that exhibited by the two Pathans who fired their guns to warn their countrymen of the British advance up the Spingwai Pass, are almost unknown.

THE FIGHTING ROUND CABUL

It was then with a feeling of joy that Yossouf related to his English friend the news of the defeat of the Afghan army. Throughout the Hindoo quarter there was deep but suppressed gladness at the news of the British victory, and this increased when, as the night went on, it was known that the Afghan army was totally dispersed, that the troops remaining in Cabul had fled, and that the city was virtually open for the entrance of the English.

When, on the 12th, with bands playing and colours displayed, the British troops marched through Cabul, Will would fain have gone out and joined his countrymen. But the Parsee pointed out to him that this would draw the attention of the Afghans to the fact that he had been concealed by him, and that in case at any time the British should evacuate Cabul and return to India, he would be a marked man for the vengeance of the Afghans. Will, therefore, wrapped up in a long cloak and accompanied by Yossouf and the Parsee, left the house after dark, and, proceeding to the gate, walked out to the Bala-Hissar.

Explaining who he was, Will was soon passed through the sentries which had been set at nightfall, and was conducted to the quarters of the general. The latter was greatly surprised when he was told that an English soldier who had been present at the attack upon the mission wished to speak to him, and at once ordered Will to be brought before him. Great was his surprise when he learned from the young soldier that he had fought under him at the taking of Peiwar-Khotal, and having been made prisoner near Ali-Kheyl had been brought to Cabul, and had joined the party of Sir Lewis Cavagnari on its arrival at that city—still more that, having been in the residency when the attack upon it was commenced by the Heratee soldiery, he had managed to escape from the massacre of that night.

After having first heard a complete outline of Will's story, the general called in several of his staff, who had just finished dinner, and then requested Will to give a full and detailed description of his adventures. After he had concluded, Yossouf and the Parsee were called in, and the general warmly expressed his gratification at the kindness that they had shown to a wounded English soldier at the risk of their lives.

He ordered that a handsome present should be made to Yossouf, and told the Parsee to call again in the morning, when the quartermaster-general would be told to arrange with him for the supply of such articles as the country afforded for the use of the troops.

"Your regiment," he said to Will, "is at present at Jellalabad; whether it will come up here I do not yet know, but in the meantime you will be promoted to the rank of sergeant, which is the least we can do after what you have gone through, and you will take your place with my staff orderly sergeants."

He then sent for one of the sergeants and gave Will into his charge, telling him he would speak further with him when he had arranged the pressing business which the occupation of Cabul entailed upon him.

Yossouf remained with Will, being at his urgent request placed upon the roll as a native follower, of whom a considerable number accompany each regiment in India. His duties were but nominal, for when Will's story was well known, Yossouf became a most popular character among the sergeants of the staff. The money which he had received, in the first place from the Ameer and now from General Roberts, would secure his future. In Afghanistan animals are cheap, and the owner of a small herd of oxen, sheep, or even goats, is regarded by his neighbours as a wealthy man. Therefore Yossouf would, on the departure of the British, be able to settle down in a position of comparative affluence.

Two days later, General Roberts, being one evening disengaged, sent for William Gale. He had been much struck with the bearing and manner of the young soldier, and now requested him to give him a full history of his antecedents.

"You have had a curious and eventful history," he said, when the young sergeant had finished, "and appear to have conducted yourself with great discretion, readiness, and courage. From what you tell me of your conversation with Colonel Shepherd, I have no doubt that he formed the same impression that I do from your manner and appearance, that you are of a respectable if not of good family, and I trust that you will some day discover a clue to your parents. It seems to me that had the authorities of the place where you were left properly bestirred themselves, they ought to have been able to find out who you are. However, that is not to the point now. It is sufficient for me that from your manner and address you would not be out of place in any position. I shall, of course, report the fact of your having fought by Major Cavagnari's side in the attack upon him here, and shall strongly recommend that a commission be granted you. I am sure that from your conduct hitherto you will never do discredit to any position in which you may find yourself. Say nothing to your fellow sergeants of what I have told you. It is possible, although not probable, that my recommendation may not be acted upon, and at anyrate some months must elapse before an answer can be received."

William Gale returned to his quarters in a state of extreme delight. The communication which General Roberts had made to him was altogether beyond his hopes. He had indeed from the very day that he enlisted often hoped that some time or other he might win for himself a commission, and take his place in the rank to which he had from his childhood believed that he was by birth entitled. The words and manner of his colonel had encouraged this hope, but he had never dreamed that his promotion might be attained so soon. It was but a year since he had enlisted, and five was the very earliest at which he had even dreamed that a commission might possibly be gained.

The next day he had been sent from the orderly-room with a note to the colonel of the 67th, which was the regiment now in quarters in the Bala-Hissar, the rest of the force being encamped in the plain below. As he was walking across the open, he was suddenly hurled to the ground with tremendous violence, and at the same moment a roar as loud as that of thunder sounded in his ears. Bewildered and half stunned, he rose to his feet, while showers of stones, beams, and other debris fell around him.

One of the gunpowder magazines had exploded. It had been known that very large quantities of powder were stored in various buildings at the Bala-Hissar, and at the moment of the explosion a body of engineers under Captain Shafto were examining the buildings in which it was stored, and making preparation for the removal of the powder. Singularly enough, no soldiers of the 67th were killed, but of the Ghoorkas who were on guard at the arsenal at the time, twelve were killed and seven wounded. Shafto was unfortunately killed. The 67th were at once called out and set to work to extinguish the flames which had been kindled by the explosion, great damage being done. The southern wall of the arsenal had been blown down and several buildings set on fire. Explosion followed explosion, and the work of extinguishing the flames was an extremely dangerous one. In the afternoon another magazine blew up; fortunately, no troops were in its neighbourhood at the time, but four Afghans were killed and several soldiers hurt at a distance of three or four hundred yards from the spot.

Although it was never proved, it was strongly believed that these explosions were caused by the Afghans, and, as large quantities of powder still remained in the Bala-Hissar, it was determined that for the present the place should be evacuated. The general, therefore, with his staff and the regiment in garrison, left the place and joined the camp in the plain.

The little force at Cabul was now isolated. Troops were slowly coming up the Khyber Pass to Jellalabad, where a division was to be formed, destined in the spring to join the force at Cabul should it be necessary to carry on further operations.

Between Cabul and the Shatur-Gardan the natives were in a restless and excited state. Two attacks by 3000 men had been made on the garrison holding the crest of the latter position, 300 in number. These bravely sallied out, attacked the enemy in the open, and killed large numbers of them. Still great numbers of the tribesmen were gathered round, and General Gough with the 5th Punjaubee Cavalry, the 5th Punjaubee Infantry, and four guns, was

"One of the gunpowder magazines had exploded."

therefore sent from Cabul to bring down from the Shatur-Gardan the garrison and all the stores accumulated there. The pass, which would shortly be closed by snow, was then to be deserted.

Several executions now took place at Cabul of men who were proved to have shared in the attack on the embassy. Some of the leading men of the place, who had instigated the troops to the attack, were among those executed. Many of the villagers were also hung for shooting at detached bodies of our troops. A proclamation had been issued by the general on his first arrival, warning the people that any attempt against our authority would be severely punished, forbidding the carrying of weapons within the streets of Cabul or within a distance of five miles of the city gates, and offering a reward for all arms belonging to the Afghan troops, which should be given up, and for the surrender of any person, whether soldier or civilian, concerned in the attack on the embassy.

The position of the British force at Cabul was that of a body holding only the ground they occupied in the midst of a bitterly hostile country.

The Ameer was powerless, and indeed his good-will was more than doubtful. He had from his arrival in the camp been regarded as a prisoner, although treated with courtesy; and after the battle of Charasia, feeling his own impotence, and being viewed with hostility by both parties, he resigned his position as Ameer, and asked to be sent to India, which was done. The abdication of the Ameer really took place on the day the troops entered Cabul, but it was not publicly known until the end of the month, as nothing could be done on the subject until his desire was communicated to the Indian authorities and their views concerning it ascertained.

From the moment of his arrival at Cabul, General Roberts had set to work to prepare for the winter. He would for four or five months be entirely cut off, and would have to rely upon himself alone. He had before him the terrible catastrophe which had on the same ground befallen General Elphinstone's army, and knew that it was possible, and indeed probable, that, with the memory of that success before them, the Afghans would unite in another great effort to annihilate the little force shut up in the heart of their country.

Fortunately he had in the Ameer's barracks at Sherpur a position which he was confident he could hold against any attacks that could be made upon him. These extensive barracks had been erected by Sheer-Ali for the use of his cavalry, but had never been used. They consisted of a large square, three sides of which were surrounded by a lofty wall, an isolated and rocky steep hill rising at the back and closing the fourth side. The buildings were amply large enough to contain the whole of General Roberts' force, and there was abundant room for the stores, baggage animals, and waggons; the only fault was, indeed, that the extent of wall to be defended was too long for the force at his disposal. Round two sides the outer wall was complete, but on the third it had not been taken to its full height, nor had it been continued so as to join the hill behind it.

Great efforts were made to bring in sufficient provisions and forage for the winter, and expeditions were made up the Logan, Maidan, and other valleys for the purpose. Winter was fast setting in. Snow had begun to fall upon the hills, and ice formed on the pools every night. The natives of the valleys near were ready enough to sell their grain, straw, and fuel, but few supplies came in from a distance, as armed bands stopped all supplies on their way. However, a sufficient amount of food and fuel was obtained and stored in Sherpur. Grain, too, was procured for the winter, and the only article of which the supply was insufficient was chopped straw, of which a very large quantity was required.

The attitude of the natives grew daily more hostile. Their priests were preaching a revolt to the death, and recalling to the people how their fathers had annihilated a British force thirty years before. Urged alike by fanaticism and a desire for plunder, the natives over the whole country were seething with excitement, and General Roberts saw that a crisis was approaching.

The Afghans could assemble at least 100,000 men, and among these would be included all the troops of the Ameer's disbanded armies, armed with weapons equal to our own, and burning to revenge the defeats which had been inflicted upon them. To oppose them the English general had less than 6000 men. But though prepared for trouble, the storm, when it came, burst suddenly upon the English. The enemy were known to be collecting in great numbers in the Maidan valley, and two columns were sent out to attack them. One was commanded by Macpherson, the other by Baker. Although they were to strike simultaneously at the enemy, their route of march lay up different valleys, with a lofty mountain range between them, so they could in no way co-operate with each other. After they had started, General Massy was directed to move out with a small force of cavalry and a battery of horse artillery, and co-operate with General Macpherson.

An hour after the cavalry had started, General Roberts himself rode out. He was accompanied by his usual escort, and by two mounted orderly sergeants. One of these was William Gale. They had only proceeded a short distance when they heard some distance ahead of them the guns of the Royal Horse Artillery with Massy at work, and the general at once rode forward at a gallop.

General Macpherson had found Mahomed Jan, one of the principal leaders of the Afghans, with 10,000 men, near Chardeh.

A fight ensued. The guns shelled the enemy, but the water-courses prevented the cavalry with Macpherson acting, and Mahomed Jan, moving across the hills, placed himself between Macpherson and Cabul. Shortly afterwards, General Massy, who had with him three troops of the 9th Lancers and forty-four men of the 14th Bengal Lancers, with four guns under Major Smith-Wyndham, came in sight of a portion of Mahomed Jan's force.

It was clear that these had in some way interposed themselves between the little force and Macpherson's column, and Massy supposed that they were a party of fugitives flying before the force of Macpherson or Baker. As they came streaming down the hill, he got his guns into action. After a few shells had been fired, the enemy advanced in full force. Four thousand men were extended in the shape of a crescent, advancing in fairly good order, while behind was an irregular mob of some six thousand men.

The ground upon which General Massy found himself at this time was singularly unfitted for the action of artillery. It was cut up by deep water-courses, and anything like rapidity of movement was impossible. It would have been prudent had Massy, when he saw how large was the force opposed to him, at once retired until he came to ground where his guns could be rapidly manoeuvred; but relying upon the effect of the shell, he remained in the position in which he had first discovered the enemy. The shell pitched rapidly into the thick of the Afghans, but no effect was produced in checking their advance. They did not waver for a moment, but came steadily on. The enemy's bullets were now dropping fast among the cavalry and guns. Thirty of the 9th Lancers were dismounted and opened fire with their Martini carbines, but the enemy were too numerous to be checked by so small a body of men.

At this moment Sir Frederick Roberts arrived upon the spot. The position was serious, and to retire the guns in safety it was absolutely necessary to check the advance of the enemy. General Roberts therefore ordered Massy to send his cavalry at the enemy. Colonel Cleland led a squadron of the 9th full at the advancing mass, the Bengal Lancers following, while Captain Gough with his troop of the 9th charged the enemy's left flank; but even the charge of Balaclava was scarcely more desperate than this. Two hundred and twenty men, however gallant, could not be expected to conquer 10,000. The three bodies of cavalry charged at full speed into the midst of the enemy's infantry, who received them with a terrible fire which killed many horses and men. The impetus of the charge bore down the leading ranks of the Afghans, and the cavalry tore their way through the mass until their progress was blocked by sheer weight of numbers.

A desperate mêlée took place, the troopers fighting with their sabres, the Afghans with knives and clubbed muskets. Many of the soldiers were struck from their horses, some were dragged to their feet again by their comrades, others were killed upon the ground.

The chaplain of the force, the Rev. Mr. Adams, had accompanied the troopers in the charge, and, seeing a man jammed under a fallen horse, he leaped from his saddle and extricated him, and brought him off in spite of the attack of several Afghans. For this act of bravery he received the Victoria Cross, being the first chaplain in the army who had ever obtained that decoration.

When the dust raised by the charging squadrons had subsided, it was seen that the enemy were still advancing. The Lancers had fallen back, and as the men galloped in, they rallied behind Captain Gough's troop, which had kept best together, and had formed up again between the guns and the enemy. Lieutenants Hersee and Ricardo and sixteen of their men had been left dead upon the ground. Colonel Cleland, Lieutenant Mackenzie, and seven of the troopers were wounded.

A second charge was ordered, but this time it was not pushed home, as a wide water-course checked the advance. Under cover of the first cavalry charge, Major Smith-Wyndham had ordered two of the guns to be taken off, and, as he now fell back with the other two, one of them stuck in the water-course. The greatest efforts were made with the horses which still remained uninjured to get the gun out, but the enemy were pressing close on. Lieutenant Hardy was killed by a shot through the head, and the gun was abandoned. The other three guns were retired 400 or 500 yards farther, but here they became hopelessly bogged in a channel deeper than any that had hitherto been met with. They were spiked and left in the water, and the drivers and gunners moved off with the cavalry just as the enemy poured down upon them.

Seeing the danger of the situation and the large force of the enemy, General Roberts had, on his first arrival, sent off a trooper at full gallop to General Gough, who commanded at Sherpur, ordering him to send out two hundred men of the 72d Highlanders at the double, to hold the gorge leading direct from the scene of conflict to Cabul. There was but a very small garrison of British troops in the city, and had the enemy made their way there, the townspeople would have risen and a serious disaster taken place.

After leaving the guns behind them, the cavalry retired steadily towards the village at the head of the gorge, keeping up a hot fire with their carbines on the enemy who pressed upon them.

"Ride back, Sergeant Gale," the general said, "and meet the 72d. Hurry them up at full speed—every minute is precious."

William Gale rode back at full speed. Until a fortnight before he had never been on a horse, but the animal which he rode was well trained and steady, and hitherto he had had no difficulty in keeping his seat as he trotted along with the escort. It was a different thing now, for the ground was rough and the horse going at a full gallop, and he clung on to the pummel of the saddle to steady himself. As he passed through the village, he saw the Highlanders coming along at a trot half a mile further on, and was soon beside Colonel Brownlow, who commanded them.

"The enemy are pressing the cavalry back, sir," he said, as with difficulty he pulled up his horse. "The general desires you to use the greatest possible speed, as every moment is precious."

Panting and out of breath as the Highlanders were, they responded to Colonel Brownlow's shout, and, rushing forward almost at racing speed, reached the village while the Afghans were still 100 yards beyond it. They instantly opened such a fire upon the enemy that the latter ceased their advance and soon fell back, and Cabul was for the moment safe.

CHAPTER XVI
THE FIGHT IN THE PASS

THE Afghan force, after half an hour's effort to carry the village held by the Highlanders, moved off to their left, and, working along the hills, took post on the heights beyond Bala-Hissar. In the meantime, General Macpherson, having dispersed a strong body of the enemy up the valley, marched back towards Cabul, and, coming across the scene of the late action, brought in the bodies of the dead officers. The guns had already been carried off, for, as the enemy advanced, Colonel Macgregor, collecting a handful of lancers and artillerymen, worked round to their rear, and, dispersing a small body of the enemy who had lingered at a village near the guns, succeeded in extricating the cannon from the swamp and carried them off to Sherpur.

From the signal-post established above Bala-Hissar an order was flashed to General Baker, who was many miles away, to inform him of what had occurred, and to order him to march back with all speed. Late that evening he arrived with his column, and the British force was again united. The next day 560 men of Macpherson's brigade, composed of portions of the 67th, the 72d, the 3d Sikhs, and 5th Ghoorkas, were sent out to attack the enemy, who had established themselves upon a lofty peak south of Cabul.

The Afghans occupied the crest in strength, and hidden behind the hill had 5000 or 6000 men lying in wait to attack the assailing party in the rear as they pressed upwards. The position was, however, too strong to be carried. After several hours of fighting, the little British force had driven the Afghans from the lower part of the hill, but were unable to mount towards the crest, for ammunition was running short, and the enemy were too strongly posted. General Roberts therefore ordered Macpherson to hold the ground which he had gained until next morning, when more troops would be sent. At eight o'clock in the morning, accordingly, General Baker moved out from Sherpur with a strong force and attacked the enemy's position in flank, while Macpherson continued his advance in front. The Afghans fought desperately, and clung to their position until the British were close up, when a desperate hand-to-hand struggle took place, and the British became masters of the position.

While the fighting had been going on, great masses of the enemy had come down from the end of the valley and threatened the road between Sherpur and Cabul. The 9th Lancers made a magnificent charge among them, broke them, and drove them back.

Several other brilliant charges were made, and the plain was kept clear of the enemy. Captain Butson, however, who commanded, was killed, and two other officers wounded. With each hour that passed the position grew more serious, as immense bodies of the enemy were seen advancing from all sides. The city was now in open revolt, and the small garrison there with difficulty held their own. One more effort was made to drive the enemy off the hills.

Early on the 15th, General Baker, with 1200 infantry and eight guns, left the cantonment. After very severe fighting the enemy were driven from their lowest positions, but, as Baker advanced, a body of from 15,000 to 20,000 of the enemy marched out across the plain towards the position just captured. Steadily they advanced, and the shells which our mountain guns sent among them, and the volleys poured down from the face of the hill, did not suffice to check them in the slightest. Reassured by their own enormous numbers, and feeling that success was in their grasp, they pressed forward and desperate fighting took place.

A position held by the 5th Punjaub Infantry was carried by their attack and two guns were lost, but the rest of the positions were maintained. Seeing that it was impossible to hold the Bala-Hissar and Cabul in the face of the hordes opposed to him, which were estimated by the general himself as numbering 80,000 men, but which the Afghans themselves afterwards acknowledged were between 100,000 and 120,000, General Roberts determined to concentrate his troops at Sherpur. Baker was ordered to maintain the position he held at all costs until the troops from the Bala-Hissar were withdrawn. This he did; and although, as he fell back, the Afghan hordes swarmed round him, he fought his way back to Sherpur, and by nightfall all the British force were safely gathered in the cantonments there.

Two days previously, General Roberts had telegraphed for the regiments most advanced in the passes below to come forward; they arrived on the morning of the 16th, and the general had no longer any anxiety as to his ability to hold the cantonments for months, if necessary, against the attacks of the Afghans. Had these attacked on the morning following what was virtually a victory, whilst still flushed with triumph and excitement, it would have needed all the efforts of the English to hold their position against so formidable an attack. The Afghans, however, contented themselves with occupying several walled villages near the cantonment and keeping up an incessant fire upon it.

Meanwhile their main body indulged in wild excesses in Cabul, sacking the Hindoo quarter and plundering all the shops without much distinction of nationality. Thus three days elapsed, the British making the most of the time afforded them by strengthening the weak points of their defences. Lines of waggons were placed in the gap between the unfinished wall and the foot of the hill. Wires were stretched in all directions and chevaux-de-frise erected beyond.

On the 18th the enemy came down in force, and for some hours a tremendous musketry fire was kept up at the position; but the fire of the musketry and guns from the walls was so hot that they did not venture upon an attack. The following day General Baker sallied out and attacked a fortified post a few hundred yards from the wall. From this place the enemy had greatly annoyed the garrison. After some severe fighting the Afghans were driven out and the place blown up.

On the evening of the 22d, the general received news that the Afghans, having prepared a great number of ladders for the assault, intended to attack that night. There had been several similar warnings, but this time the news proved correct. A signal fire was lit upon one of the heights at four in the morning, and at five o'clock the plain was covered with the enemy. Quietly they crept up in the darkness towards the walls, and at six o'clock a prodigious shouting was heard, and from the villages, orchards, and inclosed ground upon all sides the enemy dashed forward to the assault.

As they approached, they opened fire on all sides, pressing chiefly towards the weak point near the foot of the hills. But tremendous as was the roar of the Afghan fire, it was drowned by the roll of musketry which broke from the whole circuit of the walls where the British troops, rifle in hand, had been lying for three hours waiting the attack.

So terrible was the storm of lead that swept the plain that the Afghans paused in their advance. For two hours they remained around the walls, yelling, shouting, and firing heavily; but all the efforts of their leaders could not induce them to rise from the ground and hazard a charge. Many dropped within eighty or ninety yards of the wall, but beyond that the bravest dared not advance.

When morning broke, the welcome news was brought down from the outlook on the top of the hill that far across the plain could be seen the tents of the force of General Gough, who was coming up through the passes to the relief of the garrison. The news had reached the assailants also. Considerable bodies of the enemy were observed moving out from Cabul, as if with the intention of attacking the relieving force. The assailants of the British position, finding their inability to produce the smallest impression, were now beginning to waver, and General Gough ordered the cavalry and horse artillery to go out by the road which led through a gorge in a hill behind, and to sweep round and take them in the rear. This they did with immense success. At the moment that they fell upon the enemy, the British infantry sallied out from the cantonment and attacked them in front. A panic seized the Afghans; in a few minutes the whole plain was covered with flying fugitives, among whom our cavalry swept backward and forward, cutting them up in all directions, while the fire of our infantry and of the guns on the walls searched them through and through whenever they attempted to gather in a knot and make a stand.

By nightfall the whole of the Afghans had either fled to the hills or were driven into Cabul. Upon the following day General Gough's force marched in; but before their arrival, it was found that the enemy had again evacuated the city, and the British were, as before, masters of the position.

After the decisive defeat which had been inflicted upon them, and the dispersion of the great force which had gathered, confident of victory, there was little fear of any further attempt on the part of the enemy. They had brought their whole force into the field, and as this was defeated and dispersed before the arrival of General Gough with his reinforcements, it was evident that success could not be hoped for against the united strength of the English.

The time passed quietly now. The Bala-Hissar and Cabul were reoccupied, and, as the natives were cowed by the crushing defeat they had experienced, there was no longer any repetition of the insolent and defiant manner which they had before manifested.

On the 3d of January a message was brought to the orderly-room that the general wished to see Sergeant Gale. Upon his presenting himself at the general's quarters, Sir Frederick Roberts, to his surprise, at once advanced and shook him warmly by the hand.

"Mr. Gale," he said, "I am very happy to inform you that the Horse Guards have acted upon my recommendation, seconded by that which was sent in by your colonel, who wrote at once upon receiving a notification from me of the step I had taken, saying that you had distinguished yourself very highly in the attack upon the Peiwar-Khotal, and that he was convinced that you would make in all respects an excellent officer. With my despatches that have just come in, I have received a notification that my request has been attended to, together with a copy of the Gazette, in which you are appointed to the 66th Regiment. I have to congratulate you, sir; you are now an officer, and will, I am quite sure, do every credit to my recommendation."

THE FIGHT IN THE PASS

The young soldier was for a moment too moved at the tidings to speak coherently, but he murmured his thanks to the general for his kindness.

"Do not say anything about that," the general said heartily; "it is a pleasure to me to have been able to advance a promising young soldier. I am only sorry that you are not gazetted to a regiment in my own division. The 66th are at Candahar, and unfortunately they will not, I understand, form part of a column with which General Stuart will advance in the spring up the valley through Ghuzni to this place. Had it been so it would have been best for you to wait their arrival here; but as it is, you had better go down the pass to India and work round and join your regiment. It is a long road, but it is always best for a young officer to be with his regiment, especially when in the field, and it is possible that they may have their share of fighting round Candahar. And now there is one thing more. You will have to get an outfit, and there will be the expense of your travel until you join your regiment. There will be no difficulty about an outfit. This you can procure easily on the sale of some officer's effects. By the by, poor young Thompson, who died yesterday, was about your size, and you had better bid a lump sum for the whole of his kit. I shall be happy to be your banker for that and the needful sum for your travelling expenses. When you join your regiment you will, of course, be able to draw your pay from the date on which you were gazetted."

Will thanked the general very heartily for his offer, but said that he had £100 standing at his account at the bank of Hindostan, which had been presented to him by the owners of the vessel in which he arrived there, and that this would be more than sufficient for all his needs if the general would kindly authorize the staff paymaster to cash his drafts upon the bank.

This request was at once granted. The paymaster of Lieutenant Thompson's regiment estimated that the effects of the young officer would sell at auction for about £20, and this sum William Gale gladly paid, thereby obtaining a complete outfit of regimental and civilian clothes and under linen of all descriptions. Another £30 bought him a horse and saddlery; while for £5 he obtained a rough pony for the use of Yossouf, who steadily refused to leave him, although Will pointed out to him that, glad as he should be to have him with him, it would be far more to his advantage to remain among his people at Cabul, where he had means of settling comfortably.

Upon the following day, having obtained his new uniform, which he found required no alteration to fit him fairly, William Gale dined with General Roberts, who had kindly invited him in order to introduce him in his new position to the officers of his staff. He was obliged to remain three or four days longer at Sherpur until a strong escort with sick was going down through the passes to Jellalabad. His baggage was stowed upon a camel, and after a kind adieu from General Roberts, and a very cordial one from the staff sergeants, among whom he had worked for three months, he started with the convoy for the lower valleys. The escort consisted of a hundred men of the infantry of the Guides. The way down the pass was difficult, but no snow had fallen for three weeks, and the roads were fairly beaten down by passing parties. Still, their progress was slow, and late on the afternoon of the second day after starting, they were still four miles from the fort of Jugdulluk, which was held by a British force, and where they were to halt for the night.

The Guides were on the alert. A party of four men were 200 yards ahead of the little column, which was commanded by Captain Edwards. Presently a shot rang out from the front, followed by a scattered discharge. William Gale was at the moment riding by the side of Captain Edwards; he had already placed himself under that officer's orders in case of any emergency.

"Mr. Gale," Captain Edwards said, "will you ride forward at once with six men to the advanced party. When you get there take such measures as you may think fit, and send me back word as to the strength and position of the enemy."

With six of the Guides, Will at once rode forward, while Captain Edwards halted until the little column was gathered closely together, the camels and dhoolies with sick men in the centre, the soldiers in readiness for action around them. A soldier now ran up with a slip of paper upon which Will had scribbled in pencil: "The enemy are apparently in considerable force. The defile opens here. They are disposed among rocks and boulders on either side."

Will, on arriving at the advanced party, had found at once that the force of the enemy was too strong for him to attempt to move forward at present. He had posted the men behind boulders by the wayside, ordering them to pick off any man that showed himself, and they were soon engaged in a sharp musketry skirmish with the enemy. One of their number had fallen at the first discharge, and Will, taking his rifle, used it with effect until the head of the convoy arrived.

It was now fast becoming dark, and the flashes of the enemy's fire from behind the rocks showed how numerous were the assailants.

"There must be a couple of thousands of the scoundrels," Will said to Captain Edwards, as the latter came up to ascertain the state of affairs. "Hampered with the convoy, the position is an awkward one. It is fortunate they attacked where they did, for we can hold our own here; while, if they had waited till we got fairly down into this comparatively open valley and then attacked us on both flanks, it would have been very awkward. We must try and clear them out; we cannot stop here all night. It is freezing very sharp now, and the cold will be intense in an hour or two."

"I will take thirty men," Captain Edwards said, "and skirmish along among the rocks on the left. Do you take as many more, and move along the right of the path. The remaining forty shall stay here under my sergeant to guard the convoy from an attack in rear in case any of the enemy should come down the defile behind us."

The fight soon became exceedingly hot. Making their way along the rocks on either side of the path, the Guides slowly drove the enemy before them. It was hard work, however, for the tribesmen fought steadily, and as those in front fell back upon those lower down the valley, their resistance became every moment more obstinate. Eight of Will's party had already fallen; but although, sword in hand, he was leading them, encouraging them with voice and gesture, not a bullet had as yet struck him. Presently Captain Edwards, having crossed the valley, stood by his side.

"We are at a standstill," he said. "Nine of my men are killed or wounded already, and the fellows are as thick as peas. I am afraid we shall never be able to force our way through. There," he exclaimed, as a sound of firing was heard in the rear, "they have come down on the convoy from behind. We had better, I think, fall back a bit, and take post near the mouth of the defile. We must defend ourselves as best we can till morning."

The movement was steadily executed, the wounded men being carried with them as they retired. The tribesmen advanced as they fell back, not venturing to press them, however, for the rear-guard kept their faces towards them, and any who ventured to show themselves instantly paid the penalty of their rashness. For an hour the fight went on. It was night now, and dark as pitch in the deep valley in which the fight was going on, the position of the combatants being only indicated by the flickering flashes of the muskets. The Afghans were gradually creeping nearer, as the Guides could see by the flashes.

"If the fellows only make a determined rush at us," Captain Edwards said to Will, "it will go hard with us. Fortunately they are as much in the dark as we are, and will find it difficult to gather for a rush."

"I think we may hold out till morning, but by that time news that we are blockaded here will spread throughout the hills, and we may have 10,000 of them down on us. I think, if you will give me leave, the best plan will be for me to try and make my way down to Jugdulluk to bring up help from there."

"You would never get through," Captain Edwards advised. "It is a brave offer, Gale, but could not be done."

"I think it might be done," Will said. "It is as dark as pitch. I will take my lad with me, and will borrow a native cap and cloak from one of the bearers—there are some Afghans among them. I will take off my patrol jacket and leave it behind me, and my boots. We will crawl along in the dark. If, as is likely enough, we stumble against some of them, we will say we are wounded and are making our way to the rear. They cannot see us in the dark, and my Afghan will pass muster, and Yossouf will certainly not be suspected. If I am discovered and killed, he will go forward and deliver the message."

The plan seemed to offer every possibility of success, and Captain Edwards, seeing how serious the position was, consented to allow Will to attempt it.

A few words to Yossouf sufficed to inform him of the task Will was about to undertake, and he at once agreed to share the danger. A rough sheepskin cap was obtained for Will from one of the camel men. His tunic was thrown off, and a posteen or Afghan sheepskin coat was put on in its place. He took a long matchlock which the camel man carried slung over his shoulders, took off his boots, and thrust a pair of loose Afghan shoes into his belt. Yossouf needed no preparations beyond borrowing a matchlock. Wringing Captain Edwards' hand, Will stooped on his hands and knees, and, with Yossouf a pace or two ahead, began to crawl down the path.

Before starting, the orders had been sent round to the soldiers to fire at the rocks on either side of the path, but on no account to fire down the road itself. As he expected, Will found this clear of Afghans for a considerable distance. A heavy fire had, previous to their starting, been directed down this path to prevent the Afghans from gathering there in the darkness preparatory to making a rush. They came across several dead bodies, but the enemy were all behind rocks on one side or other of the road.

When they had crawled a hundred yards they were past the front line, from which the Afghans were keeping up a heavy fire; but Will knew that from their numbers they must extend far back down the valley, and indeed from almost every rock the flashes of the matchlocks blazed out as the lurking tribesmen fired in the direction of the mouth of the defile. They were nearly a quarter of a mile down when an Afghan, who had been crouching behind a rock close to the path, advanced into the road to fire, when he stumbled against Yossouf.

"What are you doing?" he exclaimed.

177

"We are both wounded by the Kaffirs," Yossouf answered, "and are making our way back to bind up our wounds. I think my arm is broken, but I mean to come back again to have a few more shots at the infidels."

"Good!" the Afghan replied. "How goes it in front?"

"Their fire is lessening," Yossouf said. "We must have killed many. We shall finish with them in the morning if not before."

The Afghan fired, and then retired behind his rock to load again, while Will and Yossouf continued their way. A few hundred yards farther they rose to their feet. Will slipped on the Afghan shoes, and they then proceeded at a rapid pace down the pass. Several times they withdrew from the road and hid beside it as they met parties of tribesmen hurrying up to join in the attack, but in an hour after starting they heard the welcome challenge of the sentry at Jugdulluk. Saying who he was, Will was at once passed forward into the fort and taken to the quarters of the officer in command.

"I am Lieutenant Gale, of the 66th," Will said, "and was on my way down the pass with the convoy of wounded and 100 men of the Guides under Captain Edwards. They have been attacked at the lower end of the defile, some four miles above, by a very strong body of tribesmen. They are attacked front and rear. I have made my way through to ask you if you can despatch a force to their rescue. Were the tribesmen attacked in their rear now they might be scattered easily enough, but they are assembling very fast, and in the morning it will be a difficult matter to reach them."

"We have fancied," the officer said, "for the last two hours that we heard distant firing, but we could not be sure, for any noise echoes so in these mountains. I will set out at once with you with as many men as I can spare."

CHAPTER XVII
AT CANDAHAR

THE garrison of Jugdulluk consisted only of 220 Sikhs. The officer in command left seventy of these in charge of one of his subalterns, with the injunction to exercise the most extreme vigilance in his absence. Then with 150 men, a subaltern, and Will Gale he started up the path to effect the rescue of the beleaguered convoy. The road wound and turned frequently among the spurs of the lofty hills which had cut off the sound of firing from the garrison, and only a faint and distant murmur was audible when they started. After marching two miles, however, the rattle of the musketry became clear and distinct. Upon the way the officer in command learned from Will the exact position of things in front and the situation of the Afghans.

When within half a mile of the scene of action, fifty men were thrown out on either side of the road, while the other fifty advanced very slowly along the centre. The orders to the flankers were to search among the rocks as they advanced, and to bayonet or shoot every Afghan they found among them. It was not long before they came upon the enemy. Then the rifles cracked out, and the wild shouts of the Afghans betokened their astonishment at being thus unexpectedly assailed in rear.

Numerous as they were, they offered but a slight resistance. Their one thought was to effect their escape; and they hurried rapidly away as the relief advanced, climbing the steep sides of the valley by paths only known to themselves, and then from the hillside far above opening a scattered fire at random down into the valley.

In five minutes all resistance had ceased. The flanking parties were ordered to shelter themselves behind the rocks and to return the fire of the natives on the hillsides, to retain the position until the convoy passed through, and then to close behind it as a rearguard.

With the fifty men in the road the officer then pushed forward, and was soon greeted by a shout of welcome from the defenders of the defile. There was not a minute to be lost, for the Afghans, when they recovered from their first scare, would renew the attack; and the party pressing down the defile on their rear, ignorant of what had taken place below, were still keeping up an incessant fire. Twenty-eight of the Guides were already killed or wounded.

Several of the sick men in the dhoolies volunteered to walk down to the fort and to give up their places to those of the wounded men who were unable to walk, and in a few minutes the convoy moved forward.

The fifty men of the relieving party placed themselves in their rear; and as the tribesmen who had been attacking them from behind rushed down through the defile with exulting shouts, believing that they were now secure of their victims, the Sikhs opened so heavy a fire on them that they fell back up the defile in disorder. As the convoy wound down the valley, the enemy again assembled on the hills and pursued them hotly. But the Sikhs and Guides kept up so steady a fire that they did not venture to approach to close quarters, and with a loss of eighteen more men, the convoy reached the shelter of the fort. Conscious of their inability to attack this position, the Afghans drew off.

On returning to his friends, Will had resumed his uniform, and now, on reaching the fort, Captain Edwards expressed to him his warmest thanks for the hazardous adventure that he had undertaken.

"I shall, of course," he concluded, "furnish a full report of the affair to the general, and I should think he would recommend you for the Victoria Cross. If any fellow ever deserved it, you do so, for it seemed to me almost certain death to venture through the pass. I never expected to see you again, and I was never more glad in my life than I was when the firing began down below in the valley, and knew that help was at hand; for had you failed, it would have been all up with us. I doubt if we should have seen the morning, and at anyrate few of us would have been left by that time."

The convoy reached Jellalabad without further adventure, and Captain Edwards reported to the general the events of the march. He was requested to give a full written report of the affair, and the general stated that in forwarding it he should certainly append a recommendation that Lieutenant Gale should receive the Victoria Cross for his gallantry in venturing through the Afghans to fetch assistance for the convoy.

Will himself, as soon as he reached Jellalabad, hurried away to the cantonment of the Norfolk Rangers, who were in a village a mile distant from the town. He was not recognized as he passed through the soldiers scattered about the village street, and was soon at the principal house where the colonel had his quarters. On sending in his name he was at once shown into the room where the colonel was at work.

"I am indeed glad to see you," the latter said, rising and shaking him heartily by the hand, "and I congratulate you most warmly on your promotion. I promised to do what I could for you when you joined, but I did not expect that it would be so soon."

"I am indeed obliged to you, colonel, for your kindness," Will said, "and am conscious how much I owe to you."

"Not at all, my boy, not at all; it was General Roberts himself who recommended you for your commission, and I was only too glad to back up his recommendation to the best of my power. We all thought you were gone when you were reported as missing at Ali-Kheyl, and we heard from the sentry that, having gone forward to investigate the origin of a noise he had reported to you, you were suddenly fired upon, and that he saw no more of you as he ran back to the picket. I was glad indeed when the report was received from poor Cavagnari that upon his arrival at Cabul he had found you there just recovering from your wounds. Then, of course, we gave you up again when we heard of the massacre of the mission; and it seemed like a resurrection from the dead when I got a letter from Roberts saying you were found again, and that he was recommending you for a commission. I see by the Gazette you are appointed to the 66th, and we were expecting to see you on your way down. Had you any difficulty in getting through the passes?"

"The convoy was attacked, sir, by the tribesmen, when near Jugdulluk, but the garrison came out to our rescue and we got through safely. But we had thirty men killed or wounded."

"A smart affair!" the colonel said. "And now of course you will take up your quarters with us for a day or two before you go on. The officers will all be glad to see you, and you will be able to tell us all about the attack on the mission and the recent fighting. Roberts has been having some hot work there. We have been grumbling horribly at our bad luck. We thought at the time we were fortunate at being sent back to India when peace was signed, instead of being kept in the Khurum valley. But the consequence has been that we have been out of it all. However, we must look upon you as our representative."

Will hesitated about staying, but the colonel overruled his objection, saying that as there would be no fighting until the spring there could be no particular hurry for him to join his regiment. A spare room was placed at his disposal in the colonel's quarters, and Will was soon made at home. The officers flocked in upon hearing of his arrival, and all congratulated him most warmly upon his promotion. An hour later a mounted orderly rode up to the colonel's quarters.

"Is Lieutenant Gale here?" he asked. Will went forward.

"A note from the general," the orderly said, and handing it to him; "also one for Colonel Shepherd." Will's note was simply an invitation to dine that evening with the general. The colonel's letter was as follows:—

"Dear Colonel Shepherd,—As Lieutenant Gale was promoted from your regiment, I think it is likely that he has found his way to you. I have written to ask him to dinner; please spare him to me. I

Letters from the general.

hope you will do me the pleasure of accompanying him. He has performed a most gallant action, and I have just had the pleasure of writing a despatch recommending him for the V.C."

Will and the colonel at once wrote notes accepting the invitation. When these had been sent out to the orderly the colonel read aloud to the officers present the note he had received from the general.

"Now," he said, turning to Will, "what is that you have been doing? You told us the convoy had been attacked and sharply pressed, but you said nothing of your share in the affair. What was it?"

"It was simple enough, sir," Will answered, colouring hotly. "We were surrounded just at the mouth of the defile. The enemy held the valley in front in great force, and another party were pressing on our rear. Things looked awkward, and so I volunteered with my faithful Afghan boy to get through the fellows in front and make my way down to Jugdulluk, which was four miles away, to bring the garrison up on their rear. It was simple enough, and in fact there was less danger than in remaining with the convoy to be popped at by the Afghans. The night was very dark, and down in the bottom one could hardly see one's hand. The Afghans had been cleared pretty well off the road by our fire, so there was no difficulty whatever in making our way down. We were, in fact, only questioned once; and my boy's statement, that we were wounded and were going to the rear, was accepted at once."

"The fact that you succeeded," the colonel said, "does not detract from the pluck required to attempt such an adventure. To my mind there is more courage required in venturing alone through the midst of the Afghans at night than there would be in charging any number of them in hot blood in the light. You have earned the V. C. well, Gale, and I am sure we all feel proud of you, though you do not belong to us now."

There was a chorus of approval from the officers around.

"I don't belong to you now, sir, but," Will said earnestly, "I shall always feel, whatever regiment I may be with, that the Norfolk Rangers are my corps. It is the kindness which was shown me here which has put me in the way of rising, and I shall never forget it."

It was now time to dress for dinner, and Will for the first time arrayed himself in full-dress uniform. The buttons and facings he would of course get altered when he joined the regiment. The general received Gale with great kindness. He had a large party to dinner; among them was Captain Edwards; and after the table was cleared, the latter, at the general's request, gave a full account of the attack upon the convoy, and Will was then called upon to relate the part which he had taken in it, which he did very modestly and quietly.

For two days longer he stopped at Jellalabad, and then, with a hearty farewell to the officers of the Rangers, he started down the pass. He again journeyed with a convoy; for although the tribes below Jellalabad were cowed into submission, many attacks were made by the mountaineers upon small parties going up or down the passes, and stringent orders had been issued that no officer should go down except when accompanied by an escort.

After a week's travelling Will arrived with Yossouf at Peshawur; then he rode by easy stages until he reached the Indus, where, taking his place on a steamer, he travelled down the river to Sukkur, where he disembarked and started for the weary march across the desert to the foot of the Bolan.

Along the road large numbers of coolies were at work constructing a line of railway which was now almost complete to the foot of the pass. It did not ascend this, but, turning to the right, wound up the hills to the plateau. It was intended to be taken on to Candahar, and its completion would have been an immense boon both to that city and to India, as it would have opened a great trade to the north, and have enabled the inhabitants of the fertile plain around Candahar to send their corn, fruit, and other products down to India. Unhappily, with the subsequent abandonment of Candahar, the formation of the railway was stopped, and the whole allowed to go to ruin. The work has, however, been recently taken in hand again.

Will and his follower ascended the Bolan, stopped a day or two at Quettah to rest their horses, and then proceeded on through the fertile plains of Pisheen and over the Kojak Pass, and thence on to Candahar. Here Will joined his new regiment and was well received by its officers.

In every regiment in the service an officer risen from the ranks is invariably received with special courtesy and kindness. Every endeavour is made to place him at his ease in his new position. This is specially so when, as in Will's case, the promotion has been earned by distinguished services in the field.

In most instances officers promoted from the rank of sergeant are a good deal older than the young lieutenants among whom they find themselves. Being often married men and having nothing but their pay to depend upon, they find themselves, therefore, unable to take much part in the pleasures and gaieties of the regiment.

In India, however, as the rate of pay is much higher, an unmarried officer can live very comfortably on his pay; and as in the field the expenses are far less than when a regiment is in cantonments at a large station, where there is much gaiety, Will found that he was able to live very comfortably on his pay in the same style as that of his comrades. They on their part were pleased to find in Will a young fellow of the same age as the other junior lieutenants, and withal a pleasant gentlemanly young man. The fact, too, that he had seen so much service, had gone through stirring adventures, and had fought by the side of Cavagnari in the Bala-Hissar, made him quite a hero among them, and Will was soon thoroughly one of themselves. When it was known that the regiment was likely to remain at Candahar for some time, many luxuries had been brought up from India, together with means of passing away the time, such as the necessary appliances for cricket, racket, and other games.

Among these too were several boxes of books, and Will, who had at first a little amused his comrades by his absolute ignorance of cricket, but who soon became a promising recruit at that game, steadily devoted three hours a day to reading, in order to improve his mind, and to obtain a knowledge of the various matters which were topics of conversation among his comrades. Above all he diligently studied the newspapers, great parcels of which arrived every week, in order to obtain some knowledge of the political state of affairs in England, the position of parties, and the various matters occupying public attention.

He had at first found his ignorance of these matters a great drawback to him in general conversation; but he discovered that newspapers rather than books are useful in enabling a man to mix with his fellows in social talk, and that the current events of the day form ninety-nine hundredths of the subjects of conversation. The fact that all his mess-mates had been thoroughly posted in the history of Rome and Greece, that they could read these languages almost as well as English, that they had been coached in high mathematics, and had a knowledge of French and German, gave them, Will found, very little advantage in general conversation; and he was surprised to discover how entirely useless from a practical point of view is much of the instruction which must be mastered by young men before obtaining a commission.

Many times, when talking with the young officers with whom he was most intimate, he inquired of them what good they found the learning they had obtained during their many years of schooling, and was surprised at the universal reply, "No good whatever!" He found, however, that some of the more thoughtful of them admitted that they had gained increased powers of thought and reasoning from their training.

"That is the good of education, Gale," Captain Fletcher, who commanded Will's company, said to him one day. "A certain time must be spent upon education, and the course of study is intended to strengthen and improve the mental powers. As far as soldiers are concerned it would certainly be of more practical use if the time we spent at school on Greek and mathematics had been expended in acquiring three or four European and Indian languages. But you see, boys educated at the same school must all work together and study the same books, whatever the profession for which they are intended is. Our practical, that is, our professional education, only begins when we go to Woolwich or Sandhurst. Perhaps some day a different system will be employed. There will be special schools for lads intended for various professions and careers. Till that is done we must all work upon a common basis, which has at least the advantage of forming the mind for the after work of acquiring the special branches of knowledge required by us in the careers we may adopt. If you ask my advice I should not at your time of life dream of setting to to learn the dead languages or to study mathematics. Read the histories of Rome and Greece, and study that of your own country. Read books of travel and the biographies of great men, and keep yourself well posted, as you are doing, in current public events. You will then find yourself able to take part on equal terms in any conversation which may be going on. You will indeed be considered by strangers an exceptionally well-informed young fellow, and you may pass through life without any person having a suspicion that Latin, Greek, and mathematics, the cardinal points of an ordinary education, are wholly unknown to you."

Will was cheered by the advice, and henceforth directed his studies only in the direction which Captain Fletcher had indicated. At the beginning of April a large diminution had taken place in the force stationed at Candahar, as General Sir Donald Stewart marched with the greater portion of the force for Cabul. The route led through a country which was the stronghold of the fanatical party, the important town of Ghuzni containing the most fanatical population in all Afghanistan. This had been the centre whence the attacks on General Roberts had been organized, and it was deemed necessary to march a strong force through the country to overawe the tribesmen and break up their organization.

The march was uneventful as far as Shahjui, the limit of the Candahar province. At this point the Taraki country begins. The Mollahs here had been actively preaching a holy war, and several thousand men were reported as having collected. The villages were found to be deserted, and everything betokened an active opposition to the advance.

When the head of the column arrived at Ahmed-Khel, a body of the enemy, estimated at from 12,000 to 15,000, were seen clustered on a semicircle of hills beyond the village. The baggage of the column stretched far along the road, and it was all-important to prevent the enemy from falling upon this long line. General Stewart therefore determined to attack them.

The two batteries of artillery opened fire upon the enemy, who at once in reply rushed down to the assault. The charge was led by some 3000 or 4000 Ghazis, as they were called, fanatics who had sworn to give their lives in carrying out their object of exterminating the hated infidel. Some of these men were armed with rifles and matchlocks, some with heavy swords, knives, and pistols; others again with pikes made of bayonets or pieces of sharpened iron fastened upon long sticks. Some were on foot and some on horseback.

With wild yells the mass rushed down upon our troops, and so sudden and unexpected was the attack, so swiftly did they cross the 400 or 500 yards of intervening ground, that they came upon the British before preparation could be made for their reception. At the moment when they charged, some of the cavalry were moving across in front of the infantry, and these, before they could be got into a line for a charge, were surrounded by the enemy. In an instant they were lost to sight in the cloud of dust and smoke. It was a hand-to-hand struggle, and in the confusion, a troop charged to the right in rear of the main line of the infantry and burst into the midst of the 19th Punjaub Infantry, who were in reserve in rear of the position occupied by the general and his staff. In a moment all was confusion.

The ammunition mules were stampeded, riderless horses dashed hither and thither, and close behind the cavalry the Ghazis with a furious rush dashed in among the broken infantry. Upon the left flank, too, the Ghazis swept round in the rear of our infantry line, and for a time it seemed as if the whole British formation was broken up, in which case the numbers of their foes must have prevailed. Colonel Lister, V.C., however, who commanded the 3d Ghoorkas, threw his men rapidly into company squares, and poured a tremendous fire into the fanatics.

All along the line the attack raged, and so hurriedly had the battle commenced that many of the men had not even fixed bayonets. Desperate was the hand-to-hand fighting, and valour more conspicuous than that of the Ghazis was never shown. Furiously they threw themselves upon the line of their opponents, clutching their muskets and trying to wrench them from their hands, while they strove to cut down their holders.

Many of them threw themselves upon the fixed bayonets and died in the endeavour to cut down the soldiers with their swords, but the three regiments which formed the line—one British (the 59th), one Ghoorkas, and one Sikhs—alike held their own and poured rolling volleys into the ranks of the enemy.

Desperately the Ghazis strove to capture the guns, which were firing case and shrapnel into them at a distance of thirty yards, mowing them down in hundreds. Not even would this terrible slaughter have checked them had not the 2d Punjaub Cavalry most gallantly charged them again and again. The general, surrounded by his escort, was in the midst of the fight, the enemy having burst in between the guns and the 59th Foot, and officers and troopers had alike to fight for their lives, several of the escort being killed and wounded. At last, however, the Ghazis fell back from the terrible fire.

The 1st Punjaub Cavalry, coming up from the rear, joined the 2d in a hot pursuit; and our native allies the Hazaras, seeing the Afghans in retreat, also rushed out after them, and the rout of the enemy was complete. The fighting had lasted about an hour, and the enemy left over a thousand dead on the field, beside the bodies which had been carried off. Their wounded of course, were far more numerous.

Ghuzni surrendered without opposition when the column reached it, the fighting men having been engaged in the battle of Ahmed-Khel, and having had enough of hostilities. On the 23d of

April a force under Brigadier-general Palliser advanced against a large body of natives who had assembled near the village of Ghalezy, again led by the Ghazis. These rushed to the attack with a courage and desperation equal to that shown by the fanatics in the previous battle. Our men, however, were this time prepared, and were able to inflict very heavy losses upon the enemy without allowing them to get to close quarters.

This was the end of the Afghan resistance. General Stewart moved on to Cabul without further fighting, and effected a junction there with the force under General Roberts.

CHAPTER XVIII
ON THE HELMUND

WITH the junction of the forces of Generals Stewart and Roberts, what may be called the second period of the Afghan war came to an end. All opposition had ceased, and it appeared probable that there would be no more fighting. Abdul Rahman, a prince of the royal house who, after for some time fighting against Sheer Ali, had been defeated and obliged to fly the country, had for a long time been a resident among the Russians.

Upon the abdication of Yakoub he had crossed the frontier and had entered at the north of Afghanistan, assuming the title of Ameer. He had been well received in that part of the country, and as no other competitor for the throne appeared to have chances equal to his, and as the British government were most anxious to withdraw their forces from the country, his authority was recognized by us. Negotiations were opened with him, and it was arranged that as he approached Cabul, the British force would retire.

The summer had passed not unpleasantly at Candahar: the country was peaceful, cricket-matches were got up between the various regiments, and horse-races established. Candahar was governed by a protégé of the British named Wali Shere Ali. He had organized a native army to support his authority upon our withdrawal. The only circumstances which occurred to mar the pleasing time were isolated attacks upon British officers and men by Ghazis.

These attacks were sometimes made in broad daylight in the streets of Candahar, where the escape of those who perpetrated them was impossible; these fanatics regarding their own life with indifference, so that they could but kill one or more of the British before being cut down.

ON THE HELMUND

One day as William Gale was walking in the principal street of Candahar at a short distance behind Colonel Ripon, an Indian official of very long standing and experience who had come up on a special mission to arrange with the Wali the details of the civil government of the province, he saw three Afghans who were loitering in the road draw their long tulwars and dash upon that officer. The first who reached him delivered a sweeping blow, which the colonel, taken by surprise, partly received on his uplifted arm, but was struck to the ground. Another of the Ghazis raised his sword; but before it could fall, Will Gale, who saw at once that he was too far behind to interpose between the assailant and the victim, drew his revolver from his belt, and, taking a hasty aim, fired.

The shot was an accurate one, the bullet striking the Afghan on the forehead just as he was about to strike. He fell forward on the colonel, receiving as he did so a tremendous blow which the third Ghazi was aiming at the prostrate man.

Before the blow could be repeated, Will had bounded forward and, sword in one hand and revolver in the other, faced the two Afghans. Another shot freed him of one of his assailants just as the other, rushing recklessly forward, aimed a blow at him which he was not quick enough to parry. His right arm fell to his side; but in an instant he threw himself upon his foe, and the two fell heavily to the ground, the Afghan striving desperately to shorten his sword so as to use the point, while Will strove to liberate his left arm, which was under the man, and so use his revolver, which he still grasped.

At this moment some soldiers of the 66th ran up, and one of them with his bayonet, which since these attacks began were always carried at the belt, brought the conflict to a conclusion by running it through and through the Ghazi's body. Will soon rose to his feet. Colonel Ripon had already freed himself from the body of the dead Ghazi and had struggled to his feet, the blood streaming from his head and arm.

"I have to thank you for my life, sir," he said warmly. "Had your aid come but two seconds less promptly they would have finished me. But I fear you are severely wounded."

Will saves Colonel Ripon.

"Oh, no!" Will answered. "It is only a flesh wound from my shoulder to my elbow. Luckily my sword partly caught the blow. I was aiming at the other fellow, and had not time to parry fairly. I shall be none the worse for it in a week's time. My wound is less severe than yours, sir."

"We are both bleeding pretty freely," the colonel said. "My quarters are close at hand, and as the principal medical officer lives in the same house, you cannot do better than come in with me."

In a few minutes their wounds were bandaged, the doctor saying that no serious harm had been done in either case, but that care and quiet lest fever should supervene would be necessary for a week or two. As the house was much more airy and commodious than that in which Will was quartered, the colonel begged him so strongly to move his quarters thither until able to return to duty that Will agreed to do so, and was soon installed, with Yossouf in attendance, in the colonel's quarters.

He was greatly pleased with the old officer, whose manner was most kind and courteous, and who from his long experience in India was full of anecdotes and information concerning the country. Ten days after the struggle the doctor told them that there was no longer any occasion for his services.

Their wounds were healing favourably and all fear of fever had passed. At the same time it would still be some time before either could take their arms from their slings. The following day, in honour of his convalescence, Colonel Ripon invited several friends to dinner, among them General Burrows and Colonel Galbraith of the 66th. All had of course heard the details of the attack on Colonel Ripon, and Will was congratulated warmly upon the promptness that he had showed.

"Do you know, colonel," General Burrows said as they were smoking their cigars after dinner, "there is a wonderful likeness between you and Lieutenant Gale. I should have taken you for father and son anywhere."

The other officers agreed with the remark. The likeness was certainly strong. Both were men of six feet in height. The colonel's hair and moustache were grizzled, and his face bronzed with the sun of many Indian summers; he was thin and spare of habit, but his shoulders were broad, and it was evident that in his youth he must have possessed much of the muscular strength which was apparent in Will's more rounded limbs. But it was in their eyes that there was the greatest similarity. Both were gray and of nearly the same shade; both had a simple, straightforward, and kindly expression; both were shaded by straight and rather heavy eyebrows. The men looked at each other.

"I suppose he is like me," Colonel Ripon said; "still more like, I fancy, what I remember myself at his age; but curiously enough, he has ever since I met him been recalling someone else to my mind;" and a shade passed over his face.

Seeing that Colonel Ripon was not disposed to talk further on the subject, a fresh topic of conversation was started. There was news that Ayoub Khan, the brother of Yakoob, who was governor at Herat, was marching south at the head of a large force with the intention of opposing Abdul-Rahman and again reseating Yakoob on the throne. He had also preached a holy war against the British.

"I fear that the trouble is serious," General Burrows said. "The troops Ayoub is bringing with him have not yet met us in the field. The population on the road is wild and fanatical in the extreme, and will no doubt join him to a man. On the other hand, the troops of the Wali are not to be depended upon, and the brunt of the fighting is sure to fall upon us."

Three days later the order was issued by General Primrose that the 66th Regiment, the Bombay Grenadiers, and Jacob's Rifles, together with the 3d Scinde Horse and 3d Bombay Cavalry with a battery of artillery, were to move out with the Wali's army towards Girishk on the river Helmund, which formed the boundary between the province of Candahar and that of Herat.

After the long period of inactivity at Candahar, Will was delighted at the thought of taking part in an expedition with his regiment; but when they reached the Helmund, life was for some time exceedingly monotonous. The news of Ayoub's advance greatly excited the population, who had been further worked up by agents widely distributed through the country, and by the exhortations of the Mollahs and Ghazis; consequently, rambling at any distance from the camp was forbidden, and the shooting parties, which had been one of the great resources of their life at Candahar, were peremptorily put an end to.

Colonel Ripon had accompanied the force as the Wali's adviser. Both he and Will had recovered completely from their wounds. When the regiment first marched, indeed, the surgeon had strongly recommended Will to remain behind until his wound had completely healed, but the young officer had so strongly begged to be allowed to accompany the regiment that the surgeon had consented.

His colonel had for a time relieved him from all duty and he rode in rear of the regiment, but within a fortnight of their arrival at the Helmund he was able to lay aside his sling and to take his turn of regular duty. The officers did all that they could to make existence tolerable on the sandy shores of the Helmund; they got up foot-races and athletic sports for the men, played cricket on the sands, and indulged in a bath twice a day in the river.

Will often spent the evening in Colonel Ripon's tent. A warm friendship had arisen between the two officers, and each day seemed to bring them closer together. All this time Ayoub's army was known to be approaching. It had been delayed by want of transport and by the difficult nature of the country over which it had to pass. The guns, too, of which it was reported to have a large number, had greatly hampered it; but by the second week in July it was near at hand. For some time the Wali's troops had been showing signs of insubordination, and little doubt was entertained that they had been tampered with by Ayoub's emissaries.

The question of disarming them was several times discussed, but the Wali maintained his faith that they would remain true to their salt; and the British force was so small that it was deemed imprudent to take any step to diminish their strength by dispensing with the services of a strong body of men who might after all be faithful at the critical moment. Moreover, it was doubtful whether they would submit to be disarmed by a force so inferior to their own. Should the attempt to disarm them succeed, they must either be escorted back to Candahar by a strong detachment of the British, or be permitted to disperse, in which case they would assuredly swell the advancing army of Ayoub.

One day Will arranged to start the next morning at daybreak for a day's shooting with four other young officers—Hammond and Fortescue of Jacob's Rifles, and Plater and Lowther of the Grenadiers. The country round the camp had been already shot over, so they were to go some miles out. Will's colonel, in giving him leave off parade for the day, had asked him to endeavour to ascertain at any village he might enter the state of the feeling of the natives respecting Ayoub, and their disposition towards the British, points on which a deplorable ignorance existed in the camp.

The party started before daybreak, putting their wiry little tats, or native ponies, into a gallop so as to reach the spot, eight miles distant, where they were to begin to shoot, as early as possible, so as to get two or three hours' sport before the heat of the day really set in. After an hour's ride they overtook their servants, who had gone on ahead with the guns and luncheon. The sun was but just above the horizon and the morning air was cool and pleasant.

Dismounting, they handed over the ponies to the servants, and, taking the guns and ammunition, set out on foot. The servants were to go on with the ponies and lunch to a village in the hills four miles distant, and to get tiffin ready by eleven o'clock.

The young officers set out on foot, keeping a short distance apart. Two of their servants accompanied them to carry the game; the other three went with the two Syces who looked after the ponies. The ground was broken and stony, and altogether uncultivated except in the neighbourhood of the villages. They had better sport than they expected, for hares darted out in numbers from behind the rocks. Some of these were bowled over, while others escaped, and there was much bantering and laughter among the young men, none of whom were first-class shots.

As the sun rose higher, the game became more scarce, and by ten o'clock the party turned their faces towards the village where they were to lunch, and which lay, they calculated, a mile or two away on their right. The sun was now blazing down upon them, and they were glad indeed when they came in sight of the village, which was not perceived until they were close to it, as it lay in a deep and rocky valley.

Yossouf met them as they entered the village.

"Well, Yossouf, where have you laid the tiffin?"

"I have spread it, sahib, on a level piece of ground in the shade of the chief's house. He did not seem disposed to be civil, and indeed I thought that it would be more pleasant out of doors in the shade than inside."

"Much more pleasant, Yossouf; and these forts, as they call them, are generally stuffy places with small windows. What is the feeling of the people here?"

"They are looking forward to Ayoub's coming, sir, when they say a holy war will be preached, and every man will rise against the infidels. When they found I was a countryman they talked freely enough before me, especially as I led them to believe that I had been taken prisoner at Cabul and forced to accompany you as a sort of slave. I should recommend that as soon as tiffin is over, you should start for the camp, for I don't think it is quite safe here."

"They would never think of attacking us, Yossouf, with our force within an easy day's march."

"I don't know, sir," Yossouf said doubtfully. "They say that the Wali's men are all with them, and that these alone are quite sufficient to eat up the three British regiments."

"They will find out their mistake if they try it. However, Yossouf, I will let the others know what you think."

By this time they had arrived at the spot where the lunch was laid out, and very tempting it looked to hungry men.

A great dish of curry made with some fowls purchased in the village was the principal dish; but there were some fish which Yossouf had caught in the Helmund on the previous day, a roast of young kid, and several dishes of fresh fruit. A large vessel of porous clay containing the drinking water stood close by, and the necks of some bottles of claret peeped out from a tub full of water, while a pitcher of cold tea was ready for those who preferred it. The young men set to with a vigorous appetite, and when the meal was over, pipes and cigars were lighted, and they prepared to enjoy a rest until the heat of the day was past. Will now told them what Yossouf had said.

"Oh, nonsense, Gale!" Hammond said. "Your boy is an Afghan, and these fellows are always dreaming about treachery. They are scowling, sulky-looking brutes," he said, looking at a group of natives who stood watching them with lowering eyes, "and of course they hate us as infidel dogs; but as to attacking us, it's all nonsense."

"Well, you know, Hammond, these Ghazis do attack us in all sorts of places, as I have found to my cost, and these villages abound with these fanatics."

"Oh, yes," Fortescue said lazily, "of course they do; but we have got our revolvers handy, and our guns are within reach of our hands. We should make precious short work of any Ghazis who were to run amuck among us. Well, I for one don't mean to move till it gets a bit cooler. If these fellows want to attack us, they have got the chance now, and there is no more reason they should do it three hours hence than when we are having our breakfast quietly."

CHAPTER XIX
THE BATTLE OF MAIWAND

THE servants were squatting in a circle near their masters and enjoying their share of the breakfast. The two Syces were Beloochees; the others were men from the Deccan, the regiment having been stationed at Poona before going up into Afghanistan. Of these the Syces alone understood the Afghan language.

After the men had finished their meal, Yossouf strolled away by himself into the village. When he returned, Will saw that he wished to speak to him, so, rising carelessly from the ground, he walked to the ponies, which were tied up near, and called Yossouf as if to give him some instructions respecting them.

"Well, Yossouf, what is it? Have you learned anything?"

"No, sir, nothing. But the people no longer speak to me freely. They must have guessed when they saw me speaking to you that I was warning you; but I don't think things are right. The children are all in the houses instead of playing about in the street. A few of the women are standing at their doors, but most of them are inside too."

"But if the men are thinking of attacking us, why shouldn't they do so at once?"

"There are not above twenty or thirty men here, sahib. They may not think they are strong enough. Perhaps they have sent to some of the villages for help."

"Likely enough, Yossouf, I did not think of that. Do you go up above the village and have a good look round. I will try and persuade my friends to be moving."

Yossouf moved off at once, and Will stood for a minute or two thinking what was the best to do. The position was not pleasant. Yossouf's suspicions might be altogether unfounded, but Will had found him to be so uniformly right on former occasions that he did not like to neglect his advice now. After a little further thought he joined his companions.

"Come," he said, "we had really better be moving. I believe we are in real danger."

The earnestness with which he spoke roused the others, who were all lying at full length on the ground.

"But as we said before, Gale," Fortescue urged, "why shouldn't they now attack us if they wanted to? We have been here more than an hour."

"Perhaps they may think we shall all take a nap after our tiffin," Will replied; "perhaps, as Yossouf thinks, they have sent off to some other villages for assistance. He has gone up the hillside to look out. Anyhow, I can assure you, I think we had better be moving."

"It is beastly hot," Hammond said, getting up and stretching himself; "but as you are so earnest about it, Gale, perhaps we had better make a move. As you say, you know no end more of these fellows than we do, and you certainly ain't a fellow to get into a funk about nothing. Come on, boys, we had better do as Gale tells us."

"That's right," Will said cheerfully. "And look here, if we get away from here without any disturbance and find it all right, we can halt again at the first shady place we come to, and stop there for two or three hours till it gets cool.

"Wait a moment," he went on, as Hammond was about to order the ponies to be saddled. "Just let us settle what we had best do should they attack us, which, if they mean it, they will do when they see we are moving off. I have been thinking it over. We have all got bullets in our pockets to drop into our guns over the shot in case of necessity. But these smooth-bore fowling-pieces are of no good except at close quarters, while the Afghan matchlocks will carry straight a long way; therefore if we had to make a running fight of it we should get the worst of it, for these fellows could keep up with us easily; besides, there are the servants. Therefore, if a shot is fired, my advice is that we should make a dash at the chief's house. Seize that, and hold it."

"Yes, that would be a good plan," Fortescue said, for they were all sobered now by Will's gravity, and convinced that there must be good grounds for his belief in danger.

"Look here, Gale, we are all senior to you in the date of our commissions, but you have seen no end of service and adventure; therefore I vote that you shall be commanding officer until we get back to camp."

The others willingly agreed.

"Very well," Will said; "I will do my best. Hammond, will you tell your servant to get ready for a start at once. Speak to him quietly and carelessly. Then as the men move up more towards the ponies, tell them in Hindustanee to go about their work quietly, but in case of any trouble with the Afghans, to out with their swords and join us in a rush at the chief's house."

Hammond carried out his instructions. The two Beloochees were not taken by surprise, for they as well as Yossouf had been feeling uneasy at the disappearance of all women and children from the scene. The other men looked startled, but they were stout fellows, and as all the native servants were armed with swords to enable them to resist sudden attacks by the country people, and as they had unbounded faith in their masters, they went about the work of packing up the plates and dishes, and preparing for a start quietly enough.

As the Syces began to put the saddles on the tats the Afghans spoke quickly and angrily together. Two or three minutes later Yossouf arrived. He had evidently been running, for his breath came quick, but he now walked forward in a leisurely way.

"Two large parties are coming, master, one down the valley and the other across the hills. They have got flags with them, and I am sure they are going to attack us."

Just at this moment an Afghan lad joined his seniors and spoke rapidly to them. Will judged at once that he also had been placed on the watch. The chief of the village, accompanied by two or three of his men, now stepped forward.

"Ask the sahibs," he said to Yossouf, "why they are in such a hurry, why they want to start in the heat of the day; they had better wait till it is cooler."

Will did not wait for Yossouf's translation, but answered direct:

"We have duties at the camp and must return at once."

The chief was surprised that one of the young officers should speak his tongue so fluently.

"It looks as if you were not pleased with the hospitality of our village," he said, " that you should hurry away so quickly."

"We are content with it so far, but we must be off now. Bring up the ponies quickly," he said to Yossouf. "Never mind those things; there is not a moment to be lost."

Yossouf and the servants brought up the ponies. The chief laid his hand on one of the bridles and drew a pistol.

"Kaffir dogs," he said, "you shall not leave us at all."

Will's hand was already on his revolver, and before the chief could level his pistol, he fired and the Afghan fell dead.

There was a shout of rage from the others, and their long matchlocks were levelled. It was well the party were prepared, or all might have been shot down at once; but the instant Will fired, his friends raised their double-barrelled guns to their shoulders and let fly the contents among the Afghans, who, thrown into confusion by the sudden and unexpected attack, fired wildly, several of them dropping from the effects of the shot.

"Now!" Will shouted. "To the house, every one of you!"

There was a rush, and before the Afghans knew what had happened, the little party had burst through those standing at the door of the house, and had barred and bolted it within. There were but two men inside, and these, running upstairs, leaped from the windows. A wild screaming was heard from the women and children.

"Yossouf, tell these women that we don't want to hurt them, but that they must be silent and keep the children quiet. We have got enough to think about without this frightful row inside. Then when you have got them quiet, put them all in one room together upstairs, and keep guard at the door. See that none of them leave the room, for they might steal down and open the door to admit their friends while we are busy. What! Fortescue, are you hit?"

"I am done for!" the young officer replied faintly. "One of their bullets has gone through my body; but never mind me now." As he spoke he tottered, and would have fallen, had not the others supported him and gently laid him down on a heap of skins which served as an Afghan bed. Then leaving his servant to attend to him for a minute, the others ran upstairs to see what was going on without.

"Be careful!" Will exclaimed. "Don't show a head above the roof or at a loophole, or you will get a bullet in your brain to a certainty. Stand well back so that they can't see you."

Already a pattering fire of musketry had broken out round the house, but not an Afghan was to be seen, every man having taken his position in shelter.

"There is nothing to do at present," Will said. "When the other parties arrive they may make an attack, but I don't think they will do so till night. Hammond, you had better go down to Fortescue at present. One of the Syces can take Yossouf's place on guard over the women, and he can help you. The lad is a good nurse; but I fear there is nothing to be done for the poor fellow."

A few minutes later a wild outburst of shouts and yells, and a great firing of guns, announced that the other parties had arrived, and the cracking fire of the matchlocks around the fort became incessant.

The defenders did not attempt to return it; it would only have been throwing away lives uselessly to approach any of the loopholes. In a quarter of an hour Hammond rejoined his companions.

"He is gone, poor fellow!" he said. "He never spoke again. The bullet went close to the heart. I think he has bled to death internally. I have handed his revolver to one of the Syces, and his gun to the other. Your man Yossouf has a revolver."

"What on earth are we to do now, Gale?" Plater asked. "You have been right thus far, and if it hadn't been for you putting us up to make a rush here, we should have been done for long ago; but we are not much better off; for here we are cooped up, and the betting is a hundred to one against our being rescued in time. No one will know where to look for us, and though we may beat them off two or three times, in the end it is likely to go hard with us."

"Couldn't we send a messenger with the news of the fix we are in?" Lowther asked. "Though I don't see how any one is to get through."

"That's what I have been thinking about ever since I first planned coming here," Will said; "but I am sure no one could get through. The Afghans know the importance of it, and when it gets dark they will be so thick round the place that a mouse couldn't make its way through them unobserved."

The situation was gloomy enough; but there was no lack of good spirits among the young officers, the danger causing their blood to course rapidly through their veins.

Will sat on the floor apart from the others. They had made him their commanding officer, and the responsibility of thinking for them devolved upon his shoulders. Suddenly a thought struck him, and he leapt to his feet with a shout. "I've got it!"

"You will get it if you don't mind," Hammond said dryly, as a bullet passed through one of the loopholes and struck the wall an inch or two from Will's head. "But what is it?"

"When it gets quite dusk we will call a parley and tell them we don't want to keep the women here, they are only in our way and eat up the food, so we will open the door and let them go."

"But what will you do that for, Gale? You were saying a short time ago that the women could be kept as hostages."

"So they might, Hammond; but it will be more useful to us to let them go. There are seven women here. Six of them shall go out, and with them, in the clothes of the seventh, Yossouf."

"Capital! Capital!" the others exclaimed. "Don't you think they will notice him?"

"No," Will said; "we won't do it till dusk, and some of these women are as tall as he is. They will hurry them away as quickly as possible so as to recommence the attack, and wrapped up as these Afghan women are, no one could see the difference. Once fairly away we can trust Yossouf for finding an opportunity of slipping away and bringing us help."

Will now laid the plan before Yossouf, who at once agreed to attempt it.

The day passed slowly, the fire of the enemy being kept up without intermission.

"Now," Will said at last, "it is getting dark enough, let us put the plan into operation. In the first place the women must be separated, and taken into separate rooms—the one Yossouf has fixed upon as nearest his height into a room by herself. Then Yossouf must tell the old mother of the chief that they are to be released, and that she must show herself on the roof and make them stop firing till they have gone out. While she is doing that he can slip down and dress himself in the robes of the woman. She must be gagged to prevent her screaming or making a row as her companions go out."

Greatly surprised was the old woman at being told that she was to be released. These kaffirs must be mad, she thought, to give up their hostages. However, she at once proceeded to carry the orders into effect.

Before raising her head above the roof she uttered a loud quavering cry, the cry of welcome of the Afghan women. The firing without instantly ceased. Again raising the cry she stepped out on to the roof and shouted that the English did not want to keep the women, and that the door would be open for them to come out, providing the Afghans promised that no attempt to enter should be made, and that none should move from their present places until the women had fairly left.

There was a shout of surprise and satisfaction, and one of the chiefs rose to his feet and gave the promise in the name of his companions.

"How many are there of you?" he asked.

"Seven," the woman answered.

"Are the children to come?"

"We may take away the babies, but the three boys are to remain behind."

Five minutes later the door of the fort opened, and seven figures came out. Not a shot was heard until they had passed down the street of the village, and had entered a house at the further end; then the rapid fire commenced again. Twice during the evening did the Afghans attempt to storm the little fort, but were each time repulsed with loss, the fire of the five double-barrelled guns, loaded with shot and bullets, and of the revolvers, proving too much for them. The second attack was made about eleven.

A quarter of an hour later wild shouts were heard outside; there was an instant cessation of the enemy's fire, and then in the silence the deep thundering sound of galloping horses was heard.

"Hurrah!" Will shouted. "Here they are!"

A minute later the Third Bombay Cavalry dashed up to the fort. The door was thrown open and the little garrison ran out.

"All safe?" the officer in command asked.

"All safe, except Fortescue, who was killed at the first attack."

"So we heard from your boy," the officer said; "he has ridden back with us as guide. Now, lads, dismount and clear the village. Shoot every man you find, turn the women out of the houses, and then set them on fire. Don't waste any time over it, for the rascals are swarming round the place. Captain Lawson, you take your troop and dismount it as skirmishers round the place, and keep them off till we have done here. Here, you four men who brought the powder kegs, carry them inside this fort. We are going to blow it up to give them a lesson."

THE BATTLE OF MAIWAND

Ten minutes later the cavalry were again in their saddles. Spare horses had been brought for the four officers, and the servants mounted the tats, which would be able to keep up with the cavalry. The flames were already bursting out brightly from the houses.

The yells of the Afghans rose high, and their bullets flew thickly over the village, but they kept at a respectful distance. The officer in command gave the word and the party set off at a trot.

Before they had left the village a deep roar was heard, and they knew that the Afghan fort was destroyed. Two hours later they arrived safely in camp, where the four rescued officers were warmly congratulated on their narrow escape by their friends.

On the 14th of July the conspiracy among the Wali's troops came to a head. They openly mutinied and marched out with their cannon and arms from the camp. This was situated at a short distance from that of the British, and Colonel Ripon was the first to gallop in with the news.

Unfortunately the British commander was not a man endowed with promptness of decision, and no steps were taken until the mutineers had proceeded a considerable distance; then the cavalry and artillery were despatched in pursuit. Had the order been given at once there can be no doubt that the Wali's force would have been completely cut up, and those who escaped would have arrived a mere horde of fugitives, for the most part without arms, at Ayoub's camp.

Late as was the pursuit it was not ineffectual. Six British guns opened fire upon the Wali's artillery, which was in rear of the retreating column, with such effect that the gunners were seized with a panic, and, cutting the traces, fled for their lives. A good many were cut down by the British cavalry, and the six guns deserted by them were brought into camp.

Colonel Burrows' little force now stood alone, for he had with him but 1500 infantry, 500 cavalry, and six of his own guns besides those taken from the mutineers—a force altogether disproportioned to that with which Ayoub was advancing, swelled as it was by the accession of the Wali's army. A message was sent to General Primrose at Candahar asking for reinforcements; but that officer, although he had a considerable force at his disposal, declined to despatch any reinforcements whatever. News now arrived that Ayoub, instead of marching direct upon Girishk, had crossed the Helmund higher up and was moving across the country by a line parallel with the road from Candahar to Girishk. By this movement he would have the option of placing himself either between Colonel Burrows' force and Candahar, of marching direct upon the latter city, or of keeping to the north and coming down upon the road between Candahar and Shahpur, and then marching direct for Cabul. Under these circumstances General Burrows determined to fall back at once to a spot where he might oppose Ayoub's advancing force. Accordingly the brigade marched from the Helmund to a village called Khusk-I-Nakhud and there encamped. General Nuttal with the cavalry made reconnaissances in the direction of the enemy.

The people of the country held altogether aloof, and no accurate information was obtained as to the strength of Ayoub's army, which was believed by General Burrows to be very much smaller than it really was. Early in the morning of the 26th it was known that Ayoub was marching upon Maiwand, a village farther to the north, and at half-past six the troops moved out to intercept him.

It was at this time believed that it was only the enemy's cavalry with whom we should have to deal.

Upon arriving near Maiwand, however, news was brought in by spies that the whole of the enemy were at hand. The force was at once halted in a position singularly ill adapted for a fighting ground. Deep ravines ran both to the right and to the left of the ground occupied by the British. By these the enemy could advance under shelter until within a short distance. On either side were ranges of hills completely commanding the position.

It is difficult to imagine a more unsuitable position than that which General Burrows prepared to hold with a mere handful of troops against an enormously superior force. What was the total strength of Ayoub's army was never exactly known, as it was swollen by enormous numbers of Ghazis and tribesmen from the villages. These were in fact far more formidable opponents than the regular

Afghan troops, as their tremendous rushes, and indifference to the loss inflicted upon them, were trying in the extreme for even the best-trained troops to withstand.

The morning was thick and but little could be seen of Ayoub's army. His cavalry, indeed, were found to be moving about in large masses, but these fell back at our advance. Lieutenant Maclean, with two horse-artillery guns and a small cavalry escort, galloped out on the extreme left and opened fire on the Afghan cavalry. His infantry at once appeared in force, swarming down towards the guns, and these were withdrawn to a position nearer to our line.

The British infantry were formed in the following order:— The 66th were on the right, the Bombay Grenadiers in the centre, and Jacob's Rifles on the left. Two guns were placed in position to support the 66th on the right; the remaining four British guns, and the six smooth-bore guns captured from the Wali's mutineers, were placed between the Grenadiers and Jacob's Rifles. The 3d Scinde Horse and 3d Bombay Light Cavalry were formed in the rear of the line.

As the enemy advanced, our guns opened a heavy fire upon them, but it was fully an hour before their artillery replied. Then thirty guns were unmasked and opened fire upon the British line. Under cover of this heavy fire, swarms of the enemy's irregulars advanced towards our position. When within 600 or 700 yards of the 66th, the British opened with their Martini rifles, and the shower of lead at such an unexpected distance checked the advance of the enemy.

For some time the artillery duel continued, but the enemy's guns were then moved on to the hills on either side of the British position and a terrible cross-fire was opened from both flanks. At about two o'clock the smooth-bore guns began to get short of ammunition. Only sixty rounds had been captured with them, and there being no reserve of ammunition fitting them, they ceased fire. The position now became most serious. From the ravines on either side the Ghazis swarmed up in vast numbers. The artillery thundered from the heights upon our troops. Some of their batteries were brought up to within very short distances; and great numbers of the enemy, keeping along the ravines sheltered from our fire, came up in the rear and seized the villages there. The companies of Jacob's Rifles on the left, after resisting for some time the furious attacks of the Ghazis, began to waver. The enemy's cavalry swept down in heavy masses, while our cavalry, for some reason which has never been explained, remained inactive. The general has stated that he ordered them to charge, but that they would not do so; the cavalry affirm that they never received orders. Anyhow, at this critical moment the 3d Scinde Horse and the 3d Bombay Cavalry remained inactive. The confusion amid Jacob's Rifles rapidly grew in spite of the efforts of the officers to rally them. The Ghazis swept down upon them and the Rifles broke in confusion and rushed among the Bombay Grenadiers, who, hitherto fighting steadily, also fell into confusion, as the Rifles and Ghazis burst into their ranks.

"This is hot work," Will Gale said to his captain when the enemy's guns on the heights on either side began to play on the line of the 66th with their flank fire.

"It is, indeed," the officer answered, "and the fire of the enemy from the edge of that ravine is very trying. I wish to heaven the general would move us farther back; he has made a hideous mistake in fighting on such ground as this."

"It would be difficult to withdraw now," Will said. "It would shake the confidence of the men. I think myself that we ought to advance and drive the enemy before us till we take up some really defensible position; but I doubt if the Afghans would wait for that. In all our history a British charge against an Indian enemy has always been successful, no matter how great the odds."

"It is a bad look-out," the captain said, as a shell burst close by him, killing and wounding five or six men. "It is quite evident that if we stay where we are, we must in time be annihilated. Our fellows will stand, no doubt; they are English soldiers and well officered. But how can one expect the two Indian regiments, with only three or four white officers each, to remain steady under such a fire as this and with these desperate charges of Ghazis upon them?"

THE BATTLE OF MAIWAND

Very steadily the 66th held their ground in spite of a flanking fire of artillery and musketry. Every time the enemy gathered at the edge of the ravine for a rush, the heavy fire of the company on the flank, which was wheeled back at a right angle to the line so as to face them, drove them back to shelter again. The regiment had suffered very heavily; still, the officers felt that they could endure till nightfall. Of victory there was now no idea; for to conquer, men must act, and here they were only called upon to suffer. Presently a wild tumult was heard to the left, and then the men of the scattered native regiments burst in a tumultuous mass into the ranks of the 66th.

"Steady, men, steady!" shouted the officers.

But it was of no avail. All was in hopeless confusion. The artillery fired until the Ghazis were within a few yards of them; then they hastily limbered up and fell back. But the Ghazis were too close at hand, and two of the guns were lost. Even now, had the cavalry charged upon the Afghans, time would have been given to the broken infantry to form again into a solid mass and to draw off from the field in good order. But the cavalry remained inactive. Both these regiments had a record of good service in the field, but their conduct on this occasion was little short of disgraceful. Among the infantry all order was lost, and, mixed up in a confused mass, hemmed in on all sides by the enemy, they fell back, each man fighting for himself, upon the village behind. Here in the walled enclosures the 66th and the Grenadiers rallied and fought nobly. Each house was used as a fortress and only carried after a desperate struggle. Here Colonel Galbraith and nine other officers of the 66th were killed, and the greater portion of the regiment shared their fate.

Some bodies of the troops entirely cut off from the rest in their retreat stood their ground in the open and fought desperately to the end, surrounding themselves where they died with a ring of slaughtered enemies. So desperate was the defence in some cases that, outnumbering them fifty to one, the enemy never dared to come to close quarters with the gallant band, which kept up a rain of fire on them till the last man had fallen. So long and stoutly was the village defended that the great majority of the broken fugitives had time to pass out behind. General Burrows, who had done his best to stem the rout, drew off the shattered remains and fell back with them in fair order.

Will Gale's company was in the right flank of the regiment, and therefore farthest from the point where the line was broken by the rush of the native troops. Seeing what was taking place, the captain formed his men into company square and fell back to the village in fair order. The company then threw itself into a house with a walled garden to the right of the village, and its steady fire in no slight degree helped to keep back the Afghans and cover the retreat. This they did until General Burrows himself rode up and ordered them to fall in.

"Your company has done good service, sir," he said to Captain Fletcher, "and it is for you now to cover the retreat."

Slowly and in good order the company fell back, and, joining the troops who still retained their formation, retired slowly, facing about and pouring volley after volley into the Afghans as they came out through the village. For two miles the enemy pressed closely upon them; but their loss had already been immense and all desired to join in the plundering of the British camp; therefore the pursuit slackened, and three miles from the village the rear-guard were ordered to the main body at quick march.

CHAPTER XX
CANDAHAR

"THANK God that is over," Captain Fletcher said, as he lifted his cap and wiped the perspiration from his forehead, "but the regiment is almost annihilated."

"I fear the worst is yet to come," Will said. "We are fifty miles from Candahar, and when we came out, we had to carry water with us, for there was none to be found on the way. We have a fearful march before us. What on earth has become of the cavalry? They have done nothing to cover the retreat."

"They have ridden on ahead," the captain said bitterly, "without having drawn a sword in this day's fight, and will ride into Candahar to-morrow morning without losing a man, save the few who were knocked over by the artillery."

Presently an officer rode up.

"Ah, Gale!" he exclaimed. "Thank God you are safe. I rode back to see." And Colonel Ripon shook hands warmly with the young officer.

"I am glad to see that you are safe, sir," Will answered. "This has been a terrible day."

"It has, indeed," the colonel said mournfully. "Terrible! There has been nothing like it since the retreat from Cabul in 1848. And how many of these poor fellows will reach Candahar, God only knows! The water-bottles were emptied hours ago. The men are already exhausted with the long day's work and parched with thirst, and we have fifty miles' tramp before us. Have you any wounded men here with you?"

"Several, sir; some of them badly hurt."

"Put one of the worst on my horse," Colonel Ripon said, dismounting; "and push on briskly, lads. There are some carts ahead. We will turn out the stores and put the wounded in. You had better

215

let the men throw away their knapsacks and all useless encumbrances," he said to Captain Fletcher. "You will have to march and perhaps fight all night, and must husband your strength."

Steadily the rear-guard followed the broken column. It consisted of men of the 66th and Grenadiers mingled together, and well did they carry out their arduous duties. A portion were thrown out on each flank, while the rest kept to the road. This was strewn with arms and accoutrements of all kinds. The men's hearts were wrung to the core by the sight of the number of wounded who had dropped by the roadside and who implored them as they passed not to leave them to be murdered by the enemy. Many of them were lifted and placed in carts, everything else being turned out to make way for them, but many had to be left behind, for it would be impossible to carry them on such a march. Slowly the long night passed. All along the line ahead a scattered fire of musketry could be heard as the villagers shot down the fugitives who in hopes of finding water straggled from the road. Sometimes sharp volleys rang out as the troops stood at bay and drove back the natives when they pressed upon them. Several times the rear-guard were hotly engaged as the Afghans, furious at seeing their prey slipping from their fingers, mustered and fell upon them; but each time they were repulsed and the column held on its way. Will was in command of a mixed band of some forty men which moved to the right of the road. Colonel Ripon kept by his side, but few words were spoken through the long night.

The men were half mad with thirst, and had there been water near, nothing could have restrained them from rushing to it; but they knew that none could be obtained until they reached Candahar. Many, in utter despair at the distance before them, threw themselves down on the ground to die. But the others kept on, stumbling and staggering as they marched, stupid and half-blind, rallying only when the order came to turn and repulse the enemy.

Two or three times in the night the rear-guard halted for a few minutes and the men threw themselves down on the sand, where they picked the scattered herbage within their reach and chewed it to quench their burning thirst. Daylight was a welcome relief. They knew indeed that with the rising of the sun their torments would grow still greater; but the change from the long dreary darkness cheered them, and they could now see from the nature of the country that they were within fifteen miles of Candahar. They marched on for two more hours, and then the officer in command of the little body saw that they could do no more.

He therefore led them to a village on rising ground a short distance from the road and halted them there. The exhausted men threw themselves down in the shade of the houses. They had the long day yet to pass and their thirst seemed unendurable; still, the halt was welcome, for there was not a man but felt that his strength was at an end and that it would have been an impossibility to reach the city.

Captain Fletcher picked out a few of the least exhausted men and placed them in the outskirts of the village to call the rest to arms in case the Afghans, numbers of whom were hovering round, should venture upon an attack. For the first hour after reaching the village not a man moved from the spot where he had thrown himself down. The officers had searched the houses and found some jars of water. These they carried round and doled out a few mouthfuls to each man. Small though the amount was, the relief afforded was immense; and as soon as their first exhaustion had subsided, the men scattered through the gardens, plucking the vine leaves and chewing them, and fortunately discovering a few gourds, which were cut up into small fragments and divided.

The day wore on, and at one o'clock there was a shout of joy, for a body of cavalry were seen approaching at a rapid trot from the town. Soon they rode up, and proved to be a regiment which had been despatched from the town for the relief of the stragglers. At daybreak the cavalry, riding in many miles ahead of the infantry, brought the news to the city of the defeat, and something very like a panic at first ensued.

It was some time before anything was done to succour the exhausted fugitives who were pressing forward to the city. But at last a force was sent out with waggons and bullocks with water-skins, and thus hundreds of lives which would otherwise have been sacrificed were saved. The cavalry had come out with full water-bottles, and relief was soon afforded to the worn-out rear-guard, who at once fell into rank and resumed their march towards Candahar, the cavalry, who had brought a few light carts with them, pursuing their journey for some distance further to succour and collect those who had fallen on the road.

The sun was just setting as the rear-guard of General Burrows' brigade reached Candahar, after having marched since the previous morning sixty miles without food, and with only a few mouthfuls of water, and having fought for nearly twenty-four hours of that time. Every preparation was made in the city for the expected attack. The defences were strengthened; the lower portion of the populace, who would be likely to declare against them, were turned out of the town, and provisions were collected from the country round. Fortunately ample time was afforded them for these preparations. Ayoub's army had been to a great extent demoralized by the tremendous losses which it had sustained in the defeat of this handful of British troops, and some days elapsed before it moved forward from Maiwand. Then by easy marches it approached Candahar, and took up its position in the plain to the north of the city.

Just as the rear-guard of General Burrows' force were starting from their halting-place for their last march into the city, Will Gale was delighted at seeing Yossouf approaching. He had not seen him since the regiment marched out from Kusk-I-Nakhud. The young Afghan had remained with the other followers in the village behind Maiwand during the battle, when, while the resistance of the British was still continuing, the Afghans had worked round by the ravines and entered the village.

Yossouf had been obliged to join in the retreat, which was at once commenced by the baggage train. Full of anxiety for the fate of his master, he had hurried forward at his best speed to Candahar, reaching the city only an hour or two after the arrival of the cavalry. In spite of the distance he had already performed, he did not delay for an instant, but set out again with some provisions, and a bottle of wine and one of water hidden away in his dress. He had resolved to push forward at all hazards until he had either joined his master, whether on his retreat or as a prisoner in Ayoub's army, or had discovered his body on the field of battle, and given him burial.

Passing through the throng of fugitives, and questioning any of the men of the 66th he met, he made his way forward. He had learned that Will's company had withdrawn in a body from the battle-field to the village, but further than this none of the fugitives could tell him; and his delight was exuberant when he saw Will marching along with his company.

The little supply which he had brought was at once served out among the men who most needed it, and Will, who had been in a state of great uneasiness concerning the safety of his faithful follower, was greatly cheered by finding him alive and unhurt.

The news of the defeat of Maiwand produced an immense sensation in India, and measures were at once taken for the relief of Candahar. A strong division was ordered to march from Cabul through Ghuzni, while General Phayre, who commanded the force at Quettah, was also ordered to advance to the assistance of the garrison. General Phayre, however, although comparatively close to Candahar, was unable to advance for some time. The same miserable economy which had dispersed the transport train after the signature of the Treaty of Gundamuk, and had so delayed the advance of General Roberts towards Cabul after the massacre of the mission, again paralysed the action of the British troops, the whole of the transport train, collected at so much cost and difficulty, having been dismissed to their homes as soon as the negotiations with Abdul-Rahman held out a prospect of peace.

Many weeks elapsed before a sufficient number of baggage animals could be collected to enable General Phayre to advance with his relieving column. In Candahar things passed quietly. The enemy from time to time fired shot and shell into the city from distant positions; but believing that no relief could reach the garrison before the supplies of food were exhausted, and that it must therefore yield to hunger, Ayoub's army contented themselves by watching the city from a distance, and by keeping a cordon of troops round its walls to prevent the country people from bringing in provisions.

Detached bodies, indeed, often crept up near the walls and kept up a musketry fire at any troops showing themselves there. But no attempts were made to batter down the walls or to make anything like a resolute assault. Ayoub's army had indeed greatly lost heart. If 1500 British soldiers attacked under circumstances of the greatest disadvantage, had killed 6000 or 7000 of their assailants, what might not be the slaughter which a greatly superior force would inflict when sheltered behind stone walls?

From one village, situated half a mile from the eastern gate of the city, so constant and harassing a fire was maintained by the enemy that General Primrose resolved to make a sortie to capture it. The affair was, however, badly planned, and resulted in failure. The Afghans, sheltered in the strongly-built houses, kept up so severe a fire upon the assailants that these were obliged to fall back with a considerable loss.

After that no further sorties were attempted, and the city remained in quiet until the relieving columns were close at hand.

The force selected to march from Cabul to the relief of Candahar under the command of General Roberts consisted of the 92d Highlanders, 23d Pioneers, 24th and 25th Punjaub Infantry, the 2d, 4th, and 5th Ghoorkas, the 72d Highlanders, 2d battalion of the 60th, the Norfolk Rangers, the 2d, 3d, and 15th Sikhs. There were three batteries of artillery and four cavalry regiments, the 9th Lancers, the 3d Bengal Cavalry, the 3d Punjaub Cavalry, and the Central India Horse. This gave a total of about 10,000 fighting men. There were, in addition, 8000 followers to feed, 7000 horses, and some 8000 transport and artillery mules and ponies.

The Ameer did his best to assist the force, which was indeed going to fight his battle as well as their own. The question was whether so large a force would be able to subsist on the road, and in order to assist them to do so, he sent orders to all the tribes along the line of march to aid the column in every way. In consequence, no difficulties were met with, and scarce a shot was fired on the way down. In seven days after starting, Ghuzni was reached, and in fifteen, Khelat-I-Ghilzai, where Colonel Tanner with a small garrison had been besieged by the local tribes since the advance of Ayoub. Khelat-I-Ghilzai stood near the lower end of the valley down which the column was advancing, and was but three days' march from Candahar.

From the day of their leaving Cabul to their arrival at Khelat-I-Ghilzai the troops had marched a distance of fifteen miles a day—not an extraordinary distance for a single regiment to perform, but a wonderful feat for a force containing some 18,000 persons and 9000 baggage animals marching through mountains and valleys. As the relieving force approached Candahar, Ayoub drew off his troops from around the city, and took up a strong position on some hills a few miles to the north. On the 27th of August, Roberts' cavalry were near enough to establish heliographic communication with the town, and on the 31st the column entered Candahar.

During the siege the duties of the garrison had been heavy. A strong force was always held ready to get under arms instantly in case of an attack by the enemy. The number of sentries on the walls, magazines, and lower important points was large. The town had to be kept in order and the inhabitants strictly watched.

House-to-house requisitions were made for provisions, and the greatest economy was used in the distribution of these, as the garrison had no means of knowing how long a time might elapse before any could arrive. The death of ten officers of the 66th, all of senior standing to himself, had placed Will Gale at the top of the list of lieutenants, and, as several officers were disabled by wounds, he was now performing captain's duty, and was in charge of a company. There were, indeed, but three companies now in the 66th Regiment, so great having been the loss that the whole of the survivors now made up but this number.

Among the other duties of the troops was that of protecting the many houses which had been left vacant by the hasty retirement of many of the native merchants and traders at the approach of Ayoub's force. Colonel Primrose, anxious to lessen the number of mouths to be fed, encouraged the exodus, promising to take charge of all property left behind. This duty proved a troublesome one, as the lower class, which still remained in the city, were constantly endeavouring to break into and loot the houses thus left vacant by their proprietors. In order to protect these as much as possible, many of the officers were directed to move from their quarters in the barracks and take up their residence in them, an order which was gladly obeyed, as the exchange from hot confined quarters to the roomy dwellings of the merchants was a very pleasant one. Will Gale was one of those who so moved, and with Yossouf and two native followers had been quartered in the house of a wealthy silk merchant.

One night he was aroused from sleep by Yossouf.

"Sahib!" the latter whispered. "I hear people moving below. I think there are thieves in the house."

Will rose noiselessly, slipped on his trousers and shoes, and, taking up a revolver in one hand and a sword in another, stole down-stairs, followed by Yossouf with his long Afghan knife in his hand. The door of the warehouse was open, and within it Will saw, by the faint light of a lamp which one of them carried, four Afghan ruffians engaged in making up silks into large bundles in readiness to carry off. His approach was unnoticed, and, on reaching the door, he levelled his pistol and shouted to the Afghans to surrender as his prisoners. In reply they dropped the lamp, and made a sudden rush at him. He fired his pistol hastily in the darkness, but in an instant the Afghans were upon him. The first man he cut down, but he was knocked over by the rush of the others. Two fell upon him, but Yossouf bounded upon them like a tiger and buried his knife to the hilt in their backs in quick succession. The last of the party, without staying to see what was the fate of his friends, at once took to his heels, and rushing to the door leading to the street, made his escape. Yossouf raised Will to his feet.

"Are you hurt?" he asked anxiously.

"Nothing to speak of," Will replied. "I am a bit shaken and bruised by the fall. Those fellows in the darkness were upon me before I could see them. Thanks to you, I have escaped without hurt, Yossouf, and had it not been for your aid they would assuredly have made an end of me. My pistol had fallen from my hand as they knocked me down, and on the ground I could not have defended myself with my sword for an instant. Once more, Yossouf, I owe my life to you."

So many attempts similar to that made upon the house occupied by Will Gale took place that sentries were posted at ten o'clock at night at the entrances to the various streets in which the houses left deserted by the native traders were situated, and orders were given that no natives should be out of their houses after that hour unless provided with a pass signed by the commandant of the city. Several messengers were from time to time sent out to endeavour to get through the enemy's lines and to carry to General Phayre the news of what was going on in the city. A few of these succeeded in getting through, but none returned, so that until the signal-lights were seen flashing from the distant hills in the direction of Khelat-I-Ghilzai, the garrison were unaware of the steps which were being taken for their rescue. Even had unforeseen obstacles prevented the advent of either of the relieving columns, it is probable that the garrison at Candahar would finally have freed itself. Colonel Primrose had at his disposal a force more than double that which had fought at Maiwand, and had the British advanced into the plain and offered battle to Ayoub on a fair fighting ground, they should without difficulty have defeated his army, whose long delays and hesitation showed how immensely their morale had been affected by the previous battle. Thus it was that Sale, after sustaining a long siege in Jellalabad, finally sallied out and completely defeated the besieging army before the arrival of the force marching to his relief.

The Candahar force was not commanded by a Sale; but had it been given a chance to retrieve Maiwand, there can be little doubt of what the issue would have been. Over and over again the subject was discussed at the messes of the various regiments, and immense indignation was felt at the force being kept cooped up in Candahar when the history of India recorded scores of examples of victories won by British troops against greater odds than those now opposed to them.

It must be said, however, that the native portion of the army in Candahar was of very inferior fighting quality to that which operated in Eastern Afghanistan. Those regiments were for the most part either Ghoorkas, Sikhs, or Punjaubees, than whom no braver men exist. The Ghoorkas are small active men, mountaineers by birth, and to whom war is a passion. The Sikhs and Punjaubees, upon the contrary, are tall stately men, proud of the historical fighting powers of their race. They had fought with extreme bravery against the English, but once conquered they became true and faithful subjects of the English crown, and it was their fidelity and bravery which saved England in the dark days of the mutiny. The Bombay troops, upon the other hand, were drawn from races which had long ceased to be warlike. They possessed none of the dash and fire of the hardier troops; their organization was, and still is, defective; and the system of officering them was radically bad. The contrast between the two was strongly shown in the conduct of the Sikh and Ghoorka regiments with General Stewart when attacked by the sudden rush of the Ghazis at Ahmed Khil, and that of the Bombay Grenadiers and Jacob's foot under precisely similar circumstances at Maiwand. There is no doubt, however, that the main reason why General Primrose did not sally out and give battle on the plain of Candahar was that in case of defeat, the populace of the city would assuredly have closed their gates against the army, and that nothing would have remained but a disastrous retreat across the Kojak Pass, a retreat of which very few would ever have survived to tell. Their enforced idleness in Candahar made the time pass slowly and heavily, and it was with the greatest joy that the garrison hailed the entry of the columns of General Roberts.

Upon his arrival the general lost no time in reconnoitring the position of the enemy.

It was well chosen for defence. His army was encamped behind the range of hills known as the Baba-Wali Hills. A road ran direct over these hills, and here a strong force was stationed, supported by artillery in position. The last hill of the range on the southwest was known as the Pir-Paimal Hill, and by turning this, the camp of Ayoub's army would be taken in flank and the defences in front rendered useless. The reconnaissance which was made by the cavalry, supported by the 15th Sikhs, advanced close to the central hill. The enemy unmasked five guns and opened upon them, and the Afghans poured down to the attack.

There was, however, no intention on the part of the British commander of bringing on a battle, and the troops accordingly fell back in good order to the main body. A mile and a half from the city stood a low ridge of rock called the Picket Hill, in the line by which the column would have to move to turn the Pir-Paimal Hill, and this was at once seized. A number of Ghazis stationed here fought, as usual, desperately, but the 4th Ghoorkas repulsed their charge and cleared the ridge of the enemy. The general determined to attack the enemy's position with his whole force on the following day.

CHAPTER XXI
THE BATTLE OF CANDAHAR

THE plan of action upon which General Roberts determined was simple. The 1st and 2d brigade were to advance abreast, the 3d to follow in support. As the 66th were to take no part in the fight, Will Gale obtained leave to ride out with General Weatherby with the 3d division. The enemy were well aware of the weak point of the position which they occupied, and they had mustered thickly in the plain, in which were several villages, with canals cutting up the ground in all directions, and abounding with hedges, ditches, and inclosures; altogether a very strongly defensible position.

It was at 10 o'clock on the 1st of September that the British force advanced. The first division on the right advanced against the large walled village of Gundi, which was strongly held by the enemy. Against this General Macpherson sent the 92d and the 2d Ghoorkas, and stubbornly as the enemy fought, the place was carried by the bayonet. On the line taken by the 2d division under General Baker, three villages had successively to be carried, Abasabad, Kaghanary, and Gundigan. The 72d Highlanders and the 2d Sikhs advanced to the attack of these. The resistance of the Afghans was stubborn in the extreme, but they were driven out. The fighting line of the two divisions kept abreast, and for two miles had to fight every inch of their way from wall to wall, from garden to garden, and here and there from house to house, and from lane to lane.

Once or twice the attack was checked for a few minutes by the desperate resistance of the Afghans at the crossing places of canals and in walled inclosures; and again and again the Ghazis rushed down upon the troops. The 3d Sikhs and the 5th Ghoorkas joined the fighting line, and step by step the ground was won until the base of the hill was turned and the attacking force saw in front of them the great camp of Ayoub's troops. Up to this point the enemy had fought with the greatest bravery, but a sudden panic seized them now they saw that their line of retreat was threatened by our cavalry, for an Afghan always loses heart under such circumstances. As if by magic the defence ceased, and the enemy, horse and foot, abandoning their guns, and throwing away their arms, fled up the Argandab valley. Everything was abandoned.

There was nothing more for the infantry to do but to sack Ayoub's camp and to park the captive guns, thirty in number. The amount of stores and miscellaneous articles in the camp was enormous: arms, ammunition, commissariat, and ordnance stores, helmets, bullock huts crammed with native wearing apparel, writing materials, Korans, English tinned meats, fruit, and money. Here, in fact, was all the baggage which the army had brought from Herat, together with all the spoil which they had captured at Maiwand.

The cavalry took up the pursuit. Unfortunately they had met with great difficulties in advancing through the broken country in rear of the infantry. Had they been close at hand when the latter fought their way into Ayoub's camp, very few of the fugitives would have escaped. As it was, they did good service in following up the rout, and driving the enemy, a dispersed and broken crowd, into the hills. To the fury of the men, they found in Ayoub's camp the body of Lieutenant Maclaine, who had been taken prisoner at Maiwand, and who was barbarously murdered a few minutes before the arrival of the English troops. The battle cost the lives of three officers: Lieutenant-colonel Brownlow, commanding the 72d Highlanders; Captain Frome of the same regiment; and Captain Straton, 2d battalion of the 22d. Eleven officers were wounded, 46 men were killed, and 202 wounded.

The enemy left 1200 dead on the field. Ayoub's regular regiments scarcely fired a shot, and the British advance had been opposed entirely by the irregulars and Ghazis, the regular regiments having been drawn up behind the Pir-Paimal Pass, by which they expected our main attack to be made, a delusion which was kept up by our heavy fire from early morning upon the Afghan guns on

Gundi carried by the bayonet.

the summit of the pass. When our troops appeared round the corner of the spur upon their flank, they lost heart at once, and for the most part, throwing away their arms, joined the body of fugitives.

"It would have been hard work, sir," Will Gale said to Colonel Ripon as they rode forward in rear of the fighting brigade, "to have taken this position with the Candahar force alone."

"It could not have been done," Colonel Ripon replied; "but no one would have dreamed of attempting it. The Afghans say that the force which Roberts brought down from Cabul was so large that they stood on the defensive, but they would have ventured to attack us had we sallied out and offered battle on the level plain round the city. Then I have no doubt we could have beaten them. However, all is well that ends well. Roberts has come up in time, and has completely defeated the enemy; still, it would have been more satisfactory had we retrieved Maiwand by thrashing him single-handed. Well, I suppose this is the end of the Afghan war. We have beaten Ayoub, I hope so effectually that Abdul-Rahman will have no difficulty in dealing with him in future; and if he really means the professions of friendship which he has made us, we may hope for peace for some time. Probably the next time we have to fight in this country it will be against the Russians and Afghans united. There are men in England who persist in shutting their eyes to the certain consequences of the Russian advance towards the northern frontier of Afghanistan; but the time will come when England will have to rue bitterly the infatuation and folly of her rulers. When that day arrives, she will have to make such an effort to hold her own as she has never had to do since the days when she stood alone in arms against Europe."

Upon the following day Will paid a visit to his friends in the Rangers.

"So you got through Maiwand safely!" the colonel said. "Upon my word, I begin to think that you have a charmed life. I hear one of your captains died last night. That gives you your step, does it not?"

"Yes, sir."

"You are the luckiest young dog I ever heard of. You got your commission within a year of enlisting; and now by an extraordinary fatality your regiment is almost annihilated, and you mount up by death steps to a captain's rank nine months after the date of your gazette. In any other regiment in the service you would have been lucky if you had got three or four steps by this time."

"I am fortunate indeed, sir," Will said. "I can scarcely believe it myself."

"Ah! Whom do I see here?" the colonel exclaimed, as a mounted officer rode through the camp. "My old friend Ripon! Ah, Ripon! How are you?"

The colonel reined in his horse, and the two officers, who had not met for some years, entered into a warm conversation, while Will strolled away to talk to some of the younger officers, who congratulated him most heartily on the luck which had in a few months taken him over their heads.

In the afternoon Will received a note from Colonel Ripon asking him to dine with him, as Colonel Shepherd was going to do so. Will replied that he would gladly dine, but must be excused for a time afterwards, as he was on duty and would have to go the rounds in the evening. There were three or four other officers at dinner, as Colonel Ripon had many friends in the relieving column. When dinner was over, Will made his excuses and left, promising to look in again in a couple of hours when he had finished his rounds. Soon afterwards the other young officers left; Colonel Shepherd only remained.

"That is a singularly fine young fellow—young Gale, I mean," Colonel Shepherd said, "and a singularly fortunate one. I feel quite proud of him. It was upon my advice that he enlisted; but if anyone had told me at the time that he would be a captain in two years, I should have said that it was absolutely impossible."

"Yes," Colonel Ripon replied, "his luck has been marvellous; but if ever a fellow deserved it, he did. I have a very warm liking, I may say an affection, for him. He saved my life when I was attacked by some Ghazis here, and must have been killed had it not been for his promptness and coolness. He was wounded too, and we were

230

nursed together here. Since then I have seen a great deal of him, and the more I see him, the more I like him. Do you know anything of him previous to the time of his enlisting? You told me he joined your regiment on the day when it arrived at Calcutta. I know nothing of his history before that. The subject never happened to occur in conversation, and it was one upon which I naturally should have felt a delicacy in asking any questions, though I have sometimes wondered in my own mind how he came to be penniless in Calcutta, as I suppose he must have been to have enlisted. Did you happen to hear anything about it?"

"Yes, indeed," Colonel Shepherd answered. "Curiously enough, he was by no means penniless, as he had just received £100 reward for the services he had rendered in preventing a ship from being captured by the Malays. I happened to meet its captain on shore the day I landed, and heard from him the story of the affair, which was as follows, as nearly as I can recollect."

Colonel Shepherd then related to his friend the story of the manner in which the brig, when chased by Malays, was saved by being brought into the reef by Will. "Naturally," he went on, "I was greatly interested in the story, and, expressing a wish to see the young fellow, he was brought off that evening after mess to the *Euphrates*, and told us how he had been wrecked on the island in a Dutch ship, from which only he and a companion were saved. I was so struck with his conduct, and I may say by his appearance and manner, that I took him aside into my own cabin and learned from him the full particulars of his story. I don't think anyone else knows it, for when he expressed his willingness to take my advice and enlist, I told him that he had better say nothing about his past. His manner was so good that I thought he would pass well as some gentleman's son who had got into a scrape, and as I hoped that the time might come when he might step upwards, it was perhaps better that it should not be known what was his origin."

"But what was his origin, Shepherd? I confess you surprise me, for I have always had an idea that he was a man of good family, although in some strange way his education had been neglected, for in fact he told me one day that he was absolutely ignorant of Latin."

"Well, Ripon, as you are a friend of the young fellow, and I know it will go no further, I will tell you the facts of the case. He was brought up in a workhouse, was apprenticed to a Yarmouth smackman, and the boat being run down in a gale by a Dutch troopship, to which he managed to cling as the smack sank, he was carried in her to Java. On her voyage thence to China he was wrecked on the island I spoke of."

"You astound me," Colonel Ripon said, "absolutely astound me. I could have sworn that he was a gentleman by birth. Not, mind you, that I like or esteem him one iota the less for what you tell me. Indeed, on the contrary, for there is all the more merit in his having made his way alone. Still, you astonish me. They tell me," he said with a smile, "that he is wonderfully like me; but strangely enough, he reminds me rather of my wife. You remember her, Shepherd, for you were stationed at Meerut at the time I married her there?"

Colonel Shepherd nodded, and for a few minutes the two friends sat silent, thinking over the memories which the words had evoked.

"Strange, is it not," Colonel Ripon went on, arousing himself, "that the child of some pauper parents should have a resemblance, however distant, to me and my wife?"

"Curiously enough," Colonel Shepherd said, "the boy was not born of pauper parents; he was left at the door of the workhouse at Ely by a tramp, whose body was found next morning in one of the ditches. It was a stormy night, and she had no doubt lost her way after leaving the child. That was why they called him William Gale. Why, what is the matter, Ripon? Good heavens, are you ill?"

Colonel Shepherd's surprise was natural. The old officer sat rigid in his chair with his eyes open and staring at his friend, and yet apparently without seeing him. The colour in his face had faded away, and even through the deep bronze of the Indian sun its pallor was visible. Colonel Shepherd rose in great alarm, and was about to call for assistance when his friend, with a slight motion of his hand, motioned to him to abstain.

"How old is he?" came presently in a strange tone from his lips.

"How old is who?" Colonel Shepherd asked in surprise— "Oh, you mean Gale! He is not nineteen yet, though he looks four or five years older. He was under seventeen when he enlisted, and I rather strained a point to get him in by hinting that when he was asked his age, he had better say under nineteen. So he was entered as eighteen, but I know he was more than a year younger than that. But what has that to do with it, my dear old friend? What is the matter with you?"

"I believe, Shepherd," Colonel Ripon said solemnly, "that he is my son."

"Your son!" his comrade exclaimed, astonished.

"Yes, I believe he is my son."

"But how on earth can that be?" his friend asked. "Are you sure that you know what you are saying? Is your head quite clear, old friend?"

"My head is clear enough," the colonel replied, "although I felt stunned at first. Did you never hear of my having lost my child?"

"No, indeed," Colonel Shepherd replied, more and more surprised. For he had at first supposed that some sudden access of fever or delirium had seized his friend. "You will remember that a week or two after you were married my regiment was moved up to the north, and we remained three years longer in India. When I got back to England I heard that you had lost your wife a short time before and had returned. I remember our ships crossed on the way. When we met again, the conversation never turned on the past."

"I will tell you the story," the colonel said, "and you will see that at any rate the boy may be my son, and that being so, the double likeness proves to me incontestably that he is. I had, as you know, been ill before I left India. I had not been home for fifteen years, and got two years' leave. As you may know, I had a good fortune irrespective of the service, and I took a place called Holmwood Park, near Dawlish, and as I had thought of retiring at the end of my leave, I was put on the commission of the peace. My boy was born a few months after I got home. Soon after I took the place, some gypsy fellows broke into the poultry-yard and stole some valuable chickens which were great pets of my wife. I chased them, and finally brought home the guilt of the theft to one of the men in whose tent a lot of their feathers were found. He had been previously convicted, and was sentenced to a term of penal servitude. Before the trial his wife, also a gypsy, called upon me and begged me not to appear against her husband. This of course was out of the question, as he had already been sent to trial. When she found that her entreaties were useless, she in the most vindictive tone told me that I should repent it, and she certainly spoke as if she meant it. I heard nothing more of the matter until the boy was sixteen months old; then he disappeared; he was stolen from the garden. A clue was left, evidently that I might know from whom the blow came. The gypsy had been convicted partly on the evidence of the feathers, but principally from the fact that the boot which he had on had half the iron on the heel broken off, and this tallied exactly with some marks in my fowl-house. An hour after the child was gone we found in the centre of the drive in the park a boot, conspicuously placed there to catch the eye, and this boot I recognized by the broken iron as that which had transported the gypsy. That the woman had stolen the child I had not the least doubt; but neither of her nor it could I ever gain the slightest clue. I advertised in every paper in the kingdom. I offered a reward of £1000, and I believe the police searched every gypsy encampment in England, but without success. My wife had never been strong, and from that day she gradually sank. As long as there was hope, she kept up for a time. I hoped all would go well, but three months afterwards she faded rapidly, and ere six months had passed from the loss of the child, I buried her and came straight out to India. I went home once for two or three months upon business connected with my property there some seven years since. That was when we last met, you know, at the club. With that exception I have remained here ever since."

"The trouble will be, I fear," Colonel Shepherd said, "for you to identify him. That vindictive gypsy woman who stole your child is not likely to have left any marks on its clothing by which it might be identified at any future time and her revenge on you frustrated."

"Thank God!" the colonel said earnestly. "If it be my son, he bears a mark by which I shall know him. That was one of his poor mother's greatest comforts. The child was born with an ugly blood mark on its neck. It used to bother my wife a good deal, and she consulted several surgeons whether it could not be removed, but they all said no, not without completely cutting out the flesh; and this, of course, was not to be thought of. After the child was lost I remember as well as if it had been spoken to-day, my wife saying, 'How strange are God's ways! I was foolish enough to fret over that mark on the darling's neck, and now the thought of it is my greatest comfort; and if it shall be God's will that years shall pass away before we find him, there is a sign by which we shall always know him. No other child can be palmed off upon us as our own. When we find Tom we shall know him, however changed he may be.' Listen, Shepherd! That is his step on the stairs. May God grant that he prove to be my son!"

"Be calm, old friend," Colonel Shepherd said; "I will speak to him."

The door opened and Will entered.

"I am glad you have not gone, colonel—I was afraid you might have left, for I have been longer than I expected. I just heard the news that the 66th are in orders this evening to march the day after to-morrow for Kurrachee to sail for England, where we are to be reorganized again."

"Gale, I am going to ask you a rather curious thing. Will you do it without asking why?" Colonel Shepherd said quietly.

"Certainly, colonel, if it is in my power," Will said, somewhat surprised.

"Will you take off your patrol jacket, open your shirt, and turn it well down at the neck?"

For a moment Will looked astounded at this request. He saw by the tone in which it was made that it was seriously uttered, and without hesitation he began to unhook his patrol jacket. As he did so his eye fell upon Colonel Ripon's face, and the intense anxiety and emotion that it expressed caused him to pause for a moment. Something extraordinary hung on what he had been asked to do. All sorts of strange thoughts flashed through his brain. Hundreds of times in his life he had said to himself that if ever he discovered his parents it would be by means of this mark upon his neck, which he was now asked to expose. The many remarks which had been made of his likeness to Colonel Ripon flashed across his mind, and it was with an emotion scarcely inferior to that of the old officer that he opened his shirt and turned down the collar. The sight was conclusive. Colonel Ripon held out his arms with a cry of—

"My son, my son!"

Bewildered and delighted Will felt himself pressed to the heart of the man whom he liked and esteemed beyond all others.

With a word of the heartiest congratulation Colonel Shepherd left the father and son together to exchange confidences and tell to each other their respective stories and to realize the great happiness which had befallen them both. Their delight was without a single cloud, save that which passed for a moment through Colonel Ripon's mind as he thought how his wife would have rejoiced had she lived to see that day.

His joy was in some respects even greater than that of his son. The latter had always pictured to himself that if he ever discovered his father, he should find him all that was good; but the colonel had for many years not only given up all hope of ever finding his son, but almost every desire to do so. He had thought that if still alive he must be a gypsy vagabond, a poacher, a liar, a thief, like those among whom he would have been brought up. From such a discovery no happiness could be looked for, only annoyance, humiliation, and trouble. To find his son, then, all that he could wish for—a gentleman, a most promising young officer, the man, indeed, to whom he had been so specially attracted—was a joy altogether unhoped and unlooked for. Morning had broken before the newly united father and son had done their long and happy talk, and they separated only to take a bath to prepare them for the day's work.

The astonishment of everyone was unbounded when Colonel Ripon announced on the following morning that in Captain Gale of the 66th, who it was known had risen from the ranks, he had discovered a son that had been stolen from him as a child. No one entertained a doubt for an instant that any mistake had arisen, for the likeness between the two men as they strode down the street together on their way to General Roberts' quarters was so marked that now that men knew the relationship, none doubted for a moment that they were indeed father and son.

The warmest congratulations poured in upon them from all sides, and from none more heartily than from the general, who was more than ever pleased that he had been the means of Will's obtaining his commission from the ranks. The same day Colonel Ripon sent off, by a mounted messenger carrying despatches, a telegram to be sent from the nearest station of the flying line, which the engineers advancing with Colonel Phayre's force had already carried as far as the Kojak Pass, to the government of India, asking leave to go home at once on the most urgent and pressing family business.

Yossouf's grief when he heard that his master was going to leave for England was very great. At first he begged that he might accompany him; but Tom pointed out that, much as he should like to have him with him, his position in England would be an uncomfortable one. He would meet with no one with whom he could converse, and would after a time long for his own country again. Yossouf yielded to his reasoning, and the picture which Will drew of his own loneliness when in Cabul separated from all his own people aided greatly in enforcing his arguments on his mind. He said, however, that at any rate he would not return to Afghanistan at present.

"It will be long," he said, "before things settle down there, and it will be useless for me to put my money into a herd which might be driven off by plunderers the next week. Besides, at present the feeling against the English will be strong, so many have lost men of their family in the fighting. If I returned I should be a marked man. It is known that I threw in my lot with the English, and it will be cast in my teeth even if no worse came of it. No, I will enlist in the Guides; I shall be at home with them, for most of them belong to the Afghan tribes. I am young yet, not fully a man, and I have my life before me. Some day, perhaps, if things are quiet and prosperous at home, I will go back and end my days there."

So it was arranged. One of the officers of the Guides had accompanied General Roberts as interpreter, and Will handed over Yossouf to him, telling him how well the lad had served him. The officer promised to enroll him in the corps as soon as he rejoined it, and also that he would not fail to report his conduct to the colonel and to obtain his promotion to the rank of a native officer as soon as possible. From Will Yossouf would accept nothing except his revolver as a keepsake, but Colonel Ripon insisted upon his taking from him a present which would make him a rich man when he chose to return to his native country.

CHAPTER XXII
AT HOME AT LAST

THE next day Colonel Ripon started with the 66th, and, at the end of the first day's march, met a messenger, who, among other despatches, carried a telegram granting him at once the leave he asked for, and which indeed had been due had he asked for it many years before. His intention was to accompany the 66th to Kurrachee and to sail with it to England. This intention was carried out, and the remnant of the regiment safely reached England.

One of Colonel Ripon's first steps was to accompany Will, or, as he ought now to be called, Tom, to the Horse Guards, and to procure an insertion in the Gazette stating that Captain William Gale of the 66th would henceforth be known by his true and proper name of Thomas Ripon. The colonel purchased a fine estate in Somersetshire, and, retiring from the service, settled down there. There was a considerable discussion between father and son as to whether the latter should remain in the army. Colonel Ripon was unwilling that his son should relinquish a profession of which he was fond, and in which, from his early promotion, he had every chance of obtaining high rank and honour; but Tom, who saw how great a pleasure his society was to his father, and how lonely the latter's life would be without him, was resolute in his determination to quit the service. He had already, as he said, passed through a far greater share of adventure than usually falls to one man's lot, and the colonel's property was so large that there was not the slightest occasion for him to continue in the service.

Not long after his return to England, Will paid a visit to Ely workhouse. He was accompanied by the colonel, and the two men walked together up to the gate of the workhouse. He rang at the bell, and a woman opened the door. She curtsied at seeing two tall soldier-like gentlemen before her.

"Your name is Mrs. Dickson, I think?" the younger said. The woman gave a violent start and gazed earnestly at him.

"It is Will Gale!" she exclaimed, drawing back a step. "They said you were dead years ago."

"No, I am very much alive, Mrs. Dickson, and glad, most glad, to see an old friend again."

"Good Lord!" the woman exclaimed. "It is the boy himself, sure enough;" and for a moment she seemed as if she would have rushed into his arms, and then she drew back, abashed at his appearance. Tom, however, held out his arms, and the woman fell sobbing into them.

"Why, you did not think so badly of me," he said, "as to think that I should forget the woman who was a mother to me. Father," he said—"for I have found my real father, Mrs. Dickson, as you always said I should some day—it is to this good woman that I owe what I am. But for her I might now be a labouring man; but it is to her kindness, to her good advice, to her lessons, that I owe everything. It was she who taught me that I should so behave that if my parents ever found me they should have no cause to be ashamed of me. She was indeed as a mother to me, and this lodge was my home rather than the workhouse inside. Ah! And here is Sam!"

Sam Dickson, coming out at this moment, stood in open-mouthed astonishment at seeing his wife standing with her hand in that of a gentleman.

"Oh, Sam! Who do you think this is?" Sam made no reply, but stared at Tom with all his eyes.

"If it warn't that he be drowned and dead long ago," he said at last, "I should say it was Will Gale growed up and got to be a gentleman. I shouldn't ha' knowed him at first, but when he smiles I don't think as how I can be far wrong."

"You are right, Sam. I am the boy you and your wife were so kind to from the time you picked him up just where we are standing, and whom you last handed over to go aboard a smack at Yarmouth. She was, as you have heard, run down in the North Sea, but I was saved in the ship which ran over her and was taken out to the East.

There, after being wrecked again, and going through lots of adventures, I went to India, enlisted there, and fought through the Afghan war. I am a captain now, and my name is no longer Will Gale, but Tom Ripon, for I have found my real father, this gentleman, Colonel Ripon."

"Who feels," Colonel Ripon went on, "how much he and his son owe to your kindness and that of your good wife here, and who, as you will find, is not ungrateful. I have just bought an estate down in Somersetshire, and I mean to install you and your wife in a pretty lodge at the gates, with enough to live upon comfortably to the end of your lives."

Mrs. Dickson cried with joy as Colonel Ripon entered into details of what he intended to do for them, and Sam, although, as was his way, much less demonstrative in his gladness, was yet greatly delighted. There was a good garden to the lodge; they were to have the keep of a cow, and thirty shillings per week as long as they lived. Before the colonel left, Sam Dickson's resignation of his post was handed in to the master.

The colonel told them that at the end of the month, when Sam's notice would expire, they were to sell off what furniture they had, as it would cost more to convey it so long a distance than it was worth, and he would take care that they should find everything comfortable and ready for occupation at the lodge upon their arrival. Tom called upon the master and matron and schoolmaster, and thanked all for the kindness that they had shown him when a boy; and Colonel Ripon left a cheque with the master to be expended in tobacco, tea, and sugar for the aged inmates of the house.

No words can express the delight of Sam Dickson and his wife when, a month later, they arrived at their new home. Tom had spared no trouble in seeing that it was comfortably and cosily furnished. The garden had been thoroughly dug up and planted, and Mrs. Dickson could scarcely believe that she was the mistress of so pleasant a home. Tom was forgetful of none of his old friends, and he wrote to an address which Hans, his companion among the Malays, had given him when they separated, and forwarded to him a handsome watch as a souvenir of his comrade.

FOR NAME AND FAME

There is no more to be told. Captain Ripon, still a very young man, is living with his father the colonel. He is one of the most popular men in his county, and there is some talk of his standing for one of its boroughs at the next election, and it is rumoured that he is likely, ere long, to bring home a lady who will be the future mistress of Burnham Park.

He is quite content that he has left the army, though he fidgetted a little, while the Egyptian war was going on, and could not help feeling a little regret that he did not take part in the storming of Tel-el-Kebir.

THE END

PrestonSpeed Publications 51 Ridge Road Mill Hall, PA 17751
(570) 726-7844
www.prestonspeed.com

Historiae Dona Repertum

Books by G. A. Henty

For The Temple
The Dragon & The Raven
In Freedom's Cause
By Pike & Dyke
Beric The Briton
St. Bartholomew's Eve
With Lee in Virginia
By Right of Conquest
The Young Carthaginian
Winning His Spurs
Under Drake's Flag
The Cat of Bubastes
Wulf The Saxon
A Knight of the White Cross
St. George for England
With Wolfe in Canada
By England's Aid
The Dash for Khartoum
The Lion of the North
Won by the Sword
Facing Death
The Lion of St. Mark
Bonnie Prince Charlie

In the Reign of Terror
The Tiger of Mysore
A March on London
Under Wellington's Command
At Agincourt
Orange and Green
With Moore at Corunna
To Herat and Cabul
For Name and Fame
With Clive in India

Other Publications

By Right of Conquest (unit study guide)
By Pike and Dyke (unit study guide)
The Cat of Bubastes (unit study guide)
A Journey of Souls
The Henty Companion

Audio Books

The Cat of Bubastes
Wulf The Saxon

PrestonSpeed Publications takes great pride in re-printing the complete works of G. A. Henty. New titles are released regularly. Both our hardcover and tradepaper printings include the complete text of the original edition, as well as all maps and illustrations.

For a free catalog call 570-726-7844
or write to us and request your free catalog at:
PrestonSpeed Publications
51 Ridge Road
Mill Hall, PA 17751
USA
A catalog may also be obtained at our web site:
www. prestonspeed.com